Praise for *A Manual fo*

"*A Manual for How to Love Us* is a collection that reads like a wolf howl, every page alive with longing and hunger and desire and rage. Erin Slaughter writes with tenderness—capturing the sweet intimacies of friendship, of kindness in unexpected places—but also with an unflinching eye for the pain that connects us, shapes us, makes us who we are. This is prose from a poet's heart."
—Allegra Hyde, author of *Eleutheria*

"The stories in *A Manual for How to Love Us* read like a cold ocean swim: salty and refreshing and sincere, each a bracing exploration of the particular blessings and burdens of womanhood in all its ugliness and glory. I couldn't ask for something stranger or more beautiful. Erin Slaughter is a masterful sentence writer in firm command of her craft, and this book is an inspiration and a gift."
—Julia Fine, author of *The Upstairs House* and
What Should Be Wild

"This deeply imagined, brilliantly ferocious debut collection sits perfectly among the fiction of Danielle Lazarin and Kelly Link. *A Manual for How to Love Us* lays bare the power and wildness of grief. It is unequivocally one of the best debut collections I've read in years."
—Peter Kispert, author of *I Know You Know Who I Am*

"Erin Slaughter's debut collection, *A Manual for How to Love Us*, is an evocative mix of strange realism and Bachelardian obsession. Slaughter is a gifted stylist who can instill the most mundane objects with profound meaning and depth. In her world, a tongue is never only a tongue, a thorn far more than a thorn, and even a fly—buzzing alone in a bedroom—harbors the impact of a father."
—Isle McElroy, author of *The Atmospherians* and *People Collide*

Also by Erin Slaughter

POETRY

The Sorrow Festival

*I Will Tell This Story to the Sun Until You
Remember That You Are the Sun*

A MANUAL
FOR HOW
TO LOVE US

STORIES

Erin Slaughter

HARPER PERENNIAL

NEW YORK • LONDON • TORONTO • SYDNEY • NEW DELHI • AUCKLAND

HARPER ● PERENNIAL

HarperCollins books may be purchased for educational, business, or sales promotional use. For information, please email the Special Markets Department at SPsales@harpercollins.com.

FIRST EDITION

Designed by Jen Overstreet

Library of Congress Cataloging-in-Publication Data has been applied for.

ISBN 978-0-06-323088-0

23 24 25 26 27 LBC 5 4 3 2 1

for anyone trying to find their way home

Love is dangerous.
        As is the world.
It isn't only loss—there's lots
Of weird malice loose on the planet.

—GREGORY ORR

CONTENTS

I

II

III

A MANUAL
FOR HOW
TO LOVE US

I

ANYWHERE

Days or weeks ago. Zell arrived at my apartment door, her laughter hollow, her hair too short. She'd lost weight since I saw her last, her jaw all angles and edges. She walked right in like it hadn't been five years since we'd last spoken, and there was a warmth in being with her that made it feel like it couldn't have been—like we'd been shadows moving alongside each other all this time. She asked me how my day was. We ate white rice from plastic bowls.

Then she offered me a new life like she was offering me a soda, and when a girl like that asks you to run away with her, you do. You take inventory of your little world, shuck off the pieces you won't miss, and betray the ones you will under the guise of *adventure*. I had no pets, no plants, no friends who would notice I was gone; my only furniture a mattress, a foldout chair, and a scratched table the last tenants left on the curb. Almost like I'd been keeping my life empty so it would be easier to discard when Zell showed up.

You leave your cell phone on the kitchen counter and throw your clothes into a bag without bothering to fold them. In the car, you catch yourself really breathing for the first time in years, maybe, and it turns out breathing feels magnificent, the glory-dance of lungs. She asked me to run, so I ran, and I didn't ask where we were going, or why, because it didn't matter. I was going with her.

◆ ◆ ◆

Four days ago, our first day gone. Miles and miles of night, the darkness like a fleece blanket wrapped around us. Zell's features were lit only by the glow of the dashboard, making it harder to believe she was real and next to me, not the hologram or half-drawn vision I sometimes willed into my dreams as I lay alone in bed. Then the febrile Nevada sun broke the spell, sizzling holes through the cool blue dawn, and she was there: solid, slack-jawed, alive.

She wanted to run so we ran, but first, she wanted to see the Grand Canyon, so we drove through the night from Carson City, past the neon rest stops and quiet drive-throughs, the overpasses brick after concrete brick on the skyline. I drove while Zell slept, the side of her face smashed against the cool glass, her hand coiled around the seat belt like an infant holding its mother's finger. We parked the car in the packed lot out front, and I bought our tickets at the visitors desk while Zell went to pee. After milling around the gift shop towers of souvenir magnets, we got on a bus and rode through the stuffy morning toward the canyon.

"I always thought you could drive right up to it," she said. "They make it look that way on TV."

"Me too." The natural tone between us still half performed.

"God, buses make me motion sick." She lifted her hair and fanned the back of her neck with her ticket, looking out the window.

Ten minutes later, we stepped off the bus and gulped fresh air like we'd been drowning. Pale sunlight broke over red-painted ridges, the farthest peaks huddled close like tiny villages, a molten river slicing through the impossible bottom of it all. Zell's mascara began to melt, from the wind or something more. Then, in one breathtaking motion, her smile bloomed over the crevasse, and I swelled with a wave of déjà vu; this was the Zell I remembered—often cynical and hardened, but every so often a childish wonder spilled out of her, and the crinkles in the corners of her eyes faded. She rolled her gaze toward the white expanse of sky and blotted her makeup. I looked away.

"Weird how we never came to see it before," she said.

"Who would've taken us?"

She was silent for a minute as her hair whipped around her face and she stood there, letting it. Zell's eyes were bright with whatever it was people came here to find, but feeling things so eloquently, so intensely, was a muscle I hadn't accessed in a while. My ponytail lolled, the tip licking one side of my neck, then the other.

She told me then about the time she was seven, when her mom took her camping on a seaweed-infested beach in Texas, the only vacation they ever had. How some muscle dude came over to flirt with her mom and helped Zell build a huge sandcastle; how it made her so happy, having a stranger do something just for her, that she didn't even notice when they left to go fuck in the RV and abandoned Zell on the shore.

"For years, that was my favorite memory." She wiped her face on her shirtsleeve, then let out a loud, broken laugh. "What kind of shitty childhood is that?"

Watching Zell look out at the wind and painted dust, I could feel wonder trickling in, inching my chest open, guiding me to a place where I could join her in this moment. She glanced over at me, and I swallowed it down.

◆ ◆ ◆

Zell at the wheel, we found our way back to I-40 and stopped at a diner for our first meal in twelve hours. I wasn't sure if it was the lack of sleep, the flooding brightness, hunger, or the elation of being with her, but I felt a little drugged. Pleasantly delirious, like moving through a dreamscape. Without the GPS on our cell phones—Zell made us leave those behind—we used paper maps to navigate. Being off-grid, untethered from daily life and suspended in the meat of living, gave us the air of real fugitives. This, too, was *adventure*, but it seemed more like finding our way back to being human: navigating the world on instinct and landscape alone.

We slid into a sticky booth where the rubber seat pinched awkwardly at my thighs. The waitress brought two sweating glasses of ice water, and Zell drew a heart in the condensation, a ritual I'd forgotten about. I didn't say, *Nothing's really changed, has it?* I didn't say, *I am so glad you're still in the world.* I smiled and said nothing. We ordered three side plates of hash browns to douse in ketchup and split between us, and a pot of coffee.

"So, what've you been up to lately? Still in Phoenix?" I asked, wincing at the cadence of small talk.

Zell and I grew up in the unincorporated town of Phoenix, New Mexico, and were used to telling people *No, not that one.* Years of insisting on the truth of ourselves, until I got older and left, and now when someone asked it was easier just to say *Phoenix* and let them believe what they wanted to.

Only fifty people officially lived in Phoenix, according to the bug-splattered sign at its limits; mostly people who worked at the factory or the small casino twenty miles north, or who trickled down from the Navajo Nation. You'd think a small town means you know everybody, but in that blip along an otherwise empty stretch of desert, Zell and I knew nobody but each other. Our moms, both basically teens when we were kids, worked as waitresses in the casino together, and then at the Flying J, then as cleaners in the Achilles Motel where we lived for a while. We learned most of what we knew in that brown-carpeted motel room, from staticky PBS and the shadows who walked by the window openly hollering their needs at one another.

She answered, "Yeah. I moved into the house when my mom got sick. Then stayed a while after she died."

A pang of guilt snaked through me when she mentioned her mom, and to bury it, I asked why she'd decided to go to New Jersey now. Her face lit up.

"*The Barrens,*" she swooned exaggeratedly. "You *know* I've always been obsessed with the Barrens." Her eyes sparked and her voice softened into a monologue about the atmospheric mist and moss, the trees, the light filtering through the leaves; a familiar refrain, this fascination she'd carried since our teen-age years. In the motel office, travelers would sometimes leave behind random books and when we got bored we'd flip through them, most interested in the ones that seemed scandalous:

paperbacks with outdated dating advice, or issues of *Men's Health* and *Cosmo*. It was there in the pile of discards that Zell found *Ghost Towns of the New Jersey Pine Barrens*. I wondered if all these years later she still slept with it at her bedside, like a talisman.

"I mean, why *wouldn't* you want to live in the only American state with an official state demon," she said. According to her, posers always cited the Jersey Devil, but real enthusiasts knew the forest harbored a whole ecosystem of folklore. She'd wax poetic about how the Pine Barrens were swallowingly lush and alive in every way that New Mexico was a place for death's leftovers: *Funny how they call something so green "barren." Can't imagine anywhere more barren than here.*

I asked her if she was in some kind of trouble, if there was more to prompt our leaving than she was letting on, and she made a face.

"I just wanna see some trees, Andrea." She crossed her arms, glancing out the window. "There are reasons to leave, sure, but they're just reasons."

I pretended to concentrate exceptionally hard on the sugar packets so she wouldn't see my face when I asked the next question.

"Are you, like, pregnant?"

She choked out a laugh, and I couldn't tell if she thought it was funny, or if she was suddenly racked by some crazed grief. "No," she said. "No, nobody I've known is worth getting knocked up by."

I felt stupid for how relieved I was, even though that in itself didn't tell me much about Zell's life since I last saw her.

"I mean, is it drugs though? Like, is it legal trouble, or— why'd you want to leave so fast, and why," I steadied my voice, hating myself before the words were out, "after all this time?" What I meant was: *Why with me?*

"You know how it is. The years roll over 'til they don't anymore," she said, affecting a twang I associated with the factory workers back home. "I just don't want to be found, is all."

She paused to take a drink, then added, "Why'd you come along, anyway?" Her eyes glittered with a fanglike spark of meanness. It made my neck flush with arousal.

I mumbled something about *adventure*, and she asked what I was going to do afterward.

"After what?"

"After New Jersey. I figured you'd hang around 'til I get set up, but what are you going to do when you go back to Nevada?"

My stomach dropped. It hadn't hit me, somehow, that after all this, I'd get on a plane and go back to the same life, same job, same old apartment, the carpet still caked with dirt from Zell's boots. The thought was unfathomable—to detox from days on days spent in Zell's presence and return to nothingness.

"I don't know," I said. Then the hash browns came and we ate them, silent and fast.

◆ ◆ ◆

When we were done eating, Zell pulled a roll of bills from her pocket and paid with the cash we pooled last night. She insisted we couldn't use our cards, couldn't leave any trail, and I'd agreed to play along, which meant trusting her fully; so before we left Nevada I drove through the ATM around the corner from my apartment and pulled out my full savings balance: six hundred dollars in crisp, coarse twenties. Zell had brought the car, the maps, what money she could scrounge up: two hundred-ish in crinkled bills, waitressing tips mostly.

I went to the bathroom and rinsed my face, hunched over the automatic sink. I wiped under my breasts and arms with a wet brown paper towel and threw it in the overflowing bin by the door. When I went outside, Zell was sitting cross-legged on the hood of the car.

"Let's take the scenic drive, go along old Route 66 instead," she said.

"How much time does that add? I thought we were in some kind of hurry."

"It's all about the journey, right? Letting the universe guide us? And mile marker thirteen is right at the exit fork, so that feels like something important. A sign."

"I thought thirteen was supposed to be unlucky," I joked, but she barely heard me.

"Anyway, it runs back to the big road eventually. Not like we'll get lost."

Zell merged onto the old road, winding and pockmarked, and I adjusted the air-conditioning vents, hoping I wouldn't get car sick. It was a truly beautiful drive, though, and I forgot my uneasiness. Dwarfed mountains sprouted with tufts of yellow and lilac, the azure sky flat above, and occasional clouds cast shadows on the ground like we were passing under a Macy's Day balloon. We were the only car for miles, and I had the sudden urge to stop in the middle of the road, get out of the car, and howl into the sunny emptiness.

But we didn't. We drove an hour, maybe, the clean-cut wind lapping through the cracked window. And then Zell said, "Oh shit, we're almost out of gas."

Out in some parts of the desert, it could be hours between gas stations. We were close enough to the highway, I figured, but who could say how far we'd veered? Once the panic set in properly, the engine began to feel like it was sputtering, slowing.

"Fuck," Zell exclaimed. "Roll up the window. I can't think with the noise."

I did, and she switched off the AC and radio, trying to save every morsel of energy. The car quickly hotboxed in the sun, and in seconds we were sweating something awful, wincing at each dip in the engine's roar. I got prepared to accept that we might have to walk, it might be our only choice. It was impossible to predict how far. Spiraling into survival mode, I took stock of how much water was left in my plastic bottle, examined the position of the sun in the sky, and tried to guess how long we'd last.

When the heat and tension were unbearable, when I was about to plead with Zell to at least open a window, we turned and saw a sign, then another: two gas stations, one on each side of the road. We exhaled and pulled into the left entrance, and I immediately unbuckled and jumped from the car, the breeze chilling dry the droplets of sweat on my face.

Zell got out and closed the door. Then she paused, fear creeping into her face.

"We can't go in," she said. "We've gotta go to the other one."

"Why? What do you mean?" I pressed her, dry mouthed and drenched in sweat. The two gas stations were identical, down to the weathered-away green paint on the pump numbers. I tried to understand how she jumped so quickly from relief to fear, but she wouldn't give me a reason, only: *Something bad is about to happen.*

"Please, come on, let's just drive across the street. It's not a big deal."

"Okay," I conceded, my annoyance overtaken by how visibly shaken she was. The ignition took a couple tries before rumbling awake, and we were able to make it out of the lot before the engine clonked out halfway across the (thankfully empty) road. Zell pulled the car into neutral and I got out to push, gliding the car to rest beside the pump at a wonky angle.

I pumped gas while Zell went inside to pay, and I watched the other station for any signs of Zell's prediction, noticing nothing of note. Minutes later, Zell emerged from around the side of the building. I was pretty sure the bathroom was indoors, but I didn't mention it.

"I don't see anything weird going on over there," I said, gesturing across the street.

"Ha, well, knock on wood." She was upbeat again, her paranoia suddenly mollified. She rapped her knuckles on the hood of the car.

"That's not even wood."

"Everything came from a tree at some point."

This time, I offered to drive. She turned up the AC, readjusted the vents, and I caught a glimpse of her hand: the grooves of her fingerprints outlined with traces of dirt. Fingernails embedded with slivers of dark moons.

◆　◆　◆

Three days ago. There was a dog in the hotel office, a weenie: sienna fur speckled with gray, the fattest creature I'd ever seen. His short paws drowned under Shakespearean layers of skin as he trotted from his owner's calf to the pillow at the corner of the desk. Every time someone entered the office and the bell on the door chimed, the hotel owner's wife reached into her black satchel and fed him a treat. Many people entered and exited a day, I guessed, though they were one of the last neon signs on an otherwise gutted through road. The blinking green letters squirmed through the incredible dark. I loved that dog.

That night we stopped near Tucumcari, and as we walked to the room, I anticipated one bed and what that would mean. Something between us had sunk back into eternal familiarity, but there were still parts of ourselves we withheld—the parts that revealed in how many ways we were nearly strangers. But the room had two beds, each crowned by a black-and-white poster of Audrey Hepburn hung on the stucco wall.

We undressed efficiently and climbed under the sheets, our psyches plowed by more than twenty-four hours on the road. There was no time to lay in the cover of dark, thinking, overthinking—flooded by that mix of anxiety and reverence I'd begun to associate with these small moments of intimacy. Sleep rolled over me quick and violent.

When I woke up the next morning, I was already braced for Zell to change her mind. For her to be awake, waiting to say, *How dumb was this idea. Thanks, though, it was fun.* But I was ripped from sleep by the sound of her shutting the door, Dixie cups of black coffee in both hands.

Zell spread the paper maps across her bed. So far, we'd been following I-40, a straight line east, but soon we'd have to navigate north on new roads. She pointed to a thick vein of blue threaded through St. Louis, then Indianapolis; places I'd never been, but that in my mind were painted with the chrome sheen of stainless steel.

We dressed, stuffed last night's clothes back in our bags, and left the room key on the desk—saving the weenie dog some calories, if only by a little. We settled into the Chevy's sun-warmed seats and returned to the road.

Here's the thing about the desert: it represents something to everyone, whether or not they've been there. To a lot of people, it means freedom, a geographic incarnation of American individualism as noble, a choice. But like American freedom, it's only presented in curated fragments: the landscape bordering the highway, not the endless crannies so far out you couldn't reach them without heatstroke. Not the ruthless drought, the parched and cracked earth warning of a future that lurks in plain sight, and not the pioneers of the past who ate their own families to drive somebody else's out of the home they'd inhabited for centuries. Walk into the frame of any promise without knowing what it's made of, and you'll get what's coming. Take the everything you're offered in one fell gulp, and it will swallow you up.

We'd watched the landscape gradually shift from one end of the Southwest to the other; mountainous bleached Nevada, Arizona streaked red, New Mexico yellow and emerald-tufted, West Texas with its brown trees like arthritic hands. The things that grow here aren't a miracle. They don't carry mystic wisdom, secrets about how to mine life from the barren dust. Survival in desperate conditions is not magic; it's a *fuck you*, an insistence on being.

Before noon, Zell at the wheel, we broke from one side of the panhandle to the other.

◆ ◆ ◆

We whittled away the days in surprisingly incident-free stretches, the landscape flattening out into miles of green. At a little bricked town square near Tulsa, we stopped for booths selling fresh peaches and cantaloupes, and Zell bought a candle from a woman with a port-wine birthmark who said it would "shield her heart from negative energy."

Often as we drove I remembered us as teenagers, sitting in the same spots in the same car, trailing through the desolate streets of Phoenix and planning how to get gone. Time folding in on itself, one page of history kissing the other. How lucky I was to live long enough to see them meet.

For me, disappearance was mostly hypothetical, but for Zell, freedom always meant New Jersey. A state that notoriously smelled like garbage and exhaust. A state Zell had never been within a thousand miles of, but spent a decade-plus idealizing into a promised land: her mythic beacon of the Northeast, grittier and more authentic than New York, and the forest that survives undisturbed at the edge of metropoles; the ruins of old mills absorbed by nature; whole towns abandoned to the bog, pulled back into the earth by vines and time; the Magic City artists' commune hidden somewhere in the depths. *Basically a glorified campground*, she'd once told me, *but that doesn't mean people didn't find magic there, or make their own.* Her eyes sparkled, inhabited by a love you can only hold for something you don't really know.

Zell, familiar as the earthy-sweet smell of my own bedsheets, still seemed to me a mythical being. Her long black eyelashes, nose with the slightest crook to it, her body all sliding tectonic plates. A tenderness that opened and then shut again before you got too good a look. Zell was a person of extremes, and she invited it, curated it: the worship and the demonization. She would allow for nothing in between.

We stopped for the night somewhere in Missouri and popped into a gas station across from the motel to buy drinks and chips to take back to our room—too tired to search for a real meal, uninterested in engaging a stranger or shopkeep to ask.

Perusing the liquor shelf, I suggested, "How about a bottle of Jack, to remember old times?"

Zell smiled mischievously. "How about stealing a bottle to remember old times?"

But I stood at the counter lamely while the clerk ran my card through the grimy machine, then discarded the bag in the trash can by the door.

◆ ◆ ◆

Two days ago. Four days gone, and we were running out of money. I knew this, even though Zell insisted it wasn't true. The brick of cash we'd left with was now a single roll of five- and ten-dollar bills, nestled into the breast pocket of Zell's flannel shirt. She ritually circled the bills around her pointer finger until they stuck like that.

An hour outside Indianapolis, Zell broke the silent rhythm of the road:

"Oh shit, we forgot about Memphis."

"What's in Memphis?" I asked.

"Memphis is in Memphis, duh." She clicked the blinker and started merging toward the off-ramp.

"What are you doing?"

"Well, we have to go. We can't just *miss* Memphis."

"Are you kidding?"

"Come on, I've never been," she whined, like Memphis was a roadside attraction and not a day's drive in the opposite direction.

"You want to get stranded in Tennessee? We'll have to sleep in the car. We'll have to *live* in the car." My face hung open, incredulous, but she took a left under the overpass and onto the other side of the highway.

Was she trying to delay us? Was she dreading that moment of arrival, as I was, when our shared bubble of *adventure* would end and I would leave? The hope—the fantasy of something to hope for—was a sugary jolt to my brain, but I couldn't allow myself to get lost in it.

"Just take a nap, we'll be there before you know it." She was trying to pacify me like a huffy child, and I found myself irritated with her—a foreign feeling, a little satisfying even, so rarely did I regard Zell with any kind of negativity. But I was a helpless passenger to her hurtling us off course for some reason I couldn't make sense of, which stung more for what it represented about our friendship—the foundation I tried not to look at, tried in my shame to distract Zell from noticing. It had been dark for hours already, and by the time we arrived, the sun would be up.

I wanted to call it out, lay our roles bare: my worshipful surrender, her manipulative impulsiveness. But I only turned away, my cheek against the rattling window.

◆ ◆ ◆

I woke on the side of the road, the world quiet. Soft purple light falling over a field, so lovely I wondered if I'd floated peacefully into death, or a dream. I looked over at Zell, and she wasn't there. Her door was wide open, the interstate rushing ruthlessly a few yards away.

I sat up, got out of the car, and looked around in panic. I was ready to trudge into the field to look for her, but then I glanced to my right and caught a glimpse: far away enough that her body looked like a deflated beach ball, squatting down by the fence. I ran, feet squishing in the damp ground, the untended grass lashing my ankles.

When I came upon Zell she was digging at the base of a fence post, rutting at the earth with her hands, fingers pointed claw-like. I walked closer and she startled, looked up wide-eyed, like an animal who realizes it's being hunted.

"What . . . what are you doing?"

"Oh, did you have a good nap?"

"I woke up and you weren't there," I said, sounding as childish and disoriented as I felt.

She held up a slip of notebook paper, torn and folded into a lopsided square. "Don't laugh, but it's this thing I do, sort of for good luck? I've been burying these notes along the trip, little snippets of secrets, or worries, or stories from the day. Or wishes. Like bread crumbs, so when someone uncovers one, they can follow my trail and know where to find me."

"Who is going to come find you?"

She sighed, as if exasperated by having to explain. "I don't know, someone important. Whoever is meant to. I mean, life is so twisty. We never know what's going to happen to us."

I turned my back on her, the road, the pastel sky melting toward sunrise's orange peak. A headache coming on.

"Don't laugh," she repeated, wiping her dirty hands on her thighs. "I know you probably don't get it, but . . ."

I looked at Zell, her features softened in the dawn light, and searched for something behind her face—a clue these notes should unlock about the person I knew, or thought I knew, or how to reconcile those people with the person she'd become. For some hint of wavering, a flicker of harm behind her impenetrable confidence. But she was walled off as ever. I was not afraid of her; I was afraid *for* her.

I said, "We should get going."

We walked back to the car and drove in silence, the radio and its nineties hits wedging space between us. Zell flitted anxious glances in my direction every couple of miles, but my eyes burned defiantly forward. For the first time, it dawned on me that running away, for her, might've been about more than *adventure*, or reuniting, or New fucking Jersey. That maybe my saying yes had given something unwieldy inside of her permission to grow.

On the edge of the city, we checked into one of those shady by-the-hour motels, and I didn't ask how much it cost. Just rolled into bed and slept, and when I woke, the sun was sinking down between the curtains. The maid knocked, tried to push open the door against the deadbolt before I yelled out, "We're still in here!" She looked confused, but went away, barely shutting the door. Zell was awake now, too, so we pulled our jeans back on, brushed our hair, and left.

She drove up to a barbecue place, and we ate pulled pork and mac and cheese from white Styrofoam trays, not talking much; Zell trying, me mumbling simple acknowledgments, her trying harder in response. I was tired, and didn't know what words I'd use to argue if I had the energy to. For the first time, I just wanted to get where we were going.

Zell moved to start up the car again, then stopped and looked at me. "I know I freaked you out, okay? I'm sorry."

"I just wish you'd help me understand what's happening," I said, not fully sure what I was asking. She looked ahead.

"What I said in Albuquerque, about the years rolling over?" she started. "When I was a kid, I never understood how people didn't grow up and follow their dreams—like in movies, how a sad housewife settles for someone fine, but who she doesn't love. Or a person who has a passion or talent, but life gets too hard and they give up on being famous, or even trying to be good at it. But I get it now: you make a choice because it's there, and you keep making it, and then one day your life is over. You only get the time you get." She paused, and I waited.

"And when I thought about the choices I wished I could go back and make again, I thought about New Jersey, and I thought about you. So I decided to start there."

◆ ◆ ◆

Yesterday. We blazed across the midlands, burning through every decaying town in our path, sweeping through cities made of glass, lights clustered behind us in the distance. The Chevy roared, devouring miles in fistfuls. We cranked the windows down by hand, blared "Going to Georgia" so loud that fifteen miles away they could feel the chords pumping through their veins. Half the country passed in a blur of melting starlight embedded across the sky.

More than a place, we were escaping lives that felt at once unbearably short and long, lives with no room for being alive inside them. Now, asphalt over Nashville, I was watching all of that crumble. I was seeing the murky red future flatten itself like a canvas, the landscape bleeding from mountain to mossy grave, the star-spangled heartstring of the stretching road. We were singing the Mountain Goats as the past burned in the rearview.

What I remember most was Zell, knuckles white on the steering wheel, hair in a flurry, dark-brown eyes lit ablaze. Screaming to the song at the top of our lungs, what I remember thinking is this: I hope we fucking crash, I hope we die, I hope it's messy and unavoidable, our flesh and bones mangled together for all eternity. Because nothing will ever be more exactly right than this—alive, electric. Free.

◆ ◆ ◆

I stirred awake in the dark. Tall, overgrown brush scraping against the windshield. Again, I looked for Zell and found myself alone. Beyond the driver's-side door where she should be: a tin-roof house slouching into the tangle of weeds that surrounded it. My gut sank into terror, then embarrassment, when I realized I'd been tricked and abandoned by Zell once more. A middle-of-nowhere darkness, the kind where stars shine diamond-cold and cast the only noticeable light.

Danger seared through my every nerve as I tried to calculate where Zell could've gone—maybe she pulled off the road to pee under cover of a bush? Or was burying secrets in the dark, cool mud? But my mind rang with her words: *We never know what's going to happen to us.* And suddenly I was terrified she'd done something—hurt herself. That this was all a warning I'd missed. My body filled with a choking urgency to find her before something awful happened. Hopefully, I'd be quick enough for it not to have happened yet.

I crept toward the house, whipping my head around to check for attackers. The foundation was held up on cinder blocks, the wood porch caved in. I climbed up, and my shoes scuffled shards of glass; as if passing through a strange portal, I climbed through the blown-open window frame, slicing my thigh on a small, jagged piece stuck in the windowsill. But it only ripped the material of my jeans, not the skin beneath.

Old records, some still intact, littered the kitchen. The living room floor had sunken in, sucking a floral sofa down with it and collecting thick pockets of leaves, and as I stepped over the orange carpet I feared snakes, raccoons. My heart pounded in my ears as I struggled to adjust to the darkness. It was a place where wild things scurried to shelter, but it wasn't hard to imagine the people who were here before—as if some echo of their living still pulsed between the walls, in the peeling wallpaper grown fuzzy with mold.

I didn't have to go looking for Zell: she was right there, beyond the sunken entry of the farmhouse, standing at the bottom of the staircase. I moved quietly toward her, braced for the chance she'd bolt—or attack.

"Zell, are you okay?"

She startled and turned around, let out a tiny squawk.

"Holy shit, I thought you were a ghost."

I opened my mouth to reply, but it was swallowed in a noise outside: a man's distant holler, and then the yell of his rifle, cracking open the night sky.

Zell's eyes went wide as they met mine, frozen in a single panicked moment.

"What the fuck—"

"Shhh." Zell clamped her hand over my mouth. We stilled and listened, leaping in our skins when another gunshot sounded.

"Sounds like he's coming from the front. If we go out the back . . ."

"We can sneak around the side."

"Then run to the car."

I nodded. Took a last, deep breath.

We bolted through the sunken kitchen, out the back door,

leaping across the overgrown yard to the car. The rifle blasted again, and Zell fell reaching for the door handle—for one sharp instant I was sure she was dead—and then she stumbled up, making tiny, strangled noises, slid her body into the front seat, and we sped off through the grass. It wasn't until our wheels found pavement again that I saw the blood pooling on her shirt.

◆ ◆ ◆

Hey, stay with me.

My foot grinding into the pedal. The intestines of the battered car gurgling under the pressure. Dirt and grass and road, skidding, a half-airborne leap from a pothole. Telescopes of light revealing only what's in front of us, almost too late to swerve. Time moving like this, in seizurelike flashes—a movie playing every third frame. Zell in the front seat, clutching her arm. A bloom of blood seeping into the black upholstery.

◆ ◆ ◆

Even over the roar I hear her silence so loud. Except for little gasps, grits of teeth. Hair damp with sweat, curling in the delicate places behind her ears and sticking to her forehead.

Goddamn it, Andrea.

That's good. You've got to stay conscious.

Find a place—

Press the wound. I know it hurts. You have to.

Pull over, or—fuck— She winces, bites down on her lower lip. More blood.

This piece-of-shit car—

Hey, don't talk shit about my car.

I don't know why she thought any of us would survive to reach the coast.

◆ ◆ ◆

A wave of panic bubbles up, sure, but I exile my body to some corner of the back seat. No time to be flesh, to feel; we slice clean through the muddy darkness.

There's gotta be a hospital—

No, I told you. I won't—

I want to say: *You're a grown-ass woman. No one's going to call your mom and drag you back home.* But my voice is too wobbly, the metallic smell of her blood perforating the car, and her mom long dead. Irony she'd appreciate in a less compromised state.

It's a gunshot. We'll get fucked for trespassing.

What other option—

She expels a scream. Feral kinetic energy ripping through her. Her eyes are black and wide, the look on her face animal, otherworldly. It scares the shit out of me. I don't know what's inside her, but it's this. The reason she digs in dirt. The reason without a reason.

Come on—just give me this. We'll figure it out, alone, together, like we always did. Please just get us someplace safe.

I keep pinned to the road but feel her eyes pleading a hole through my skin, and shiver.

Okay. Hold on.

◆ ◆ ◆

No way to know where we are. Back roads, pitch dark beyond three feet of ghostly searchlight. How to find a hospital without our phones; too dark for maps, no X marking a spot where we arrive and are saved. It could be hours. If we ever got there. Whose fault would that be? Whose fault was any of this?

I don't know, just know we have to stop the bleeding. Get the bullet out. Sew her together. Put her back how she was before.

The wheels pound relentlessly against the asphalt, a kind of lullaby.

What other option?

◆ ◆ ◆

What does it feel like?
   Like a white-hot cut. Like sunburn giving birth.
   She's almost gleeful behind the pain.
   Like a goddamn supernova is gushing from my body.

◆ ◆ ◆

Dark and dark and dark and dark. Zell's labored breath, the engine, deep vegetal stench of blood. Just over the Kentucky border, a sign for a town called Bugtussle. All black forest and road. Until.

◆ ◆ ◆

Twelve minutes later—what could've been seconds, or an hour, or days—a dollop of yellow light breaks the landscape ahead: a dilapidated Days Inn.

I leave Zell in the car, ask for a room, and pay with cash. The room costs eighty dollars, almost half of what we have left, and as I hand the money to the receptionist I get an uneasy feeling I shove down, remembering the crazed look on Zell's face. How she begged me to do this with her alone.

I pop the trunk, the plastic room key clamped between my teeth, and sling both duffel bags over one shoulder. I slip the half-empty bottle of Jack Daniel's into a zipper pocket. Zell is gray-skinned, ragdolled over the dashboard, and for a second I'm frozen in bottomless dread or longing. The fabric of her flannel shirt shines oily under the security lights.

"Come on," I say, helping her from the car with my free arm. "It's all right, I got you."

On the long trek through the parking lot up the metal staircase to the motel room, time begins to speed up again, the minutes catching up all at once and knocking me nearly breathless. The white paint from the railings chipping under my palms.

Zell slumps onto the mattress, on top of the bedspread—brown with jade slivers, like leaves at the bottom of a lake. Her shirt is ruined, a patch of dark liquid spreading down her sleeve. I bend down to take it off, my fingers intentional, trying hard to be merely whispers on her skin. She winces anyway.

The wound is a crater the size of a quarter in the flesh of her upper arm. I've seen things like this in movies, of course—worse even—but in front of me, it's terrifying. I cross the room, come back to the bedside with a wooden chair and my duffel bag.

"Here," I say, placing the bottle of whiskey in her good hand. "Drink up."

She doesn't question it, takes a gulp. Amber sloshes against the glass. Another gulp.

"How're we gonna do this?" she asks.

I take the pocketknife from my bag and begin ripping Zell's shirt into strips. Her watery eyes shine in the yellow lamplight, waiting for an answer.

◆ ◆ ◆

Half our lives ago. We were thirteen, maybe, walking the mile and a half to the gas station to buy frostbitten popsicles with spare change we collected from the hotel vending machine. Zell led the way, as she always did, her darker skin a marvel beneath the sun, while mine just reddened and peeled in ugly patches of freckles. The sand that veiled the sidewalk kept getting kicked into my sandals and going sludgy on the sweaty soles of my feet.

"What flavor are you going to get?"

"Hmm. I think guava. Ooh, or watermelon, if they have it."

"They never have watermelon."

I tried to get up the courage to start our game, but then, thankfully, Zell did it on her own.

"Imagine," she started, a smile in her voice, though she was still walking ahead, not looking at me. "Imagine how good the air is going to feel when we walk in."

I responded, "Imagine getting some of those ice flakes on the backs of your hands when you slide the freezer open."

"Imagine they have watermelon. Like, just tons and tons of watermelon. And we each get two because the gas station guy feels so bad for us."

"Imagine it's already a little melty, so you have to suck the juice off your fingers."

"Imagine licking all over it, and getting your face sticky and your whole mouth stained."

"Imagine it's gone but you can still feel it melting inside you."

The "Imagine" game wasn't just about popsicles; we were addicts for the future, teasing each other with fantasies of whatever small desire there was to look forward to quenching. It didn't matter if it would never be ours.

I didn't see it slither out of the wild brush before I felt it; I fell to the ground, scraping my elbows on the concrete. Zell turned around and her face morphed from confusion to panic.

"What happened?!"

"I think I got struck by lightning," I gasped. The sky was unwaveringly blue above us, but it seemed to be the only explanation.

"Where? Show me," she commanded.

I struggled to pivot my body so I could see what had become of it. Below the raw, rock-embedded patches on my knees, my ankle was swollen and red.

"Let me look." I winced as she pawed at the swell and pointed. "That's fang marks."

"I didn't see a snake." I started crying, sobs knocked loose from my chest. It wasn't an excuse but an apology: for ruining our momentum, for falling like an idiot, for making Zell join me on the dirty, snake-infested ground.

"It could be poisonous," she said. "We need to call your mom."

"It's too far," I whined. "By the time we get to the gas station, the poison will get me."

Zell considered this. She spit in her hand.

"What are you doing?"

"It's okay, I saw it on Discovery Channel."

She circled her saliva over the wound with two fingers, washing away the dust, then wiped her hand on her jean shorts. She took an audible breath before she leaned over and closed her mouth over my ankle. She sucked at the swell, and even though it ached a sharp bolt of pain, I was rapt with the sudden sensation of the inside of Zell's mouth, the wet and fleshy slide and strangeness of it, her flickering tongue.

She came up for air and spit into the dirt.

"There," she said. "Can you get up?"

I wasn't sure she'd sucked anything out of me, or if it was poison to begin with, but she helped me to my feet and I dusted the sand off. She slowed down to walk beside me and I hobbled the rest of the way to the gas station. With each step I imagined the woosh of the AC, sliding open the freezer to reveal clusters of bright pink watermelon popsicles, imagined Zell and me cradling the cold and crinkled plastic in our palms, imagined it as if I already knew it to be so.

◆ ◆ ◆

I have stopped apologizing. I pour the warm whiskey over Zell's wound, and she yelps like a hurt puppy. I dip the tip of the knife into the angry red hole in her arm and she jerks it away, and I have to cuff her wrist to the bed with my free hand and watch as she writhes like an animal trying to escape from its skin, all the while biting my tongue to hold back the *Sorry, I'm sorry, I'm so sorry,* worrying the skin of my cheek between my teeth until I taste blood.

Thankfully the wound isn't that deep, but the flesh around it puckers, clinging to the bullet. I try to keep my hands from shaking and hope Zell doesn't notice. My eyes flicker to her, but her own are pressed tightly shut. The blood covering my fingers smells like sour fruit, sticky and hot. I hate it, but I can't help but think of roadkill—the bloated bodies of deer that line all roads far enough from town, their twisted necks and punctured-through limbs, congealed innards streaming from each cavity. How the animal becomes less of an animal with every piece of flesh split from bone.

And there's a part of me, as I slice new little gashes into Zell's flesh—a monstrous, greedy part I'm ashamed of, though not entirely surprised by—that is ecstatic to find myself here. In awe as the pages of history overlap yet again, throwing us back together in another shitty motel. Even if we pull this off, Zell could rot from infection or die from blood loss, but still I'm fighting back a grin, feeling ridiculously lucky that fate ricocheted us to this room, provided an irrefutable excuse to hold her in place and put my hands on her for as long as I want. It's a deep, dark sensory overload, like gorging past the point of sickness: the walls oozing with the near transcendent banquet of desire, and the visceral focus, and how dangerously close it all is to slipping out from under us.

But for however long the bullet throbs under her skin, Zell and I are as close as two people will ever be: our sweat, blood, and spit stitched through by the inseparable past and the uncertain thread of the future. And after, there will always be a scar where I'd had my hands inside her. A reminder of me she can never walk away from.

The blood keeps coming and I keep wiping it away, trying to find the source, the bullet nestled inside. I keep offering Zell whiskey, her free hand trembling as she struggles to tip the bottle to her mouth. She is making noises that I will promise not to remember. We are drowned in ocher light, the dislocated feeling that a whole season has passed through the curtains of the hotel room.

She's quiet for a minute, my focus narrowed to the blunt tip of the knife, when I feel her tense and try to sit up.

"Andrea—" She has a look on her face, pain moving in a different direction than the obvious pain.

"Don't."

The whiskey baptizes the wound and the blood keeps coming. I am still carving her open, still searching for what's hidden there, shirking from the light.

◆ ◆ ◆

Two years ago. I moved to Nevada and took a job at a customer service call center, and the only thing I remember about those months of dial tones and sanitized headsets was the map of North America on my gray cubicle wall. While I typed reports and sent out free coupons, I was tracing the highways with my gaze, formulating some kind of personal manifest destiny. I opened a savings account. I was good at my job. I thought a lot about faking my death.

I came home every evening and climbed the four sets of stairs to my studio apartment. I lay in bed and listened to the train howl in the distance. Darkness came and sunlight came on a loop, without reason. It all returns in images like this, days recycled and melded into weeks.

One day, I was getting into my car to go to the grocery store, and I realized it was Zell's birthday. I'd forgotten. I stared at my phone for a while, not sure what to do. I knew how it would play out: I'd overcome my pounding pulse to call her, then wait all day, all week, for her to not call back. I would know she didn't intend to call back, that it didn't matter anyway, but still something would come open in me, staining the weeks afterward with an unbearable cosmic desperation. I put my phone away, and I was proud of myself—proud for having forgotten her birthday to begin with. It was raining, and I sat in my car, watching the sky's blues and oranges melt across the windshield.

I wondered what Zell was doing.

◆ ◆ ◆

I wipe the sweat from my forehead with the back of my arm. Zell is clammy, but she's still occasionally cursing and fisting the sheets. She's tired, we both are.

Her skin grows hot in the lamplight. *This bullet isn't coming out*, I think, for what truly feels like years, until with the pocketknife and a pair of tweezers, I purge the pebble of lead. It's so small I nearly want to laugh.

"Wait. I want to see it," she says.

I hold it up to the lamp. Zell smiles weakly with one corner of her mouth, then falls backward on the bed.

◆ ◆ ◆

Five years ago. I wish I could tell you this story was not about me. That I could funnel it into a caricature of some previous self, a made-up person who never learned what to say or where to rest her hands.

I'd come back to Phoenix for a funeral, planned to stay a couple days, and I was at a party, the soft melody of voices cooing in a starlit backyard. Whiskey calmed my muscles, and in the corner of my eye a couple swayed barefoot in the sparse grass. I went inside the house to grab another drink. Zell had invited me, but I hadn't seen her all night. In fact, I hadn't seen her in almost a year.

I was already drunk, too drunk, when I spotted Zell in the dark hallway. My legs felt like stilts, my mouth numb. I hugged her and felt her earring scratch a faint mark in the flesh of my cheek. Zell's body was so soft wrapped around mine, and when I pressed my mouth against hers I didn't know what I was doing but nothing else made sense, nothing but this, and Zell pulled back like she was looking through me at someone else entirely; a half smile of shock pulled at the corners of her mouth, the way children instinctively smile when they're about to tell a lie.

I had ruined everything. I knew this.

I couldn't breathe so I ran out into the road. The chilly air stung. I lay down in the gravel, smelling gasoline, the sky spinning. There were no cars.

Zell didn't follow me.

Yet.

◆ ◆ ◆

"I owe you," Zell says. She's bandaged, strips of her shirt wrapped around her swollen arm, tight enough to stop the bleeding for now. She's lying on the bed in paint-stained navy shorts and a tank top, sipping sink water from a Styrofoam cup.

"It's fine," I say. "Don't worry about it."

"I mean, I literally owe you my life after that," she says. There is a part of me I hate, a part of me that feels like I've won something when she says it.

"You would've done it for me," I say, trying to smile because I want it to be true. "We'll call it even."

"When we get to New Jersey, you know, maybe you could hang around for a while. You might like it. Did you know it can even get cold in the summers there? Can you imagine needing a jacket in the summer?"

I want so badly to believe in her. Not to have seen what I saw. I wish she would've let me believe in the version of her I'd wanted to believe in.

"Maybe," I say, turning away.

I don't say, *You promise things, but they're just words that make you feel good.* I don't say, *There's a difference between feeling something and meaning it after the moment passes.*

I say, "I'm going to take a shower."

In the bathroom, I strip off my shirt and bra, wipe my stomach where Zell's blood soaked through. The adrenaline is quickly draining from my body, and I feel weird and fragile. Sickened. Even the air is too much, sensitive on my naked gooseflesh.

By the toilet, there's a blocky beige phone attached to the wall. Zell in the other room, still bleeding, half a continent away from everything we know. Quietly, I pick up the receiver, test for a dial tone. It works.

But: half a continent away from everything we know, and nothing to go back to. No one to call, even if I decided to. The cops? A hospital? Zell would never forgive me. Neither of us has anyone who'd cross the country to retrieve us—well, no one but each other. There's a reason she chose me: because I would do anything for her, no judgments, no questions asked.

Whoever she was now, is that still who I was?

People are just people. You can't open them up and crawl inside to shelter yourself from the world. But there should be a way to draw near to the light of a person, to discover in them something like a home. There should be a way to have both: to give Zell what she wants, to be what she wants, and to do what she needs, even if it makes her hate me. But the world doesn't work that way; you don't get what you want simply because you want it.

I sit down and finger the cord, feeling plucked. Topless in filthy jeans, hugging my arms over my chest.

◆ ◆ ◆

Years and years and years. Zell's hands ruffling methodically through her hair in the dirty mirror. *Elegantly disheveled*, she called it, like she'd named a planet, discovered a cure. The buttons that stuck on the TV remote, and Zell's fingers: angry, tireless, gentle without trying. Playing tag in the motel courtyard, our socks damp and dirt-stained knees. Zell at fourteen handing me a cigarette behind the grocery store, nicked from her mom's stash at the back of the mini fridge, holding it up to her lips as if she knew how. Zell's feet rustling under blankets on the couch as she tried to fall asleep. *A comfort thing. It's hereditary, evolutionary*. Zell's fingernails, small and dirt-embedded after, as punishment, the motel owner made her pull weeds from the harsh soil in front of the office. We were twelve. We were twenty when she showed up to my grandfather's funeral holding the hand of a blond townie. They sat in the back pew, whispering almost-laughter, and left before the service was over. And at twenty-three, it was her mom's funeral, and I didn't show up at all.

◆ ◆ ◆

When I get out of the shower Zell is asleep on top of the covers with the TV on, the room bathed in shades of flickering blue. An old cartoon plays on the screen, and with the sound turned off the characters scramble around, looking frightened.

I lay down next to her and I can feel the warmth coming off her skin. She smells of sweat, of sweet wildness. A bruise the size of a fist purples beneath her collarbone. She has always been pretty, anyone could see it, but you wouldn't understand how exactly *alight* she was unless you saw her up close this way, unguarded. She is blinding.

I shift to my side, careful not to disturb her. Her eyelash flutters against her cheek.

There's a bullet on the nightstand, the blood of a girl I love under my nails, each pulse a time bomb flowing through her as she sleeps. If only I could find my way back, fold the memory in half, make the stories cancel each other out. Create a new map to move forward.

We could be anywhere, but we are still here: lost in the heart of the wrong forest, each second a yellow notch falling away behind us.

So what do we do now? Where do we begin?

YOU TOO CAN CURE
YOUR LIFE

The video chat connected and both women smiled from their screens, Melody's name rolling off the woman's tongue, each syllable like a bead on a silver abacus.

From her living room in Hickory Fist, Georgia, Melody took a moment to dial into the woman's internal state. They focused on taking three deep breaths at the same time, Melody fanning her eyelids at the scuffed spot on the wall behind the woman, trying to ignore the video lag and picking at her nail polish beneath her desk; the woman beaming expectantly up at Melody under sallow cheekbones, her head wrapped in beige silk, grinning with a desperate light that rippled the smile lines around her lips. Melody was careful to stay measured in her responses and facial expressions, to project dignified warmth from within; people tend to distrust the openly charismatic, including the charismatic themselves.

The woman had been housebound for thirty weeks now, but assured Melody that since she stopped chemo and started following her guidance, she'd never felt more on the brink of recovery. *On the brink*, that's how she'd put it, *of my whole long life*. At Melody's instruction, the woman had begun making vision boards, cutting out photos and word fragments from the dusty magazines in her storage closet and pasting them to neon-colored posters that she hung wall to wall in the bedroom where she was confined. Melody assured her it was a good sign that the newest vision boards contained pictures of mountains and aquamarine seas, that it meant her body was *incubating the energy to escape its limits*. Some of the earliest vision boards were crowded collages of mascara ads and eyeballs with spidery false lashes, layered until the whole thing looked like a series of furious black claw marks made by a small rodent.

The woman's own lashes had fallen daisy-petaled from her eyes, ironically, as soon as she decided to abandon chemo. Almost two years later, the only hair left on her face was a translucent beard that sometimes caught the hazy backlighting from her apartment window when she shook her head on-screen.

Melody asked how much Life Cure she'd been drinking, and the woman assured her it was a lot, though she'd slacked on journaling because she'd been sleeping something like fourteen hours a day lately, waking heavy and hazy to plod to the bathroom, and then to the kitchen to blend up Melody's recipe of various kales and buckwheat grounds and algaes, sourced from countries whose names the woman still hadn't learned to pronounce without hard American vowels. The woman said she sometimes coughed up green lumps after sucking it all down with a glass straw, and sometimes she shook afterward—curled in bed like the time in college when four IPAs poisoned her into the fetal position in a bar parking lot, gripping her sides while she pressed her face to a Volkswagen's oily tire.

She knew what Melody would, did, say: *You've become so used to medicine that wasn't made to love you, to even consider you human, that when something finally comes along to draw out the toxins and Repair You Whole, it's going to be intense. That's proof it's working.* On the screen, Melody widened her black-lined blue eyes with sympathy, her lashes sticking in straw-blond bangs that were a decade and a half out of style—making her look both older and younger than the woman discovered, via online sleuthing, she really was. At the end of the conversation, Melody would send her the name of a new ingredient to complete her personalized Life Cure, with an accompanying link to a foreign wholesale website, and the woman would send Melody $250 via PayPal.

The woman's breath caught in her throat as she waited for the payment to go through, but she knew Melody was right: traditional medicine was made for men, tested on men, was not made to care for women's bodies the way Melody cared for women's bodies. Melody had helped her realize this: to be a woman in this world was to crouch unseen in a dark tunnel all your life, and to be a sick woman meant to open your mouth, and for the first time, notice the shadow of flame curdling inside. Then decide how to harness it.

◆ ◆ ◆

The woman woke on the floor. She arched and flexed her foot, then the other, wiggled each of her fingers. She did this whenever she was confused: made sure her body, at least, was still there. Once she knew that, she had somewhere to begin, something to build on. She took stock of herself, each disparate bone and joint, until she figured out where the pain was coming from. Dried blood crusted her forearm, but she couldn't find a cut. She tried to lift her head and winced when her neck spasmed and snapped back like she'd been shot with a rubber band.

She sat up carefully, shifting her weight onto her thighs—those dependable, sagging lodestars. Something thick and sweet, like the odor of maple syrup, was stuck in her nostrils. There was a muffled hissing sound coming from behind her, and the woman turned to see the television flicker: close up, a tall cake spun and spun around the blunt edge of a knife, getting frosted in thick layers of sky-colored buttercream, and each time it spun back around it retreated further into the blanket of frosting, shrinking away from itself in all that blue.

The woman sat and watched the remaining light disappear through the curtains. A bird cried out in a long, strained arc that pierced the world outside. Then the room fell black.

◆ ◆ ◆

Melody grimaced as the heater in her SUV kicked on, grinding a smell like burnt graham crackers and Everclear into the car. Her husband, Jeff, had bought the new car for her with his Christmas bonus, but she suspected it was just a ploy to get leverage at the dealership where he worked. He'd unveiled the monstrosity in front of everyone when she was already three glasses deep in supermarket-brand champagne, smiling through numb cheeks at the owner's wife, who was sucking down a plate of tiny cocktail sausages. Melody chuckled, imagining them piling up directly in the plump woman's breasts and bouncing around her pillowy flesh, all those little thumbs of meat rioting to get out.

When Jeff pulled her over to him and she realized she was suddenly standing in the middle of the room, everyone watching, her smile turned icy. She wanted to pinch him and have him squirm away back to his office, like she'd once heard they do on sets of movies to make babies cry on cue. She squeezed his forearm, but he just squeezed her back, mistaking it for a sign of excitement.

The car was huge and square and too shiny, like a gaudy piece of jewelry she'd never choose for herself. At first, she waited for someone to step out—a hit man, perhaps, or a stranger serving legal papers. She waited for Jeff to open the door of the car and bring out a small box that contained her real gift. Then everyone started clapping, and she realized she was supposed to be happy.

At a standstill in the car line at her sons' school, she could feel the other moms' judgment penetrating through their vehicles, as if she alone were greedily hogging the last breath of clean air on the planet. As if it were all her fault the forests were burning and bees froze solid in their hives.

At the front of the line, the door slid open and her twin sons barreled in like clumsy foals, shoving their backpacks below the seat. Their teacher, a young, frizzy-haired woman of ambiguous heritage, peeked her head into the car.

"Jasper and Ethan had a great day today. They colored some *awesome* pictures that I put in their homework folders for you." Melody smiled the way she knew she was supposed to: warmly, generously. The teacher always hung around too long at pickup, like she was waiting for a tip.

"Are you and their dad able to make it to parent-teacher night next week?"

"We'll try," Melody said. "Their dad works long hours, and I'm an independent business owner, so I get very busy."

"You're not going to want to miss this one. There will be a raffle! Mrs. Klepman is donating a whole basket of her homemade jams," the teacher said. Melody wondered if she was Brazilian, Italian, maybe Mexican? Melody had always conceptualized Brazilian people as particularly tall, and thought Italians more aloof. Maybe the teacher was just tan.

"We know it's very important," Melody said, feigning a smile. "We'll try to make it."

On the drive home, Melody put on an audiobook and turned up the volume to blot out the boys' giggling and whining. Other than the occasional jabs to the back of her seat, as she stared forward at the road, she could almost pretend she was alone.

◆ ◆ ◆

The woman woke on the couch, not sure how she'd gotten there. She unwove her legs from the blanket, got up, peed, and smelled the sour wave drift up between her legs. Her shirt was crusted with green splatters from the last Life Cure she'd mixed—before, she suddenly remembered, the blender had shorted out. She swore into the empty room, knowing she'd have to find a way to get a new one as soon as she could. She was already feeling airy inside her skin, wavering slightly when she stood, a sensation she associated with her body's natural craving for the Life Cure now that she'd transcended the recognizable pangs of hunger.

She made a mental note to look on Craigslist for a cheap blender. Maybe someone on there would even bring it to her, if she explained her situation. People did all kinds of things for you if you told them you had cancer. At just a mention of the word, heartstrings were trained to rile so thoroughly that people usually forgot to ask anything else, even how long or what type.

She figured since she was fully awake for the first time in who knew how many days—the idea of checking the calendar to find out filled her with nauseous dread—she might as well do something productive. She rifled through the spare closet in the hall, clawing through cardboard boxes to find the extra stick of glue she knew should be there. She'd been thinking about making her next vision board spring themed, cutting around the limp, bronzed bodies of the models in magazine ads to extract the flowers and tree branches in the background. She guessed she must have had the idea while she was dreaming, that hope manifested would look something like a garden. She never remembered her dreams, but they always led to smart ideas. This would be her most inspiring vision board yet, a true sign of healing from within. She couldn't wait to show Melody.

Digging through the bottom of the closet, she stuffed back the shirts that hung above, men's cotton sleeves grazing her head as if she were being incessantly pet by ghosts. She knew they probably retained some toxic echo, and that Melody would tell her she should be taking vitamin A to shield her before she handled the shirts, but she just held her breath when she walked past and hoped that would suffice. Or, in moments like this, she pretended to ignore the items—pretended they were *only* items. Pretended to forget they were dangerous. She told herself that she'd definitely bag them up soon and drag them to the curb for someone to take away, then pretended to believe it.

The woman's partner had left so much shit in the house for her to deal with. She scowled, a smile forming behind the scowl, as she imagined telling her partner off for *leaving all his shit for her to deal with*, wagging her finger in his face like a broken-down old wife in a movie.

The woman's partner, a man who'd held her as she trembled

and howled into his chest the day she got her diagnosis, left her just before she started chemo. He said it was better for both of them to make a clean break "before things got messy." As he left their house for the last time, he'd looked back at her from the doorway and grinned sadly, the way one might look at a hotel room they'd spent a long and meaningful vacation in.

She stood there dumbly, not hating the man but wishing she did. She couldn't say much; she'd told him, when she found out, that he could leave and she wouldn't hold it against him. That she didn't want to force him through the fear and vomiting and smell on her skin like an unwashed animal—all the dramatics of disease she'd learned about from TV and blog posts. These stories had now, surprisingly, become hers, too; sickness and its processes hers to claim like a long-anticipated cultural inheritance.

The man hadn't responded, just wrapped his long arms over the woman, trapping her to his chest and shushing her, the way people did to horses. She took this to mean he would stay and comfort her through her troubles, but she realized now: he just wanted her to be quiet.

Not three months after she saw him for the last time, he was dead. Ravaged by pancreatitis in just a few weeks as the woman watched him whittle away in hopeful, emoji-filled social media posts from his teenage niece, with pictures of him smiling weakly beneath his bones. Those bones she'd touched and slid her mouth and fleshy parts all across, lazily or urgently—those bones she'd loved so much she often stared at his clavicle as he snored into her hair, feeling a great wave of sorrow that she'd never be able to actually reach up through his rib cage and slip his body over hers like a sweatshirt, to lie warm and protected beneath those bones. Those bones, at least, were left when he wasn't.

The woman felt betrayed. Even illness, which was supposed to be hers alone, had chosen him first. It was she who should be wasting away in a hospital bed, weakly smiling like the portrait of a saint. She should be surrounded by everyone she'd ever known, being told she was a "fighter," that she was "winning" just by virtue of lying there and continuing to exist. The man who had been her partner was supposed to watch her die, marvel at her new body as she shifted position and her joints turned like carousels under her pale skin. Now, she would have to grieve herself by herself.

She'd worn her most colorful headscarf to her chemo appointments, hoping he'd catch a glimpse of her in the crowded hall as she flitted past his door. She didn't know what floor he was on, but she knew the hospital liked to keep sick people clumped together, hidden away so their death aura didn't leak into the sterile white of the maternity ward or bother people recovering from boob jobs. She still had her eyelashes then, and if not for the IV in her arm, she could be mistaken for a model; bald was in fashion, and she had the right neck for it, the nurses told her. She pretended the chemicals being pumped into her blood were the man's own life force, and she was soaking up the toxic essence that remained of him, three or four or ten doors away. When she got home, she puked up yellow bile and imagined exorcising him from her insides. In those moments, she thought about how a coworker years ago had told her people puke when they do ayahuasca, sometimes even shit themselves, because the drug purges the demons you've collected unknowingly throughout childhood. After, when the woman rested the side of her face on the cool white toilet seat, her teeth caked with sour grit, she felt an ecstatic calm sweep over her. She felt purified.

When the man died, she didn't go to the funeral. She'd wanted to see him, to say goodbye to those bones she'd loved. But the thought of facing his mother, having to hold her clammy hand during the service and exchange glances with his uncles and cousins as if he were someone she still had the right to love, the right to mourn—someone who hadn't left her to shrivel and expire alone without any of the fanfare a cancer patient was due—disgusted her.

She stopped going to her chemo appointments too. There was no point. She had already sucked and purged whatever was left of the man on this earth. She woke one morning to see her eyelashes littering the pillowcase like dead ants.

The woman began to think of her cancer as an arranged marriage: a slow, bumbling fellow who would nibble at her insides over the course of many years, so that she barely noticed what was being done to her until one day she looked down and a whole organ was missing.

She was comparing the prices of mausoleums and beach houses when she came across one of Melody's videos online. When she pressed play and Melody began to speak, the woman's face relaxed, her chapped lips parting into a silent, primal O.

◆ ◆ ◆

Melody was researching new potential distributors to add to her ingredient list when the sound of the front door knocked her out of her work trance. When she heard Jeff drop his briefcase on the table and the boys stampeding to the front door, she sighed and reluctantly logged off, making sure to lock the desktop screen.

She found Jeff in the kitchen, drinking a glass of blue Kool-

Aid. The boys had already lost interest in their dad's homecoming and had run off to play with their robots and plastic rifles.

"How was work?" Melody asked, a rote pleasantry that he never returned.

"Not too bad, sold a couple sedans and a Rover," he said, a blue droplet slithering from the corner of his mouth down to his chin. "A decent day, commission-wise."

She steeled herself to sound firm, but not too firm: "So, I need you to get off early next week to go to the boys' parent-teacher thing."

"Why can't you take them?"

"I've got a client meeting that night."

"Jesus, Melody, I thought we decided you were going to stop this."

"I am! This is one of the last holdovers from before, it was scheduled out months in advance."

"You can't cancel it? I thought you were in charge of your own business, or whatever."

"She lives in *Guatemala*, Jeff." Melody sparked with rage, then swallowed it back down just as quickly. "I can't just let these people down. Sorry if it's not convenient for you to be married to a person of moral conviction, but I keep the promises I make."

He just stood there, thinking about how to respond. His thoughtful silences only further enraged her.

"Well, anyway, the deposit's already spent, so I have to take it now."

"Fine, but this is it. No more. I mean it."

"Okay, fine. But you can handle Thursday?" She gathered her blond hair in both hands like she was going to wring it into a weapon.

"Sure, yeah, okay," he gave in. "I can try to make it work." He poured another glass of the unnaturally blue juice and took it away with him to the bedroom.

Melody began gathering ingredients from the cabinets in preparation to cook dinner. Though she took little pleasure in the act of feeding her family, as she knew mothers were supposed to, she enjoyed how time slid away while cooking. She put on an audiobook and zoned out to the blurring cadence of someone else's voice. She chopped carrots, split celery, pounded away at a pink chicken breast as if it were any old flesh at all.

She almost hadn't lived through giving birth. People knew this about her now—it was a featured part of her business's story—but for a while, the fact that so many people had witnessed her undeniable frailty was a shame she held secret. Her uterus ruptured pushing out the twins, sending her into preeclampsia, and she almost bled out on the table. The delivery doctor, a thin, redheaded man with a mustache like a janitor's broom, wanted to cut her uterus out rather than spend the extra time repairing it, but she refused. She didn't want any more children. She just wanted to leave with everything she'd brought into the building.

Postpartum, sitting in a diaper of her own blood and organ tissue, she looked around and noticed for the first time that her husband, even her male doctors, seemed to feel so little, while she felt so much it made her want to claw her skin open, to wail and bolt away from herself. Even her infant sons cried only for practical reasons—to let her know they hungered, or thirsted, or had wet themselves. Otherwise, they slept or just lay there, staring up at the popcorned ceiling with blank blue eyes. How was she the only one who squirmed and suffered, while these men around her went on about their lives as if their bodies didn't matter, as if the few, measly stirrings of their hearts had nothing to do with them?

This is not me, Melody thought. *These emotions are not of me. They snuck inside me from somewhere else.*

She began to research toxic shock syndrome, leaky gut syndrome, and all the other syndromes. Now that she had clarity around the problem, she was relentless in her search for answers.

The answer came to her in the dark center of the night: the babies began to yowl and Jeff shook her awake, then rolled back over. She sobbed and begged Jeff to go instead—offering money, housework, sexual favors—but he just lay there, turned away from her, pretending to be asleep. Melody felt a sharp shock run the length of her spine, electric and abundantly painful. But as soon as she opened her mouth to cry out, it disappeared. As she nursed the boys, glaring over at the lump of Jeff beside her, it was startlingly obvious to her, so obvious she wanted to laugh. It explained the tragic life of every woman she'd ever known.

Women's bodies were like sponges, and men's were like cell towers; men radiated their emotions, toxic discharges—everything—outward, and women absorbed it all. This was why men moved through the world as if nothing were holding them back. They'd given away all their burdens, and women, by animal instinct and without their knowledge, had sucked them up and hoarded burdens inside themselves that were not their own to carry.

Before she was a mother, Melody worked as a paralegal, and she used those skills to double down on her research, sleeping only a few hours each night. Eventually, she came across a clean-eating forum where some woman with the username Kamiii2313 posted a green juice recipe that she claimed put her breast cancer in remission. Usually in these forums, "clean eating" was code for a morally zealous form of anorexia, but food as a balm for disease intrigued her. She'd already been keeping a list of antioxidant foods, such as lemon rinds and organic goji berries, which she made sure to eat each morning before she came in contact with her husband or her sons, whose combined toxicity she sensed building like a storm cloud. When she attempted to hug the twins, she was put off by a faint buzzing from their bodies. The buzz emanating from Jeff was even stronger; she could hardly stand to occupy the same room as him anymore.

She drank the green juice, altering the recipe to add ionized rock salt (for its ancient protective properties) and kelp powder (an anti-inflammatory), and she found after just a week that her feelings became less intense. Her emotions retreated into the new shadows forming in her hip bones and hamstrings. Emptiness was her safe place, and the green juice was her armor. Melody could finally choose not to feel, as was her human birthright.

And now that she had the Cure, she decided, she would use it to build a life that was all her own. She would make a career out of healing womankind.

◆ ◆ ◆

Within an hour, the woman located a used blender online and got in touch with the person who owned it, who offered to bring it by later that day, claiming they had errands to run in the woman's neighborhood. Even if she'd been in the practice of leaving her house, she had gone too many hours without a drop of Life Cure in her system to trust herself out in the world. Who knew what she might encounter, or who might, as Melody had warned, *thrust their brain waves up against hers and contaminate her with their sorrow, anger, desire, guilt*—any of those old knaves she'd worked to weed out? Without immunity to her body's impulses, those sensitive frequencies the Life Cure cauterized, she was an open sore inviting infection.

Her phone pinged with a text from the blender Samaritan that read: *It's Reesa Have your item At the door now*, like they were friends who'd long ago passed beyond the social graces of punctuation.

Reesa was a hearty, midwestern-looking lady, a head and a half taller than the woman. Her short, bleached white hair was gelled into points all over her head, and she held the blender, ten dollars and advertised as "basically new-ish," in her arms like a baby doll. A young, chubby boy in a marshmallow-green T-shirt and shorts stood beside her in the doorway.

"Thanks for coming all this way," the woman said, and slid Reesa the cash through the cracked door.

"Not a problem at all," Reesa said, placing jovial emphasis on every other word. The woman prepared to shut the door, but Reesa cleared her throat loudly.

"Do you mind if Arnold uses your bathroom real quick? I told him to go before we left, but . . ." She shrugged. "Sorry."

The woman didn't want anyone in her space, particularly strangers who, for all she knew, could be a mother-son grifter team, but she found herself a little queasy at the idea of being the reason a child wets their pants.

"Real quick," she echoed. "Okay."

"Ah, thanks, it's a big help," Reesa said, and little Arnold in his sweaty monochrome bumbled into the house alongside her. The woman pointed down the hall, and Arnold went wordlessly.

The woman found herself unable to look Reesa in the eyes, feeling awkward and unsure what to say. One symptom Melody's treatment hadn't been able to relieve was the guilt that compelled her to entertain whoever was in front of her, to be cordial and accommodating, no matter what *she* wanted in the moment. The woman could barely gather the energy to stand firmly on her own two haunches, much less whip up small talk, but Reesa enthusiastically filled the gaps.

"So, the thing about this blender—sometimes if you put something hot in it, like soup, the lid wants to come up, so you've gotta make sure you press it down hard. Otherwise you'll get a mess on your hands. Had to learn that the hard way!" Reesa chuckled, and the woman couldn't help but imagine Reesa's pointy hair splattered in tomato soup, her wide mouth comically agape. Having known her for two minutes, the woman strongly suspected Reesa would respond even to this with a bellowing laugh.

"Thanks," the woman said. "I'll probably just use it for smoothies."

Reesa lit up. "You going on one of those smoothie cleanses? I tried all that, the protein powder, the celery-juice diet—that one cost me a whole hunking hundred-dollar machine I never use either, should probably put the juicer up for sale, too, at this point—or that one where you only drink spicy lemonade. I was on that *kee-to* for a minute, but I couldn't handle the grease, got indigestion all the time. It's true what they say, it's so much harder to lose weight after having a kid! Do you have kids?"

"No."

"Well, it is. Anyway, I hope the smoothie thing works out for you. Not that you need it." She looked the woman up and down approvingly. "You look fantastic. So slender."

"Thanks," the woman mumbled. It surprised her to realize, hearing Reesa tangled up in the anxiety-vacuum of dieting (a pastime the woman had also been a faithful devotee to, for all the eras of her life before she got sick), that it had been a long time since she'd concerned herself with what her body looked like. She supposed the Life Cure made her thinner, but she barely noticed herself in that way anymore, and mostly avoided touching her body directly if she could.

"So, no kids, then," Reesa went on, a too-friendly tone in her voice. "You have a husband?"

"No," the woman replied. "I have cancer."

The woman braced herself, almost pleasurably, for the look of shock on Reesa's face, the sugary, exaggerated display of sympathy that was about to flow forth. Instead, Reesa frowned slightly and cocked her head.

"Oh, honey, that must be so hard."

The woman didn't know what to say, how to respond, how to communicate that no one, not a nurse or chaplain or by-stander in all her doctor's appointments, or the texts she got from well-meaning friends who stopped sending them when she stopped chemo, had acknowledged that yes, it was hard, so fucking scary to feel your days draining out of you with no way to plug the hole, no one who saw terror beyond their own when they saw you, so hard.

The woman opened her mouth to respond, but then the toilet flushed loudly, and Arnold shuffled out of the bathroom. She watched the boy being herded dutifully out the door by his mother, and felt tenderness toward Reesa and her small, awk-ward son. There was an emotion that slid through whatever part of the woman was still cracked open to feeling, and it was a little golden *yes*, a little warmth. It was gone before she registered its presence.

When they left, it took the woman a long moment to blend back into the silence.

◆ ◆ ◆

After the boys had been put to bed and Jeff was planted in front of the TV in the den, Melody returned to her desktop and performed the reluctant ritual of checking her social media. Quickly, like digging through the trash for something important that fell in, she held her breath and clicked through the notifications: DMs bearing dick pics and rape threats, a few messages of thanks, spam, and requests for promos sprinkled among them. Mentions in strangers' statuses that she only let herself catch glimpses of before untagging her name and closing out the tabs: *scammer, liar, changed my life, wacky cunt, fraud, savior, tag twenty friends for discount Ray-Bans.* She didn't even look anymore at the videos that popped up when she googled her name, the ones labeled *DOCTORS REACT*, with thumbnails of fame-seeking naysayers contorting their faces in exaggerated shock over Melody's YouTube lectures.

That Melody was not especially apt at social media was to her benefit. She didn't brand herself as an influencer, like those young Californians who made money posting their slim limbs folded into yoga poses, gaining millions of shame-ridden, jealousy-crazed fans. She was a regular person, *a mom*, who spoke to a particular group of silently desperate women. She never gave advice outside of private meetings, she was not flashy, and though petitions to remove her account occasionally popped up, the virtual authorities—whoever they were—assumed someone like her was ultimately harmless. Melody might have imagined her lack of publicity know-how would hurt her business, but on the contrary, it seemed to make clients all the hungrier to meet with her. She was controversial but mysteriously so, enough like them to feel approachable but different enough to spark admiration; the clients who found their way to her felt they were getting something exclusive and were willing to pay more for it. In terms of internet wellness culture, she was practically a shaman in a cave.

The online militia who formed parallel to Melody's career were always there, it seemed, complaining in all caps about the price of her Life Cure ingredients, her appearance, the tenor of her voice, her lack of medical training. (She did give in once and explain in a lengthy comment that these days, with all of human knowledge at their fingertips, anybody could become an expert if they asked the right questions. And anyway, she'd stated outright on her website that she had no medical training, which was exactly why women trusted her; traditional medicine was created by men who regarded women as property to lay their burdens upon, not experiential beings who would carry on the energy of those burdens. The medical establishment carried sexism in its DNA, failing women time and time again, so obviously the "experts" could not be trusted.) Melody's small group of decriers were just measly shouts in an endless sea of people with endless opinions on how strangers chose to live.

And sure, there were the more serious claims: two or three people who'd tried Life Cure—only one of whom had been a paying client, Melody made sure to point out—claimed it caused them numb hands, vomiting, kidneys hardened like lumps of agate, *acute* seizures, and whatever else their bodies saddled them with that they blamed Melody for. Then, when one of her clients died, a woman with terminal colon cancer she'd met with twice a week for two months, the husband filed a lawsuit; when that didn't stick, he filed a child endangerment suit against Melody for encouraging the woman to feed Life Cure to her daughters.

It was then that Melody was invited to appear as a guest on a talk show. An opportunity to explain the misunderstanding and "gain exposure to a captive audience of the American people," as the producers put it in their email. She accepted immediately.

At first, she planned to keep the whole thing a secret from Jeff, like most of her work had been so far—due more to his disinterest than active manipulation on her part, which sometimes felt more disappointing than being forced to lie. Even when she was served the lawsuit, Jeff didn't seem too concerned; she'd assured him it was just a grieving wacko from the internet lashing out. But as the weekend of the taping drew closer, she couldn't resist telling Jeff. It's not that she *just* wanted to gloat (although it was satisfying to finally have a reason to), she wanted him to see that what she was doing mattered to people, that she was important too. Maybe even more important than he was.

But he didn't give her the response she'd fantasized about. Instead of being impressed, he seemed annoyed at her for leaving him alone with the boys for a full day and night, on the weekend no less, when he planned to claim the relaxation he was owed. He offered a flat "Congratulations" and a dry kiss on the cheek, as if that were worth a parade in itself.

As soon as the cameras began rolling and the host began to question her—a bald white man whose eyebrows were drawn on so harshly he looked nearly rabid with excitement—and the audience booed on cue while video of the dead woman's husband played on the screen above, she realized she was not there to tell her side of the story. She was there to burn: a sacrificial effigy of every disease, every bombing, every bankruptcy, every unacknowledged terror that humans can't control.

She could hardly hear what the talk-show host was asking her under the sizzle of the heat lamps, but she sat up straight and spat out that yes, she'd heard reports of the handful that died, most of them deathly sick before they'd even heard of her, many of them from drinking bootleg Life Cure recipes they scrounged up online to avoid paying for a consultation. And no, she did not feel responsible, because what killed them wasn't her Life Cure, it was their life.

"Look," Melody said, raising her voice into a register that might be perceived as charming, "nobody is trying to cure their life if their life is already healthy. There are other factors, things that are too deep-seated for even the *client* to recognize when I begin treating them."

The audience jeered and shook their fists, and the host clapped a little clap along with them, one hand slapping the cue cards he held in the other. He stared her down under those arched gashes, a purplish light cast over them both. He asked if she was saying, right there, for all the viewers across their land of the free and brave to hear, that she blamed the woman for her own death.

The audience shushed, whispers clicking around the room as they lay in wait to flay her.

"I think *blame* is the wrong word," Melody began hesitantly. The crowd's mouths hung open, teeth at the ready.

"Some women, I think, have been conditioned to become comfortable in pain. And usually, if they're having a reaction to Life Cure that they don't enjoy, it means they can't push through to a place of anti-feeling—they're too used to being guided by Female Toxic Burden. They give up because suffering is their normal, and healing is uncomfortable."

Within minutes of the episode airing, the deluge of messages began. The couple of social media accounts she did have, though she barely used them for Life Cure, all got pummeled with threats and expletives, then flagged and temporarily suspended.

That was worrisome, but before the weekend was over, it spread beyond her: strangers got ahold of her private Facebook friends list and sent unhinged screeds to her in-laws, even her old boss at the legal office from a decade ago, informing them they were murderers by association. Someone made a fake profile and catfished as her late mother's uncle Rand, messaging Melody to pry her address out of her, with the excuse that it was to send a "Chrissmass card" in May. Though she blocked them and didn't allow herself to follow the thought through, she shivered to consider who would've shown up if she'd given it, and what they would've done.

Jeff was close to clueless a lot of the time, but even he saw that things had gotten out of control. And Melody couldn't deny it had become an all-consuming hassle either. She looked over her shoulder everywhere she went, listening carefully for an extra set of footsteps echoing hers. Not to mention that her neighbors, friends, the parents at her sons' school, even the working men around town whose eyes usually followed her like anxious puppies—they all avoided looking her in the face. It turned out Jeff had told his coworkers at the dealership all about Melody's impending appearance on the talk show. He'd been proud of her after all—or wanted to tack Melody's new status as a TV star onto his own reputation, she guessed. Anyway, those people had all watched the show, too, and went out of their way never to mention it, except in hurried, jolted whispers.

Yes, it had gotten out of control, threatened the ease of her life, her family's. She admitted as much to Jeff, and when he asked her to shut down the business, she agreed to. But with the swarm of malice also came an untapped hive of new clients, and she continued to schedule appointments in secret.

It was just when she thought the harassment had begun to die down, after two or three relatively peaceful days, when the

vacant accounts of her former clients were hacked: social media profiles abandoned by the dead were commandeered into an
anti-Melody collective. A handful of these zombie accounts still
swirled around somewhere on the internet, circling her from a
distance. Harmless as de-winged wasps.

It wasn't that Melody didn't care. Of course it saddened
her to know she couldn't save everyone. But sadness, thankfully, was a feeling that no longer penetrated her without her
permission.

After she flew back from the talk-show taping, on a night
much like the one she sat in now, her children already asleep, Jeff
snoring above the looping theme of a DVD menu, she searched
for the woman who died. The woman had been making vlogs for
twenty-three days leading up to her death, and with each new
video she claimed to be more hopeful, to feel her cells regener-
ating, while on-screen her eyes grew more bloodshot, and her
gums protruded farther from her teeth. In one of the videos, a
child walked into frame to tug at the hem of the woman's shirt
hard, as if trying to pull her into the child's small world, de-
manding she stay right where she was.

Melody felt her face contract, her chest opening like a great
cloud. She ran to the kitchen and ripped a paper towel off the
roll to muffle what was almost a scream—it surprised her, how
the noise came out of her like a long train screeching away from
the rails, then petered out in a trembling whine. To be there,
and then not. How did anyone know which part was which until it was too late?

She held the paper towel to her tear ducts, precisely, until
the itchy cotton was wet with black-tinted liquid. She had a
video meeting scheduled for later that night. There would be no
time, no time at all, to fix her makeup.

◆ ◆ ◆

One of Melody's most popular videos was titled "You Too Can Cure Your Life Banish Female Toxic Burden and Repair You Whole," and at night when the woman's head swirled with static and the muscles in her legs cramped and burned until she couldn't sleep, she'd watch it on her laptop, piled to the neck with blankets in the dark theater of her bedroom.

FTB is the disease we are born into, Melody's voice rang out through the tinny speakers, *but it is not an incurable one. You have the choice. Do you choose to be sick, or do you choose to rid yourself of toxic matter and make your body a clean place to live again? Do you want to be a sponge for all the world's grief—which many women do, by the way, live and die this way without knowing why they're always in pain—or do you choose to lay down those burdens, tell the world "You carry it now," and thrive in your body?*

The woman knew the words by heart, to this video and another called "Life Cure's Healing Properties Fix Marriages Women and Their Offspring." She also knew by memory all the outfits and accessories Melody wore in her videos. During one of their sessions early on, Melody had worn the same gray pearl earrings she had on in "Take Charge of Your Personal Life Force and Rid Your Flesh of Biological Dis-ease," and the woman had to stop herself from squealing or reaching out to touch Melody's earlobes on the screen. She couldn't believe that not only did she have a personal relationship with a celebrity, but also that Melody saw something in the woman that was important enough for Melody to dedicate her time to helping her get better. When she thought about it like that, it nearly made the woman's eyes swell with tears—it would have before the Life Cure worked its magic in her, sweeping her heart clean as an empty ballroom.

Now, when she began to have an emotion, when her mouth got slobbery and the itch in her throat rose, her body snatched it away from her, drug the feeling back down and dissolved it in the medicine of her Cure. She had gotten so much better, since Melody started helping her, at not feeling. Panic, hope, or yearning were no longer forces that possessed her, just gray blurs on the map of her mind that she could watch drift past, observing them without believing they had anything to do with her. At this stage, she was almost reduced entirely to physical sensations—and though much of her body sensed itself in pain much of the time, she reminded herself it was temporary. That was the goal: to snuff out Female Toxic Burden until there were no emotions to bear, just sensations to experience. A person could thrive that way—not just have a life, but live.

The woman shut her laptop and lay back, the mountain of blankets fossilizing her in soft and swallowing warmth. With her eyes closed, she imagined herself hidden in a glacier, waiting to emerge through the cracked ice when the time was right.

She listened to the fan panting above, her breath sliding out in slow streams. She took stock of each of her limbs, her toes, her torso, her eyelids. The ache that answered back meant she was still there. For too long she believed she only existed for certain in the contrast of pain, but now she knew she deserved better, and that she could have it. She inventoried her sharp wheeze, brittle fingernails splitting away from the raw, shiny skin beneath, pellet-size lumps that bruised and never faded—and slid out from under it all. The toxins of men, their messy needs and desires that devoured hers until she was a stranger to herself, she imagined bleeding out of her body as a mustard-colored gas. Then she envisioned the white light that would come next, burrowing through the microscopic cracks in her bones until she was lit from within.

She would be whole: her body, her bones, her light to live inside. And live, and live.

THE BOX

Here's a fun fact most people don't know about us: in our basement, we keep a box that's exactly big enough for two people to stand inside of. We call it The Box. It's an idea my therapist from a few years ago came up with, and she said it works very well for some couples. The idea is that you stand in The Box and say the things you don't want to say in the rest of the house, in the rest of your life. It's an exercise in communication. Also, my therapist said it's a good idea not to argue in front of the children. That's another thing The Box is good for. She was actually a couple's therapist, but I was the only one who went to the sessions. I don't see her anymore, and I wonder if she's still in favor of The Box. I wonder how many Boxes there are in how many basements in this neighborhood alone. It's not the kind of thing you can bring up during polite conversation.

At first, it was hard to get the kids not to play in The Box, so I told them it was a house for monsters. Lilac said, *If the monsters' house is inside our house, what is our house inside of?* I told her, *The ozone layer. Or America. It depends on what your point of view is.* Lilac is eight, and I imagine her insides are crisp and white like the long, sterilized hallways of a hospital, lined with painted doors that could hold anything behind them—escaped convicts or brick walls or literal magic. Charlie is four, and I imagine his insides are piles of golden lions basking in sunlit fields.

Matt went along with the story because it kept the kids out of the basement, where his power tools are, and now he doesn't have to worry about anybody slicing off a finger while he's not paying attention. This has always been a concern for him, and I think it's been a big weight off his shoulders since the monsters came into the picture. Paying attention isn't always his strong suit.

■

There are reasons I fell in love with Matt, but they all feel like stories now: Once upon a time I was in the park feeling so impossibly lonely that I thought my bones were going to fall out of my body just to escape from me. I was very, very young, but I didn't know it at the time. If someone had come up to me then and said, *You are very young, don't you know there are all kinds of situations and emotions you haven't experienced yet?* I might have punched them in the face or flipped them off with both hands, both middle fingers.

That's a lie; I probably would have just looked over their shoulder and mumbled in agreement, then resented them for the next couple of days. Or cried with joy and later come to believe they were some kind of guardian angel. That day at the park, my nerves were so raw with melancholy that I could almost feel them sizzling and curling up under my skin, like when you light a piece of your hair on fire just to see what will happen.

Once upon a time I was lonely in the park and it doesn't matter why, but I found a penny on the sidewalk with a piece of gum stuck on one side of it and picked it up anyway. I closed my eyes and threw it into a fountain and wished that any human being would talk to me so that I knew I actually existed. When I opened my eyes, Matt was bent down on one knee in front of me, tying his shoe. That is one of the reasons I fell in love with him. There must have been other reasons, but I don't remember them now.

■

Dinner is like prayer: we are all hoping for different things when we say it. Lilac wants green beans on the left side of her plate and plain spaghetti noodles on the right. Charlie wants chicken nuggets with ketchup. This is unacceptable to Lilac—tiny, excited vegetarian. *You're eating people!* she shrieks at her brother. I remind her chickens aren't the same as people, and she retorts, *Chicken people are people to each other. Just because they don't have hands and can't make buildings* . . . Charlie begins to cry. Matt tells Charlie to eat spaghetti, and Charlie haggles, *With hands, then,* to which Matt and I sigh and say fine, just this once. I rinse Lilac's noodles over the sink to *Make them all the way plain,* and Charlie stuffs his between his grin like a feral child feasting on worms. Matt stands by to collect stray pasta in a napkin, rescue stains from the floor with superhuman speed, and now he wants to be done. I assemble my own congealing plate of food while he rinses the dishes, then takes his chopped-up spaghetti to the bedroom. The kids get bored and run off. As I sit at the table alone, there's a soft pulsing through the carpet, an almost imperceptible vibration traveling up through the soles of my feet. A slight, magnetic tug that redirects my center of gravity downward. The Box's reminder that it's right below, sitting alone too.

What do I want from this temperamental god named Dinner? To see this moment from the vantage point of myself ten years ago, like I've just slipped inside the most perfect dream. To see the light in my eyes as more than the glare of waning fluorescents.

■

This is what The Box looks like:

The Box is not one box, but two. Two individual refrigerator boxes merged with a staple gun, the glinting metal in the sides like hospital-grade stitches. The Box is plain, cardboard-colored brown, and says MILK HUT in big white letters up the side, which is the brand of refrigerator that went inside it. Matt says it is *not* actually a play on the word *Malkhut*, which to Jewish mystics means *the worldly emanation of the divine*. The name just means a fun place to store your milk.

From the outside, it looks like a discount time machine, or a place to hang extra clothes you don't need except for that one week per year of undeniable winter, because most of winter isn't cold enough for a sweater anymore. Nowadays a sweater is more of a symbol, a story we tell ourselves about familiar, nonthreatening transitions. But The Box also looks like the kind of box that could be saying: *What's a family without sweaters in the winter, which is coming any day as it always has, and anyway, we have all this storage space!* Or it might just look like a piece of trash no one needed but no one knew how to remove, so it stayed in the basement and now wild animals rummage around in it.

On the inside, though, The Box is painted light blue, like the sky. Like standing in a sliver of cloud on a shiny, North Carolina morning. Matt painted it that way. But Matt didn't think about what happens when you close the cardboard cutout door. When you close yourself inside The Box, everything is pure black, even your own hand in front of your face.

The trick is this: You have to try really hard to remember the color of the sky right before you close the door, or else it's gone forever.

James William, aka Jim-Bill, is Matt's father. Jim-Bill comes over to our house to garden in the backyard every other Sunday, even though weeds don't grow that fast. He calls it his place of worship. I don't know how I feel about that. I'd prefer he call it something more neutral, like sanctuary, but Matt says it's something he's always said about nature in general and doesn't have to do with our particular backyard.

When Jim-Bill comes over to garden, he tracks mud into the house, which I will usually clean up. Matt's mom doesn't tell Jim-Bill not to track mud into the house, and also doesn't come over to our house at all, because she died of a brain aneurysm when Matt was seven. She was at the grocery store when it happened, which seems so 1960s, so housewife. Pictures tell me she was the kind of lady who, from birth, looked like she was meant to die in a grocery store.

Matt told me his father said his mother was buried in their backyard, under the flower bed, and Jim-Bill would go there to whisper into the soil. Matt believes this story proves his father is a liar, but all people are liars at least half the time, and who's to say which half Jim-Bill was occupying?

Jim-Bill comes over early on Sunday, and Matt makes pancakes for breakfast and we eat them on a blue car-tarp on the ground, like a picnic. Jim-Bill brings a wiry pear tree with him and digs a hole for it, but for some reason or another he can't plant it today. He puts Charlie in the hole and pretends to plant him instead. Charlie lifts his arms and pretends to sprout. Matt plays trees with them for a while, then goes inside to do work on his laptop. I give Lilac some leftover bread crusts to feed to the stray cat that hangs around, a gray tabby she named Little Belly, because his little belly sways when he walks. Little Belly is technically a stray, but every house on our street feeds him on occasion. I'm sure each house has a different name for him too. Little Belly has lived a multitude of lives, beyond just the nine that cats are supposedly endowed with.

This time, Little Belly gets rowdy with her and scratches and Jim-Bill kicks at him, calls him a rodent and tells him to scram. Jim-Bill gets in Lilac's face and scolds her for feeding him. Jim-Bill comes from a different generation, where communal pets were a nuisance and not a beautiful learning experience in interspecies compassion. Anyway, it causes a big scene, and Matt comes outside because of the noise, and tells Lilac and Charlie to go to their rooms because they're not in trouble, necessarily, but everyone needs some cooling-off time. Jim-Bill tells us bye and leaves. He says he will be back next week to finish planting the pear tree.

■

I remembered one of the other reasons: At the beach, Matt told me for the first time how his mother died. I was wearing a floppy yellow hat, which suddenly felt wildly inappropriate. He laughed after he told me because he knew how ridiculous it all was: the sand, the waves, the birds, his dead mom, the sun, my floppy hat pretending to be the sun.

He laughed and his eyes sparkled green, and I couldn't imagine that I would ever be capable of loving someone whose eyes weren't so perfectly green. He had brown hair that day and still does, but now it's less brown, like some of the color has been washed out from being a person for so long. His hair was so brown then, and his eyes were so green they made my teeth ache.

He grabbed my hand and pulled me toward the waves, and we dove in with our full clothes and bodies. Our fingers remained laced, salt water running between them as if to say to each other, *I have come all this way to know you.*

■

Sitting up in bed, I gently drag my fingernails over Lilac's back. This is our ritual, something my mother did for me, and my grandmother did for her. An inheritance for the women of our family.

Beneath our fingernails are murky slivers of rainbow, left by the nontoxic paint we used on plastic stained-glass hummingbirds that afternoon. Charlie wore himself out and fell into bed hours ago. He will be up with the pale blue echoes of morning, his small heart pounding the rhythm of wild horses, jumping on the bed and begging for cereal.

I still my scratching, and Lilac wiggles to let me know she's still awake. She says, *What are tendrils?*

I don't know, exactly. Something like tentacles, but not quite.

We learned about octopuses, how their hands suck to hold on, she offers. *They vomit black.*

It's ink, I say, *to keep the ocean from bleaching in the sun.*

Why do people honk cars?

Because it's hard to remember other people are living their lives too. Especially in cars.

Do pigs have inner lives?

Probably.

They're smarter than dogs. Dad said.

I didn't know that, but I'm sure he's right.

I'm going to close my eyes now. Don't leave.

I don't, because I know it's hard to believe other people are still there when you can't see them.

I sit and wait patiently for Lilac's breathing to grow slow and heavy, like waiting for whipped cream to clot into white clouds under a whisk. In the calm vanilla girl-scent of Lilac's bedroom, my mind strays. I am thinking about how my high school history teacher told me after her divorce she bought a wedding dress at a thrift store, how it struck me still—that desperate thrust between delusion and hope. I am remembering a book I read when I was fourteen, about a woman who was smart and beautiful and worked hard to have the best haircut and like good music, and then she became a mom and stopped reading *National Geographic*. I hadn't known until then that I should fear outliving myself.

The story goes: She left her family, drove out to the desert, and lived in an adobe cottage. There might have been a man named Javier or Roberto or Todd who cooked her chili, or she might have been alone. All those years later, she met her kids in a diner, and instead of telling the daughter her hair reminded her of raw honey, the woman kept talking about the wallpaper and the train and how she learned to whistle. Forgiveness was there but no one said if it was a gun or a blanket or the outline of something underneath a blanket, which direction it was moving in. I don't remember what happened to the kids, who were grown up now and didn't look like her except in sleep. I read somewhere that people start to look like their pets. I hope that woman's children were happy.

After a second, I add, *Octopi.*

What kind of pie? Lilac asks.

Never mind. Sleep, now.

Think of the last time you drank coffee alone. Think of the last time you held a real seashell in your hand. Think of the last time you sat in an empty room with the lights off, reminding yourself that you're here, you're still right here.

We're watching TV after the kids are in bed when I ask Matt if he ever thinks about Savannah, and he knows what I mean but he doesn't say anything.

When Matt is not speaking, The Box is aching underneath our feet. An audible emptiness, the static yawn of a portal to what can't or shouldn't be said. In the most blaring silences, it slips its dark hooks in me, and I can almost feel myself aching back at it.

I would never mention Savannah in The Box. Even though it was the reason for the therapist, The Box, this whole ritual, I'm afraid if I brought Savannah up in there, where he couldn't escape it, the contract would be broken; Matt would clam up, go silent, and stay that way. We sit on the couch saying none of that as the TV flickers with glimpses of different people's lives, light washing over our bodies and away.

Think of all the people you'd never get the chance to meet, even if things had turned out differently. Like Marie Curie, or Vincent van Gogh. Van Gogh could have been your soulmate, if he'd only been alive in the same sliver of time and space as you. You could have lived for the sight of his fiery orange hair and windmill eyes, his arched brow like a crooked wheat field. He could have painted sunflowers and named them after your smile. Or he could have been your best friend and given you advice on warm, wine-drinking nights about how to talk to a boy you think is cute or which new city to move to next.

When I say Savannah, what I mean is: *That time we were visiting my parents in Savannah and our last child died.* It was less than two years after Charlie was born. I was six months pregnant. There was a shock of blood, then the hallucinatory hospital, and the baby was a girl. She was stillborn. Still, born.

Impossibly tiny fingernails, impossibly tiny dark eyelashes. The doctors wrapped her in a white-speckled cloth they usually reserve for babies born alive. Even in its slack incompleteness, her face was lined with Matt's face and lined with another face that didn't seem like mine. My mother's? Her skin blotched floral in purple and red. Almost violets.

I had never seen Matt cry so easily. The tears just fell out of him, and he was nearly smiling. He had seen a glorious glimpse of *what-if* and then put it back inside a dark drawer, and I could see in his face that he would set the entire house on fire before opening that drawer again. He touched her forehead and left the room, and I didn't cry, I just stared at the silence.

I think of my violet baby and wonder if she would have been a painter. Would she fall in love with van Gogh, or shun Impressionism for something more practical? Maybe she would think art was boring and ask to be sent to math camp in the summer.

I wonder if Matt saw her as a painter. Or if he thought she'd grow up to be a teacher or a lawyer or a trophy wife. It's impossible for two people to see anything in exactly the same way, especially a person, especially if that person is dead. Think of all the flowers you spent long days planting, only to see them ice and wilt. Touching the inevitability of winter makes it easier to forgive the summer.

■

The phone call is for Matt, and I don't realize it's one of *those* phone calls until it's already over. *It's Dad,* he says. I think he means that was who was on the phone, but he doesn't.

There's been—I don't know. We have to go to the hospital. His panic holds steady with a rooted calm that's almost more unsettling.

Wow is all I can think to say. The shape my mouth makes is oblong and too raspberry. *I'm calling Gloria.* The neighbor. *To stay with the kids,* I realize. *Yes.* Matt is good in a crisis. Probably because his mother died when he was young. I wonder if this is what he heard grown-ups say then, if that's how he learned what he should do now. I wonder which neighbor came to stay with him when Jim-Bill went to the hospital to retrieve his already-dead wife. If he knew before he left the house that the situation was hopeless, or if he thought he was running toward some window of goodbye that had already shut.

This doesn't seem like the right time to ask, so instead, I offer to drive.

■

"What was the last thing he said to you?"

"He said he'd come back. To plant the tree. He ran out of mulch."

"That's it?"

"Yeah. And 'love you.' Pretty sure he said 'love you.' He must have. Right?"[1]

"Are you crying?"

"No. What do you remember?"[2]

"I don't know if it was the *last* thing, but in the yard he was telling me about a dream he had. Something like, 'I had a dream about the future,' and I asked if it was, like, a general future, with flying cars and a woman president, or if it was our particular future—"

"Jesus, just. What did he say?"

"He just shook his head—you know the way he does. Did. And . . . actually, I don't remember what he said."[3]

---

1 If I were to tell the full, honest truth here, if that's what this space is for, I don't actually remember if Jim-Bill said "love you" to his son the last time he'd ever see him. But sometimes it doesn't matter if the story is true if it feels true. I wanted to give Matt that story.

2 Dying is normal, especially parents dying, everyone says that. By everyone, I mostly mean Dr. Phil and some bookstore workers I asked about it once.

3 But I realized: Matt is an orphan now. And being a thirty-seven-year-old orphan probably isn't any better than being a seven-year-old orphan. Maybe it's worse, because you had time to get used to the idea of yourself as a parented person. Present tense. Maybe the whiplash of the past tense is the hardest part.

"Are you kidding."

"No, I'm really sorry, I just realized—that's when the whole thing happened with Lilac and the cat."

"Why would you mention it in the first place, then?"[4]

"I don't know. I'm sorry."

[...]

"I guess sometimes I worry if I don't keep talking, you'll never talk at all."

"Yeah. Well. Some things are worse than not talking."[5]

---

4 *If it's just one more thing we can't know,* he meant.

5 He was crying. I could hear his soggy breath. I did not want to kiss him, but I wanted to give him something. A way to understand what I meant without me needing to mean it so much. A way for him to walk out of here free.

The first time we saw each other naked was ten years ago on a pullout couch in the middle of the afternoon, and then we fucked for days, weeks, years. We fucked like we were making up for all the seconds in time and history that we hadn't spent fucking each other. I sucked the skin behind his earlobe like, *I'm sorry I will one day become a ghost that is separate from the ghost you'll be. Put your fingers inside me and pretend we can stay.* He tangled his hand in my hair and flicked his tongue into my mouth like, *I'm sorry I didn't know you sooner. Let me dissolve to dust beside the bare light of you, making sure you never again feel anything less than completely necessary to the ongoing existence of the universe.* The degradation of years can't free us from this thirst. It's almost too much to bear.

On the morning of Jim-Bill's funeral, the sun is unnaturally bright and everyone is sweating into their black clothing. On the car ride, Lilac complains she feels car sick and no amount of air-conditioning can soothe her, so she sticks her head out the car window like a panting dog and I let her. Matt drives. Charlie sleeps. I forget how little he is until I see him with his eyes closed.

The room where the wake takes place is covered in a mustard wallpaper that's almost furry with dust. I anticipate a sneeze just looking at it. Matt says nothing, moving to the opposite side of the room. He says nothing almost the whole day.

He walks away and I expect to feel The Box shaking behind the walls, to sense its slow, hollow moaning. While no one is looking, I actually reach out and touch the wallpaper, surprised by my hunger for the familiar heavy darkness to greet my touch. But here, there is no Box; Matt's absence is an empty thing, like a tote bag you carry around all day only to realize it has a hole in the bottom, and everything you owned fell out onto the street blocks ago.

Charlie is still sleeping, and Matt carries him over his shoulder right up to Jim-Bill's body, planted in the coffin like a maggot in a wooden chrysalis. Waxy under the lights, the eyeliner makes his gruff mug almost pretty. Old ladies approach Matt for hugs with angular bodies.

This windowless room is a kind of Box, though; funerals and coffins are contained places where people will forgive you for the truth, or pretend to forget. No one knows what to say, all hushed whispers that absorb into the wallpaper. It's impossible to tell what anyone is really thinking, to know who they are inside their own bodies—and then, when you need the answers most, bodies are the only evidence left.

Charlie hides his face in Matt's shoulder. Even he can see that whatever shell of his grandfather lies there is not the person he knew. That person is gone, if they were ever there, if they were ever the person we thought we knew to begin with. But maybe Charlie doesn't realize any of that and is just generally startled by all the black clothes and strangers crying.

I ask Lilac, *Do you want to go look at Grandpop? Over there?*

I nod.

If you want to, she says, unsure.

It's up to you, I say. *It's the time, if you want to say goodbye.*

Lilac motions for me to bend down and she whispers in my ear, *Don't tell Dad, but I'm scared of dead people.*

I am suddenly surprised that she has never asked about her little sister's body, the baby who was born dead, although I know she remembers. Explaining my empty arms when we came home from the hospital was the most heartbreaking thing I have ever had to do. Perhaps even harder than the deafening silence after the birth, the stillness and dread before the doctor confirmed what we'd immediately known, and Matt walked out of the room. Sometimes it feels like he never came back in. Like only his body did.

This is how I explained it to Lilac, because someone had to; she was six then, and deserved at least that much. Like telling a bedtime story, I said: *Sometimes babies are born into people bodies, but they're not people at all. They're clouds, or oceans, or wind. Or tree branches shuffling in the wind. Or sunlight, or pure impossible starlight, and people bodies can't contain them. We were lucky just to have had the possibility of her. But she wasn't meant to be a person. She had to go back where she came from.*

Back to her home?

Yeah.

She could have a home here. She could share my room.

I know. It just . . . It's sad, but that's how it is.

Could she be flowers?

I guess so. I guess she could be anything.

Can we plant flowers so that she can stay with us? Even if it's just pretend?

Sure, I think that would be a beautiful idea.

Matt has never talked to Lilac about her dead sister, and Charlie was too little to remember. Matt has spoken of it only twice over the past two years, and only in the briefest terms. Maybe there are some small cracks in the wall he puts up, but to him, even the promise of warmth can seem like a siege of flame. Communicating isn't always his strong suit.

That means I get to decide how to tell the story.

■

"I don't want to come down here anymore."

"Wait, no. Why are you doing this?"

"It's too horrible."

"Well, that's the point—"

"No. Not today. I can't do this anymore."

[…]

[…]

[…]

[…]

"I'm sorry. I love you."[1]

[…]

[…]

---

1   What does all this love amount to?

■

Today Matt's shoelaces are making me sad. Today, he rolls up the sleeves of his flannel shirt to wash a dish in the sink and each shift of his shoulders is another sharp tug at the noose inside my stomach.

When we were younger, I used to feel this way constantly, like I was watching him tenderly in retrospect from outside of time. He sat at the edge of the bed and pulled his shoes on, and before he left he'd grab my face in both hands and kiss me on the forehead. I'd close my eyes.

In moments like that, I was aware we were the youngest and freest we would ever be. That it would soon be time to start letting go—that life meant learning to run before anything you'd sacrifice your own world for sunk its claws into your idiot heart.

I forgot to let go. He raises his arms to reach high into a cabinet and I glimpse the parenthesis of his hip-bone, the forest of dark hair climbing his stomach, and I want to swirl my tongue in those frail hairs. I want to burrow my body into the hole still gaping hollow in our backyard, meant for the pear tree Jim-Bill died before planting. I imagine the empty hole growing tentacles, ghost roots, reaching down into the earth until it meets the basement, merging with The Box to create one big darkness. The Box looms below us, a shut-away wound, but the unfinished hole is a gouge everyone can see. I wish it were a different kind of hole, one I could plant all our time together in, until it sprouted something gnarled and knobbed that I could chop down and burn for warmth. They say the truth is supposed to reveal itself in these hollows, but in the dark, people just disappear.

We avoid the backyard now, blaming it on the kids' frail ankles, if they were to trip over the edges of the hole. Early morning and late evening, Matt goes outside alone to scoop out dead leaves and debris.

The kids run laughing around him in circles and I am untethering. For all of us, I am fraying into splinters. He calls everything in the room *honey* but me. His eyes catch in a cold fragment of sunlight and I am unrooted. The hole deepens, barrens the earth. It grows, it grows.

■

There are many days and nights. I know this to be factually true, but they all begin to clump together; thatched huts of days and molded casseroles of nights. Everything feels like the same long thing as everything else. Every morning sandwiches are made and telephones are answered and spoken into. Every day Matt passes further into silence, and the spaces his voice used to inhabit are replaced by the noise of The Box growing ever louder. Every late-night cable rerun of *Friends* is the same episode: The One Where Everything Is Meaning-less and Everyone Pretends It's Not. Or: The One Where Ross Slits Rachel's Body Open with a Kitchen Knife and Leaves Her to Bleed Out in the Streets. Or else: The One Where They Pretend They Are Actually Friends Who Will Spend Their Lives Together, Making Jokes and Raising Children and Having Meaningful Conversa-tions, and Not Just a Collection of Strangers as Dissoci-ated from Each Other as They Are from Their Sense of Reality and Concept of the Future.

I can feel it all the time now—not just The Box convulsing in the basement darkness, wailing like a maimed fox left to die, but the weight of every nook and cranny in the house. As if the house were my own flesh, I feel the thrum of completeness when my family moves from room to room, and the gaping space when they leave. And the pull below, too, is a physical ache, like marionette strings have been sewn through my feet and palms, dragging me closer to the basement door.

The refrigerator sighs through a wall, and The Box sings its big dark emptiness up through the floor. Matt sleeps. I begin to make a list.

It's the kind of list a women's magazine might call "How to Get Your Life on Track Through Goal-Based Journaling." I name it "The Ultimate Key to Processing Change: A List," but the only thing I can think to write down is: *Allow bitterness to gleam inside me. To sear the hallways of my insides with acid and leave me squeaky clean.* Obviously a dead end, I begin a new list, called, more modestly, "Ideas."

One is: *A cure for loneliness.* But by the time I found a doctor willing to research possible vaccines, it might be too late. The loneliness might have spread internationally (by way of airplane travel) or developed into a new, resistant strain that would make any previous cure obsolete. Plus, there would have to be grant writing and FDA approval. So that's a no-go.

The second idea is: *Take a vow of silence and become a street mime.* This is impractical for obvious reasons— the kids, my lack of miming expertise, etc.

Third is: *Go get inside The Box.*

I put on socks and tiptoe to the basement door. Then I turn around and walk back to the bedroom, quietly open the sock drawer, and put a pair of Matt's socks on over my socks. It feels like a betrayal to go inside The Box without some part of him involved, even though I already feel a strange relief trickling into my blood with every step toward the basement. I don't bother switching on the lights, because as it turns out, I've gained night vision like owls and raccoons. I am unsurprised. This is the kind of thing that happens when you watch too much late-night TV.

■

1

2

3 4 5 6 7 8 9

10

11

12

13

---

1 I sit on the floor inside The Box and wait. I do not think about the color of the sky. I focus in on the blackness, the big overwhelming empty, like it's someone I'm trying to remember from long ago.

2 As a child I hid in spare closets for hours, waiting to be found. I used to have a reoccurring dream in which I was in a furniture store hiding from everyone I had ever loved who had ever loved me back. And it was a little bit like fun, and a little bit like deep, looming fear. The point of the game is that I wanted to be found, except I didn't. Or maybe the point is that someone came looking for me, and it didn't matter what happened next. If they murdered me or hugged me or whatever. What mattered most is that I could lie still and quiet for years, long after they had given up looking.

3 I know what it's like to wish for a kitchen peeler made of razor wire, to exfoliate away all your previous selves, so that when true love touches you it can be wholesome as a glass of cow's milk resting on an oak table.

4 Love doesn't just happen to people, though. Love is a trap door built into our psyches, and to find it, unlatch the lock, and open it up takes a certain vulnerability; a willingness to let being human hurt. You have to be willing not to flinch.

5   For a second here, divorce sounded like a good idea—a peaceful, mature resolution, the purity and freedom you might feel after stepping off a cliff into the sea-glass-blue Mediterranean—the same way suicide can sound like a good idea in theory. A clean break on your terms. An ending you get to say you wrote.

6   When does The Box become only an incubator for pain, and when does pain exist only for the sake of having something, anything tangible to hold on to.

7   Like divorce, committing suicide is only romantic in theory. For instance, the "committing" part; suicide is probably not for someone who tries fad diets, or fails fad diets, or regularly has trouble deciding which brand of toothpaste to buy. And in the end, you have to be ready to get cold and dead and know that everyone will forget you eventually, except when they are desperately, embarrassingly sad.

8   What difference does any of this make if the whole goddamn world, quite literally, is burning?

9   Fuck it. I was wrong, all wrong. There's nothing noble about being open, being vulnerable. It's just emptying.

10 We think of another person as a thermos we can store our love in, but that's not how it works. Love incubates inside you, until one day you recognize someone with a splash of light behind their eyes and a gentleness you didn't think was possible. Then there is the bursting open, and you are reduced to little more than a walking, pulsing lesion. People say this is supposed to be beautiful, and it is. It is so beautiful it almost makes you wish you were dead, because nothing you experience going forward will be able to measure up to that initial, golden blur of days—and even as you leak and flail and grasp, remade prenatal by love, you know this. Suddenly there is a person outside of you that you want to give more to than is humanly possible. You want to make them happy more than you've ever wanted anything, more than ice cream or to go on being alive, and your organs are replaced by imploding magenta ripples that hemorrhage out of you like sand.

11 A self, too, is an hourglass; in every version of the story, we realize this too late.

■

When I return to the bedroom and slip into bed, the air is gray and noiseless. I feel hot and light-headed, almost hungover. Matt is planked on his side, facing away from me. I've never told him, but I love the dark, round freckle in the center of his back, and falling asleep next to it has always felt like coming home. *Good night, little freckle*, I think. I have been saying good night to it for years without saying anything. *Good night, little black star.* When I look at it, even if Matt is looking away, I feel like some part of him still sees me. I briefly wonder if by this time next year, Matt will be sleeping next to someone else, and I wonder if she will ever be able to love this freckle as much as it deserves, but even the hypothetical makes me almost actually vomit. I swallow bile and blink. I think, *I will miss you and remember you always.* I close my eyes and hope it understands.

■

12 And what are we left with if we give away the pain, the familiar
    wound The Box allows us to enter? What else tethers us to home?
    What does all this love amount to?

■

Matt.

His name a hoarse whisper crackling into the dark. I reach out to rub his back—first gently, then pressing firm between his shoulder blades, his warm clammy skin. Holding my hand there and shaking.

Wake up, I say, and eventually he does.

Some things are inevitably left unfinished. We leave our bodies in the middle of the day, in the middle of a thought. We leave with decisive plans for dinner and mail that needs to be opened, objects we hope to buy, cats and dogs waiting dutifully at home to be fed. And when the earth goes or we go from it, when we leave its scarred, dazzling surface finally and all at once, there will be lights left on. There will be holes unfilled, and abandoned possibilities knitting their dark matter inside.

We stand outside in bare feet in the grass, quiet shuffling animals of the night. Matt digs. He raises the shovel and plunges it into the ground, grunting with the effort. I offer to help, take a few solid tries, but end up merely scraping loose dirt from the edge before handing the shovel back. It turns out digging a hole is harder than it looks, the act of it usually driven by superhuman grief or constraints of time: before the sun rises or sets, before the unburied begins to smell.

By the time Jim-Bill's hole is wide enough for a person to lie down comfortably, plum-colored clouds are creeping across the sky and we are both sweating through our shirts, skin streaked with tawny dirt.

Matt hands me the shovel and disappears inside, and while he is gone I stay with the hole. Of course someday I will go into the ground and it will be unlike this but it will be the same ground, the same dirt as flower beds are dug from, and I hope whoever opens the earth for me will stand awhile. Watch before it's sealed over like a skin graft; before the grass heals the seams, then forgets the wound.

Matt returns, dragging The Box behind him. The white lettering of MILK HUT visible in the dark, like a jawbone starred with teeth.

I help him turn The Box on its side, and it makes a hollow thud as it hits the grass. Matt carrying one end and me the other, we position it into the hole and jam the cardboard down where the sides are uneven, slotting it in place.

He adds water to the gray powder in the wheelbarrow, the dented green one Jim-Bill bought used, and stirs with a painter's tool we took hours ago from the basement. We'd piled it with the other paint supplies in a corner when we moved in, and then like all objects we fear we can't live properly without, we pick the tools up again and find ourselves at least three lives removed from the people who set them down.

When the concrete is thickened till it almost swallows the plastic handle, I pick up a small gardening shovel and we take turns slabbing wet concrete into the hole. We spread thin layers over the sides of the box, shellac the ridge where the metal sutures overlap. When the box is packed into the earth tightly, we pour gray slop in the hole around it, and the last visible lettering sinks away.

I rip open the cardboard door at the top, freeing the sky inside. Matt bends down and cups the bottom of the pear tree, the veiny ball of roots and soft soil. He lifts it gently, carries it slow, like a small hurt creature whose organs must be carefully held inside. He places it in the center of the open box, and we bury the tree in dirt from Jim-Bill's hole, leaving a slim horizon of blue.

For once, Matt and I stand on land not speaking, comfortable in the lovely emptiness. There are no thoughts, except perhaps a swoon in the chest for which there is no language, comparable only to music, or that sacred ache behind music when we recall the first memory it wove through.

And then: *What do we tell the kids?*

A sculpture?

Will they even care what it is if they can draw on it?
We can buy chalk.

Good idea. We can let them think it's for them.

Isn't it, though, sort of?

Sort of, I smile.

It doesn't matter what we call it; children will climb and color over the concrete and surely bother the tree, and there will be insects and communal cats that stop to rest on their layovers from scavenging, tender green leaves latticed by caterpillars, branches split by heat. It will disappear into the backdrop of all the living that happens to it, and that's what gives it meaning: We don't decide what the world takes, but we decide what we make of the things that are here—which parts to keep and which parts to destroy. We don't know what the box means now, but it means something that we chose to put it here together. We don't know what the tree will become, but it will grow regardless.

■

In the last week of summer, we take the kids to the hot-air balloon festival next to the high school. The sky is stiff and shiny, and the wind smells like cinnamon sugar. Charlie is complaining that his shoes hurt, and Matt picks him up and carries him on his shoulders.

Charlie says *Giddyup* and giggles. Lilac says, *Mama, can I giddyup?* and I scoop her up and hurl her over my shoulders.

We arrive at illumination, the hot-air balloons filling themselves with heat and light. The kids harass each other with playful nudges before becoming transfixed as the baskets lift off the ground and the balloons journey into the deep blue sky.

Lilac says, *Where will they land?*

Matt tells her, *We don't know. That's part of the fun.*

She asks, *Will they be lost?*

I say, *Not today.*

Matt looks at me and his eyes are green as the grass, which is green as leaves that have not yet succumbed to fall, which is green as everything I am not yet ready to let go of. He smiles directly at me and I know that no matter what happens next, this moment will go on being beautiful long after we're gone.

Charlie points at the glowing orbs floating above, and I can see his heart blossoming with some new animal he doesn't have a word for. He says, *Sissy, pretend we can eat them.* Lilac and Charlie chomp at the air, and we watch them, their faces beaming fireflies, mouths open to the alien light. Everything rising, rising.

WE WERE WOLVES

After Banjo died is when me and Bright found out that we were wolves. We were lying on beach towels in the backyard, staring up at all that overwhelming nighttime, stars hanging in the blue-black sky like sharpened teeth. Our naked toes were wiggling right near the notch in the fence where we'd dug a hole to put Banjo's body in, back when we thought we were burying a dog's body instead of a wolf's. We were careful back then not to get too near the notch, because Bright brought up how, if Banjo decided to come back alive, he might not be quite the same or lovable anymore. His bones might be poking through his gray fur like someone's grandma's lace doilies, and we might see his wires and meat and blood holes, all those things wolves are made of. I knew that even if Banjo exposed his wires to us, I would still love him. It would not be his fault. But I kept my mouth shut, because back then I really was afraid of blood holes, and the insides of bodies were as mysterious to me as the names of all the countries, knowing which ones had mountains and which ones had which color dirt.

We had to keep our rejoicing howls and growls down because of my dad's bedroom window being so close to the backyard, and how he didn't know that sometimes Bright snuck over. Bright wasn't supposed to be out in the nighttime, but his parents had only boy-children and slept soundly. Besides, we were wolves, and wolves are not afraid of getting in trouble.

◆ ◆ ◆

Nobody else really hung out in the backyard, so it became me and Bright's place. It was technically my place, but when you spend enough time with someone nothing feels like yours alone anymore. Sometimes not even your own name feels like yours if someone says it too much. I used to play out there with girl-friends and have swimming parties in the sprinkler when I was little, when we first moved in. But that was a long time ago, and I don't relate to it anymore. Now, I feel weird wearing a swim-suit just to stand in the grass, and none of those girls come over, on account of how they grew up to be strangers. Banjo was an alive puppy dog back then, but most recently he has become a dead, grown dog in the ground beneath the fence.

My dad is always complaining about that fence, and it's true the fence does have trouble keeping stuck in the ground when the rain gets away from itself, usually knocking flat over into Next Door's backyard. Next Door came over hollering in the morning after one of those times, saying Dad should pay for the grill that got knocked over by the knocked-over fence. I was asleep when it happened, of course, because I don't like the morning. Morning reminds me of chores, and chores make my head feel like summertime, all hot and empty-bellied. I didn't hear Next Door come over, but I can imagine him talking calm and serious while pulling at his scraggy, foolish beard. Me and Dad think Next Door is a dummy and a loon. He stays up late watching sports TV, and when his kids come to visit they're wild haired and bang on pots and pans, causing a ruckus. Dad said he laughed right in Next Door's face and told him no, he would not pay for something he hadn't wrecked with his own two hands. I'm not sure what kind of laugh, but I bet it was the kind you don't want to get in the way of.

Bright says my dad is kind of cheap. Bright is my best friend, but when he talks judgy about my dad, it makes me want to grab the white part of his arm and twist hard. My dad is a good dad, and silly in a fun way, and he has "done the best with the given circumstances." That's what he always says about himself. Still, Bright's theory would explain the fence.

I'd started wearing Banjo's collar to school soon after we took it off him and left his body under the fence. It was red and smelled earthy and mysterious, like mud and like some kind of creature that hides in mud, breathing slow and deliberate. Kids at school made fun of me for wearing it, but the smell kept me calm. Or sometimes when they made fun, I picked my fingernails until they bled so I could go to the nurse and get a Band-Aid, except I'd never actually go there, just wander the hallway, lapping up water from the fountain until I felt slimy and sick to my stomach.

Bright doesn't talk to me at school either, but I'm okay with that, because we have an understanding. No matter how he acts around other people, I know that he knows we are wolves. People mean nothing to us anyway, all their talking nonsense and fancy clothes. They might as well be raw walking steaks with eyes, that's how us wolves see them. When I see Bright's face passing by, pretending to ignore me, I can hear the inside-truth of him howling and howling.

◆ ◆ ◆

I'm the only girl in my house, but Dad tries his best to respect me. He tries to give me "breathing space," which is why he doesn't come into the backyard when Bright is over, and he even lets Bright come in my room if we keep the door open. That way he knows there's no tomfoolery. I don't know what tomfoolery he means, but once when he was gone at the Policeman's house down the street, me and Bright microwaved a whole lemon and set it on fire, and he got pretty mad about that.

I'm not the only girl in my family, though. My sister, Moss, is older and lives at College. Dad is always talking to strangers about how smart Moss is and how she's learning to be a doctor. When he meets new people he always says, "I knew I had to do whatever I could, with the given circumstances, to get that girl to College!" He says it like it was the best thing that had ever happened to anybody, Moss being gone, but I miss her and wish she still lived with us. Every time Moss comes home to visit, she eats all our Froot Loops and sleeps for three days.

Sometimes when Moss is home she lets me hang out with her in her bedroom. Sometimes it's to watch a movie, or sometimes for no reason at all. Dad gets real weird and happy when he sees us together. He calls our hang out time "girl-talk," but the way we girl-talk is with silence.

If Moss is in a good mood, she'll let me sit behind her on the bed and brush her hair. This is absolutely, apart from doing wolf-stuff, my favorite thing in the world. One time, Moss sat there for an hour, or just a few minutes, and she let me brush her hair so long that she started falling asleep. I loved touching all over her hair and the white parts of her head underneath her hair so much that I started feeling dizzy with sleep too. Then I started getting hungry, like I wanted to eat that hair. It was dark and shiny like chocolate, the kind Bright's mom brought back from her business trip in Germany that I could never get my hands on, and smelled like the cherry candies you can take for free at the bank. I was grubby for it. I just wanted to lie next to her all night and smell her, drooling into her hair like a dumb, wild baby.

My mom is the other girl in my family, obviously, but she's dead like how Banjo is dead, except sooner and in a different way. Sometimes I secretly think Mom might not be dead at all, that maybe she just went somewhere else because she wanted her life to be different. I would never say it to Dad, but maybe she's like the people we see when we visit the city, the people with dirt on their hands who prop themselves up in the shadows of buildings. Sometimes those people tell you things, but Dad walks fast when they come near us and tells me not to remember the things they say. I want to be a good daughter, so I let their words fall out of my head and onto the sidewalk like loose paper clips.

Dad says Mom vomited every day I was inside her until she turned gray. Then when I came out of her, all her blood slipped away from her and she died.

There are a lot of things I don't know, but I know I will never let anything get inside of me and take my blood away. I will guard my body like Egyptians did for the dead in their tombs, making sure nothing slips in while I'm not paying attention. I decided a long time ago that even if I have to cover myself in garbage and holler like the people in the city, nobody is allowed to curl up and make the bones of me their home.

Moss doesn't like to talk about Mom or Banjo. She doesn't like dead things, which is why she's trying to be a doctor, so she can keep things alive and never have to talk about them. When Moss visits, she spends a lot of time in her room with the door locked. She thinks we don't know what she does in there, but I know it's her and her boyfriend making noises on the phone with each other. Her boyfriend's name is Josh, and he is no one good. He is from Delaware. Me and Moss basically can't relate anymore, except when we girl-talk with our silence.

◆ ◆ ◆

I guess I should tell you how me and Bright realized we were wolves, but I'm not sure it would make sense to someone who has never been a wolf before. Basically, we never knew where Banjo came from, on account of how he was found, and everyone knows you can't trust someone you didn't see born to be what they say they are. Banjo had lived with us a long time, and all that time, we thought he was a dog. But me and Bright realized that night in the backyard, after Banjo died, that he was truly a wolf all along. It was the purest thing we had known in our whole lives.

A strange wind rolled through, and from some other, distant backyard, wind chimes carried a strange song. Right then, we heard a howl from far away, almost like the animal was singing along, and we both understood the meaning. It was a song of wildness. It went: *They will kill a beast and they will eat it / walk like a wound and they smell you by blood / the tenderest things accept the most teeth.*

We knew because of the wind and the special song from nowhere that Banjo was trying to tell us we were wolves like him. How else would we have heard the same words at the same time? How else the wind? You might not believe me, but I don't need you to believe me. If I met you I would say with my face right to your face: You've never been a wolf, so how would you know? You would come to see I have a pretty good point.

◆ ◆ ◆

We figured we should start practicing wolf-things, so if we ever met other wolves, we would know how to be. As far as we knew, we were the only ones in our neighborhood, the only ones in town, maybe. At least the only ones who walked around all human-like. But out past the neighborhood and the big road beyond the neighborhood, there were forests. Kids from school went camping there with their families, if their families were outside people. We knew for certain that forests existed, and surely wolves lived in them, crouching in bushes with eyes like haunted lanterns, waiting for something to eat.

The way wolves eat is messy, like they don't care at all who sees. Wolves are ravenous. That's one rule about them. When they hunger, they feel it rippling through every inch of their insides, from the tips of their fangs to their mud-caked claws, electrifying their meat and wires. When they find themselves hungering, they chew up the first thing they notice, and they don't care what any person or creature thinks about it. A wolf's favorite things to eat are bloody things, because of how juicy, and also the color. Blood can be beautiful, just so you know. Movie blood doesn't count. If you've never seen it in real life, you have no idea what a pretty color blood can be. Imagine someone plucked a whole backyard's worth of the most gorgeous, prize-winning roses and smashed them up into soup; even that's only half as pretty as some of the actual blood I've seen.

Blood can be different colors, though, and some people's blood looks nicer than other people's. It's not mean to say. That's just how it is. Once, Bright fell skateboarding and scraped open his knee on the pavement, and what bloomed there was thin and streaked, measly and rust-orange. It was fine blood, I guess, but it wasn't anything exciting.

Bright is maybe my favorite person, besides my dad and Moss. I maybe like him more than my dead mom, even, because of how I never met her in real life, but I hang out with Bright all the time. I like him so much that I sometimes get delirious from smelling his sweat, dizzy-headed like I'm heavy with poison, and sometimes, for no reason at all, I have a craving to get my face close to his face and pull on the pale baby hairs at the back of his neck until they snap off around my fingers. Bright is great, really, but when it comes to blood, I just don't care all that much for his particular kind. It doesn't do much for me, is what I'm saying, compared to other, better blood I've seen.

Wolves don't care if blood gets all over their fur, because if it does, other animals will see them and realize a wolf is someone powerful. There's nothing that will make a creature love you more than if they know you could swallow them up with one simple flick of tongue and fang. Another name for love is "worship," like what people go to churches to do on the weekend. Even if they're tired and it's their only day to sleep in, even if it's too hot outside to be alive, they dress up fancy so maybe God will notice and pay them some attention. Those church people are always trying to get God's attention because of how much they love him, and the reason they love him is he's so big he could crush your whole house with his pinky toe. That's why wolves are the leaders of the forest; because they're the biggest and hungriest, they get to do whatever they want.

Wolves have friends, which they call a pack. A pack is a family made of friends, tied together forever until they all drop dead like flies. When a wolf dies, its pack rips their body limb from limb and eats them up so they can keep their dead friend with them in all their bellies forever. At night you can hear wolves feeding in the forest, gnashing and writhing in joy for how wild they can be, how no one can stop them from being exactly themselves.

◆ ◆ ◆

I started eating wolf-like, slurping up green beans with my face and gobbling mashed potatoes until white mush was all up my nose and in my eyelashes. Dad was shocked, I think, by how enthusiastic my hunger became. I licked my dinner plates clean for two nights until he drew a line called "enough," and my tongue was forbidden.

Bright never got in trouble for eating messy or ransacking the fridge for whatever he was hungering for at the moment. Maybe his mom and dad knew, somehow, about his true wolf nature. Maybe they kept it a secret because they were drenched in fear by how fiercely they had grown to love him.

Another wolf-thing we started was howling. Howling is the most important part of being a wolf: it's how they sling their voices up in the air so other wolves will understand how they feel about some particular thing. They don't speak words to each other, so without howling, they basically can't communicate at all. Without being able to howl, they're basically trapped alone inside their bodies. It's sad, when you think about it. I bet someone who is not a wolf would weep for a whole hour if they knew.

Me and Bright howled regularly in the backyard, and we got pretty good at understanding what each other was feeling. When Bright howled like a TV coyote, round-bellied and skyward, it meant he was feeling festive. When he howled guttural and echoey, it meant he was hungering. When he howled high pitched and silly with longing, it meant *I wish we lived in the forest, sleeping in green leaves forever and ever*. If we howled at the same time, it sounded out over the neighborhood in ripples, like a song swing dancing with itself. We howled so fearsome once that it scared off a flock of birds, and we fell to the grass and cackled joyous till our bellies were sore.

Something I've learned about myself as a wolf is that I can get very into my howling. I can get so obsessed with the way it feels to howl that I lose time and come out of my body a little bit. If you have never been a wolf, this is an example of how it feels: like a thousand wild paws and claws and talons and hooves shredding up the length of your throat, shredding it like stained old wallpaper in the hallway of an old wooden house, and the bones of your chest are an old brick house collapsing in on itself, burying all the silly, stupid people who live there in rubble and dust, and the hooves and talons are blazing fires, and the paws and claws are named freedom. That is how it feels, if you are a wolf, to do howling.

When I get lost in my howling, Bright has to shake me to settle me back in my body. He gets a weird look on his face about it, then says he wants to go do something else, like watch TV or skateboard in the driveway. He says sometimes I get carried away and we need to do human-stuff to glue me back in my body again. I'm always getting carried away about things, wanting to keep going when Bright wants to stop. Like when I find some word or phrase that makes him laugh, I'll keep repeating it over and over until he tells me it's not funny anymore. Or when he said he wanted to walk around the neighborhood pretending it was

Pilgrim Times, but wouldn't drink water out of the ditch by the model homes.

Bright can get filled up so easy by just a little morsel of something, but I need everything, all at once, to feel like life even makes a dent. Moss said boys are scared, which is why they always want to stop right when a situation gets exciting, but if Bright is scared of anything, he doesn't tell me. He keeps it locked up behind his teeth all secretive.

◆ ◆ ◆

Once at nighttime I went to the bathroom and thought I heard Moss howling in her room, and I got excited, thinking maybe she was a secret wolf, too, and we could be wolves together. We could be part of the same pack, rampaging through the trees and feasting on creatures with bloodsmile smeared across our faces. But actually, she was just making noises on the phone with her boyfriend, Josh. I listened through the crack in her door for a little while, but then I started feeling creepy and tingly in my belly, like someone was watching me from up above. I don't mean like God, I mean like a monster or a ghost. A ghost that maybe had long, creepy white fingers and long, creepy black hair fluttering out of its skull. And chunks of flaky purple-blue skin, like the ghost had been dead and lying on the carpet for such a long time before anyone noticed it.

I ran fast to my room and flopped on my bed and slept with the light on all night. When Dad came to wake me up for school, I pretended the light was an accident, like I was so stupid exhausted I couldn't even use my legs to get up and turn it off. I felt bad for lying to my dad and for being fearful, because a wolf isn't afraid of the nighttime, a wolf can gash the night sky open with one screech and kill a beast dead with one visceral chomp. But wolves must be scared of some things, like the apocalypse, or hunters who go into forests to take their heads off and use them for decoration on a wall. When I rationalized it that way, I didn't feel bad anymore.

I wanted to tell Bright about my ghost, but I knew it would have to wait. If I tried to talk to him at school, he would just stare at me crazy, like I was talking in some other jumbled-up language. Kids didn't talk to my face at all anymore, even to make fun, on account of how I was still wearing Banjo's dirty collar around my neck. But at least with Bright, I knew that as soon as we were in the backyard he would become himself with me again.

◆ ◆ ◆

I was getting restless since we'd been practicing the same wolf-stuff every day for a while. We'd gotten very good at howling and eating messy, even at walking with our hands down, crouched in the dirt and grass like wolves do. I got to where walking like that, all crouch-backed, felt as natural to me as the human way. Sometimes I walked like that in my room when Bright wasn't there. If I was feeling lonely or angry about the kids at school, or anything at all, I'd crouch-walk on all fours in a circle, just to remind myself that I was truly a wolf and those silly people meant nothing to me. Sometimes as I circled I'd start clawing at the carpet, sometimes even biting at it, which did not taste like anything good but felt like a parade sparking in my belly. When my dad was sleeping, I'd sneak down the stairs real quiet and walk around the whole house that way, prowling in the dark.

One day, Bright had the idea that we should try eating creatures. I think he was afraid if I kept on being restless, I might not come back in my body anymore. More often after school we barely howled before he wanted to watch TV or walk around the neighborhood like humans. But I knew how important it was that we stayed in touch with our animal nature. We'd talked about not going to College like Moss when we grew up, but going to live in the forest together instead. I wanted that so bad it made my teeth pulse and ache inside my skull. So I had to make sure we were ready, when the time came, to live full and wild as our true selves.

We started practicing on already-dead creatures, like the big hunk of ground-up meat that lived in my refrigerator. My dad noticed if food went missing and got grumpy about it, so we could only eat a little bit of the meat-hunk at a time. It was dark pink and slimy and mashed up so you couldn't tell what kind of creature it came from or where the blood holes had been. I was thankful for that, because of how blood holes still creeped me out to think about, even though actual blood was one of my favorite things. We each pressed a finger into the carcass and pinched out a small chunk of the raw meat, sticking it in the crook of one cheek. It tasted like metal and burnt cheese, and a little like the hot, sticky smell of the backyard after rain. Me and Bright chewed the animal up, chomping loud and open-mouthed. There was a little bit of watery blood-juice in the bag, and Bright dared me to drink it, which I did. I peeked over at his face while I lapped it up, and he was crossing his eyes in wonder.

Afterward, I started sneaking bites of the meat-hunk from the fridge at night, mushing it back together to cover up the hole. It's a good thing my dad cooked that meat the next week, because there wasn't going to be much of it left soon. I'd gotten ravenous for that creature's flesh, whoever it had been.

◆ ◆ ◆

Bright rode his skateboard over on the weekend, and we flopped around in the driveway for a long time, smooshing ants on the concrete. We couldn't do any wolf-stuff since the whole neighborhood was awake, walking around like the stupid humans they were, so concerned with groceries and car seats and getting the best pool floats that they didn't even know they were living among wolves. Or at least, that's how I felt watching them. Bright just kept skateboarding, and without our howling, his feelings were locked up behind his face.

We were bored, so we decided to go bother Next Door's kids, who were visiting that weekend. We knew Next Door wouldn't be home because of how his truck wasn't in the driveway, and his garage was filled up with old couches. We could hear the kids hollering inside when we rang the doorbell, scurrying so frantic to answer.

The Tall-ish One answered: "Hello."

"Hello," we said back.

"My dad said not to let strangers in while he's gone," she said. She was chewing bubblegum and the smell of her breath made me want to sneeze.

"We're from next door," Bright said.

She let us inside. I'd never actually seen the inside of Next Door's house, only certain rooms through the window. It was pretty much like my house, except different floors in the kitchen and different furniture, obviously, and sort of dirty. The Red-Haired and the Little One were climbing all over the couch, not watching the too-loud TV. When they saw me and Bright they came running.

"I know you," the Red-Haired said. "You have a dad over there who fights with my dad."

"My dad has a particular taste in people," I said, not wanting to break the news to him that his own dad was a sloppy-faced buffoon.

Me and Bright stood in their kitchen like that while the younger kids squirmed around. I was worried Bright was getting nervous about us being seen together as friends, like he did when I passed him in the hall at school. He always moved over to the lockers, making a force field between him and me so we couldn't accidentally touch, no matter how crowded the hallway got. But because Next Door's kids went to some other school, they wouldn't know the difference between school-Bright and home-Bright like I did. They looked at him and only saw one person.

"Why you wear that?" the Little One asked, pointing at my neck.

"My dog died," I said.

"It's just for, like, a joke, you know, not serious," Bright told them. I looked at him real hard until my eyes started feeling haunted, but he didn't notice.

He said, "We're bored. What are you guys doing?" He said it looking only at the Tall-ish One.

"I dunno," she muttered. "TV and stuff." She seemed bored with us being there, like we were just some buzzing flies hanging around. The Little One started climbing her arm, but she wriggled it off.

"Penelope died," the Little One said, real droop-mouthed.

The Tall-ish One bopped it on the head. "Stop telling everybody," she said.

"Who's Penelope?" I asked. I was thinking maybe a dog or a cat or maybe even their mom, and I really wanted to know the answer.

"My pet mouse," the Red-Haired said.

"Ours!" the Little One shrieked.

"Okay, ours together, but mine the most."

"Where is she?" Bright asked.

"In the cage," the Red-Haired said. "We're going to bury her in the backyard tonight."

I said, "Don't bury her near the fence. It's bad luck."

My skin bristled at the thought of some ridiculous mouse getting buried near Banjo, and how if it came back alive it'd be chomping on him underneath the ground.

"That's good to know," the Red-Haired said foolishly.

"Can we see?" Bright asked.

The Tall-ish One shrugged, and the Little One grabbed Bright by the hand and tugged him. I followed Bright and those kids into a blue bedroom. There were big painted fishes on the wall and their closed mouths made it seem almost like they were smiling, which I liked at first, but then I started getting creeped out.

The cage was sitting on a dresser. Bright peered inside, then looked away fast. I started thinking maybe he was just a scared boy after all, like Moss said.

I put my face over the cage and saw the mouse, a gray smudge of fur, lying on its side. Its tiny mouth was open sideways with the teeth and whiskers all peeking through. There were marks in the plastic bottom of the cage where it had tried to chew and claw its way out.

"Dare you to touch it," Bright whispered to me, all mischievous. The way his eyes looked directly at my eyes made my head go electric.

I slid my hand through the open slot in the top of the cage, hovering my pointer finger over the mouse. The Little One gasped loud, and the breath of the Red-Haired got caught in his throat. Even though I knew it was definitely a hundred percent dead, I started getting that creepy feeling in my gut again, like it might raise up its snout and bite me all the sudden, so I poked it real quick and then jumped away. It happened so fast that I started giggling like an old witch, cackling so hard I couldn't even stop myself, even though the Red-Haired looked like he might cry, and even though my finger felt a little bit diseased. I expected Bright to burst out laughing, too, at least out of nervousness like he usually did when my laughs went witchy, but he was quiet, his eyeballs floating between the cage and the ground.

"What it felt like?" the Little One asked.

"Cold," I said. "Kind of hard, like a gummy bear."

The Tall-ish One made a face like gagging. I thought for a minute her gum was choking her, and we would have to do a rescue mission. Then Bright started laughing, and the Tall-ish One rolled her eyes and smiled, and I felt a burning gladness that I was absent the day our school did the CPR assembly.

"Come on, we need to get out of here, move it," the Tall-ish One said, herding us all away from the room like we were some dumb cows on a farm. I wondered how come if she just brought us in there it was so important to leave all the sudden, but I didn't say anything. On the way back to the living room, I tried to wipe the mouse-touched finger on Bright, playful-like, but he stepped away and acted all grossed out. I wiped it on my jeans instead, even though I was pretty sure there was no mouse goo on it or anything.

In Next Door's living room, we went over to the brown corduroy couch, food crumbs tumbling into the creases when we sat down. The little kids stood on the love seat in the corner, poking each other and whining, then getting distracted by the TV, then snapping out of the trance to poke each other again. The Tall-ish One was scooted all the way to the far side of the couch, her long tan legs pulled up next to her, like it was so casual how she could bend them up to her body and still be comfortable. I tried to cross my legs the way I'd seen fancy businesswomen do on the boring police shows my dad watched, but my leg was too chunky to hoist up, and my foot slipped and hit Bright. He gave me an annoyed look and moved closer to the Tall-ish One.

At that point, my feelings were basically locked up in my brain, and I couldn't tell Bright about it because we couldn't do our howling around these dumb humans. Something got me thinking that even if I howled, Bright would pretend not to know what I was saying, even though he knew how to translate my howling better than any other wolf alive. Something got me thinking that maybe he would even lie about being a wolf and pretend I was being crazy, like he did at school. But this was home-time, which meant it was supposed to be our time, and that made me feel an awful sickness deep down in my belly. It wasn't fair how Bright could just decide which self to be whenever he wanted to, or that he even got to have more than one self, when all the time I only had one person I could be, and that person was his friend. Even if Bright wanted to pretend like he wasn't a wolf anymore, I knew I could never walk around among humans and feel at home, pretending I wasn't ravenous for flesh and power, like I hadn't heard Banjo's special song and didn't hold the secret of it in my heart. I wanted, then, not to howl, but for my insides to be so loud that Bright and everyone alive knew the awful ruckus in my head for themselves, like when lightning cracks the sky so loud it makes your house shiver.

"You guys should probably go soon," the Tall-ish One announced at the third commercial break. "My dad is coming home any minute, probably."

Bright looked kind of disappointed as he got up to leave. I stayed planted on the couch, and then I got an idea. I sprung up.

"Can I use your bathroom first?" I asked.

"Whatever, sure. It's across from the bedroom."

I tried to make my face look really grateful at her for telling me where it was, even though inside I was cackling because, of course, I already knew.

I went into the bathroom and turned on the light and the fan, then closed the door in front of me, so it sounded like I had gone inside. Then, I slipped across the hall to the bedroom, creeping with the lightest prance of a paw, imagining how a wolf creeps up on its prey in the forest without crunching any leaves. The fish on those walls were egging me on, grinning sleepily at my arrival.

I reached into the cage and picked up the mouse's body, cold and limp and heavy in my hand. I let it settle in my palm and got it up near my face, smelling mulch and rotten flowers, sickly sweet.

The smell of the dead mouse mingled with the smell of Banjo's collar, and I knew then that Banjo had planned this life for us all along. He'd given us this beautiful, rabid freedom. I imagined Bright's face twisting at the corners, and I waited with delight, dreaming of how he would look right at me so amazed, how he would see crimson streaming from my fangs and have no choice but to topple over with the crippling weight of his love. I lifted the mouse to my lips and took a grateful, fearless bite.

THE DRAGGING ROUTE

The only piece of herself the first wife left was a pair of porcelain salt and pepper shakers, shaped like ducks and painted in bright, mosaic swirls, and occasionally Cora will walk into the kitchen and the salt duck will be thrown across the room, lying whole somehow on the wood floor, Cora unaware how it ended up there. Perhaps the first time it scared her a little, but she knew it was only because she thought of being scared, the way she only craves potato chips after she sees someone on TV eating them. She does not tell Samuel about how the ducks behave, which is one definition of love: to distract each other from the tiny horrors.

◆ ◆ ◆

If it comes down to it, there are reasons: because when Samuel and Cora were married, she knew she wasn't marrying a man, but a patch of earth equally ripe and festering. Because her wedding dress was found in the attic of an old house with no staircase now, and she had chosen this. Because Samuel's blood was yoked to the dirt and the muddy roots that sprung from it, as was his father's, and his father's father's, and the lineage of faceless Appalachian-shaped men whose hands by necessity could never stay gentle.

Because Samuel's grave, he made it known to her one night in bed, after their bodies had returned to them from the machine trance of lovemaking, was to be the cave on the other side of the thick woods. It was her duty as his wife, the one thing he asked of her, to make sure of this. Whenever his ghost fled his form, she was to drag what was left across their property, along the river-bank, through the dark thicket, to the hollow in the limestone ridge. It was tradition, he told her: the only way for men of his kind to lie in the earth that made them and rest.

They'd been married near-about four months then, and with his cheeks kindled to pink, his eyes sapphire beneath the brown and silver twine of his brow, Cora was partway lost to the tangled beauty of him and barely gauged his meaning. Though Samuel was twelve years older and would surely meet his end before her, she couldn't imagine herself growing so old as to drag her husband's limp flesh out into the wilderness, lay him in a nature-made tomb where his human muscle would be rended from bone by coyotes and lost grizzly cubs. No matter how old she was when Samuel went—and certainly she would be young enough still to walk, to drag, to walk away—she could not imagine herself in the finality the act required, for surely that is a thing one does not come back from. One does not ever again make coffee or drive to the store or walk into their house and shut the door behind them as if it mattered.

Because love crawled through her like a horrible fever, Cora shut her mouth up like burial. Samuel took Cora's silence for understanding and wrapped his arms around her, squeezing in a way that for both their bodies felt like a sigh. It would not be the last promise marriage made for her without her knowledge. That was the night they conceived their daughter. How could Cora know that for sure? She knew.

◆ ◆ ◆

There are geese in the yard, picking the pieces of something—a squirrel, Cora guesses—out of the grass. Their daughter, Abbie, seven and walking with the droopy old hound that hangs around sometimes, who shows up at the back door when the doorframe has just thawed out like nothing after being frozen shut for two days. The memory of a winter storm in March, erased.

At Samuel's urging and the world's, Cora has stopped trying to protect Abbie's innocence. To do so would be futile, like being nervous on an airplane. Once you're in it, there's nothing to do but let go, so Cora reminds herself, *Let go, let go*. Despite the letting go, she hopes Abbie will not come upon the geese. She hopes Abbie will continue to think of these animals as good a while longer and leave them to be what they are on their own, in private.

Samuel's job is to care for his blood kin and what they leave behind, which includes the houses no one lives in. There are three of them along their road: one is called Blue Tree, one is called Eda Jane's, and one is Down-to-Almost-Dirt. Samuel mows the grass and tends the bramble and kills snakes as they rise up between old floorboards. He shoos raccoons out from the rusted sheds. A job can be different than a thing you make money from.

Blue Tree, named for the cedar out front, sits across the gravel road and can be seen from the bay window of Samuel and Cora's house, so that Cora has begun to think of the gray cottage as an overly friendly neighbor she reluctantly accepted. Samuel says this is the oldest of the houses no one lives in, that no one has lived in it longest—no one Samuel has a name or story for. Wagoneers brought it to stand there, Samuel reckons. Despite its age and emptiness, Blue Tree held best to its tending. The floor inside holds the weight of any of them three, in any of its three small rooms.

Eda Jane's lies farther up the gravel road, behind the curve of poplars. The tin roof has rust and holes and its walls slouch toward the weedy barren. Eda Jane was some twice-great cousin or aunt of Samuel's, who kept chickens around the side of the accompanying barn, where a possum or fox can still be trapped in the wire coop if the venison in their basement freezer runs out and they grow desperate for game. Eda Jane's belongings are still inside: the rose-printed couch cored by vermin, sliding to the center of the living room where the orange carpet caved in. Dirt-marked trails made by the shoes of two travelers who'd taken to exploring, and the bullet gash in the doorframe that resulted when Samuel chased them out. The staircase to the attic separated from the floor but clung sturdy to the foundation for decades; when Cora first moved to Samuel's, he took her up those stairs to choose one of the vintage dresses to wear when they wed. Surprisingly, they were all untouched by cobwebs, and all her size. She chose something crepe and eggshell blue, and five days later, the staircase crumbled to the ground.

Down-to-Almost-Dirt is farthest back, at the overgrown junction where the river crosses the woods: a log cabin impaled by the branch of a lightning-split tree. Cora has never been inside Down-to-Almost-Dirt.

The world has thawed, so Cora decides she will take a quick walk down the road to bring Samuel a thermos of coffee at Blue

Tree. She spots him faintly through the kitchen window, a blur of motion and old clippers. She boils too much water but pours the extra water into the coffee, anyway. It's better to have too much than to want and be left with too little.

◆ ◆ ◆

The Cumberland River is muddy and green and its banks littered with things that don't belong. Branches of trees that don't grow within a hundred miles. Little bodies of silt and creature—a fish face, a bird's arm. A wet, red T-shirt choking around itself. Cora wonders how deep the river is as she walks its shores, counts the things that ended up there, stayed, became features of her mornings and nights.

She once asked Samuel where the river ends, and he said Ohio, but Cora has never been to Ohio. She can't imagine it has anything to do with the ugly, crawling river she knows, where sweet gum tree prickles dangle against the gray sky like medieval flails or angry stars.

Not to mention that rivers don't end, not really. They dump themselves out into something larger, take on another name. Like veins that cradle blood for what must feel like miles before they empty out into the heart—it doesn't make them the heart. Even the heart is barely itself: the shape of a fist all echo on the inside. For centuries the Shawnee called this river by a word no one can translate now, and then some man named Walker came along and gave it the name that stuck. When the river drags strangeness onto its banks and threatens to rage above the shoreline, it seems to those who know the story like retaliation.

That's one problem with rivers: they are so full of remembering.

Cora does not feel loyalty to a particular place the way Samuel does; she grew up landless, shuffled from house to house, each one with a new, uncomfortable smell. Each with a new system of strangers you had to make feel sorry enough to feed and clothe you and keep out of your bedroom at night. When people ask her where she's from, she tells them out West, which is close to the truth. She couldn't imagine even if she'd grown up belonging that she would have chosen to spend her life staying like Samuel, churning old ghosts.

But her husband was raised from the stubborn tobacco fields and is as brambling beautiful as the thorns Cora has learned to navigate from memory. His ghosts are acceptable because they're his. Because they are rooted to the earth, Cora tells herself, and he is only their caretaker. When he dies and goes to the cave to dissolve his human body (*goes* as if he'd walk there, Cora thinks, but no, there would be dragging, Cora was always thinking about the dragging, how to do it, if she'd be able), there would need to be a new caretaker, a new gardener for the rotting homes, the moth-eaten memories. She supposes it would be her. Who else was there?

Samuel and Cora met at the post office the year that Cora was thirty and stopped asking questions. He had kind eyes and very few answers. He bought her ice cream, like some kind of old movie. She moved into his house a week later. There are some benefits to a flimsy life, to having nothing to second-guess leaving behind.

In the first year, even before she got pregnant with Abbie, she learned how when you build a home, the memories begin to layer themselves. When you walk into a room, you can't just be a person walking into a room; you think and feel everything that happened in that room before, each shadow and corner its own breathing animal.

But in a new place you can *un-be*. Feel your chest bones expand and the choking cloud of personhood rush out of you like the clean smell of a city after rain. Sometimes on this land Cora feels absolutely flooded by the eight painful, gorgeous years of her own remembering.

A flood is just a metaphor for what life is, which is everything ending all the time and you never know when. Without the cave, the bodies of Samuel's kin would be swept downstream when the river gushes to life. Swept away like all things time takes—except what somebody sticks around to preserve.

The Cumberland floods every couple of years, swallowing Nashville, Clarksville, for days at a time. It floods other places lately, especially in spring, gagging and heaving of itself in a way that makes Cora wonder what the river's old name was.

◆ ◆ ◆

Cora walks up to Blue Tree and Samuel greets her with his mouth. Yes, they are very much in love, she remembers.

"Thankin' you," he says, throws his head back to receive a bitter slosh from the thermos. Samuel takes his coffee unsweetened. Cora has learned to drink it that way.

Long ago, something like a friend told her that coffee has a half-life. She never found out what it meant, but she imagines tiny, round caffeine molecules sticking in the thermos lid and in Samuel's mouth and gut. Breaking down in hour increments, like a virus being drowned out. Samuel's skin is gray with sweat and dust, and Cora wants to lick at it, just to remember what's underneath. Like those candies that change color in your mouth. Samuel's body could be like that to her, if he'd let it be.

His eyes are pale and soft in the backdrop of the day's weather, a kindly gloom. In most of the places she was raised, not even seasons were promised, only storms that came hurtling down where something hopeful should be. At least Tennessee turned on an axis of change, even if the scenes repeated themselves year after year. When the sky broke its fury over Samuel's home, at least it promised to come to an end.

"Gettin' Abbie?" Samuel asks, returning to rip browned weeds from the ground. Chains of tiny roots dangle at the ends like upturned baby teeth.

She'd forgotten what time it was, and wished she didn't have to walk the mile to meet her daughter at the bus stop. Strange how you can love something so much you cleave your body for it, yet it still ends up a footnote to your own self-interest.

"Way to it," she says, smiles. She notices where the bark has been clawed away at the base of the blue atlas cedar. By a pothole in the yard, she sees the body of a common crow—black feathers stabbed through, pinned to dirt with the quick shine of a corkscrew.

"Done that?" she asks Samuel. He shakes his head no.

"Some different thing," he says.

Cora nods and puts her lips together.

◆ ◆ ◆

Cora can sometimes feel the ghost of Samuel's first wife occupying the alive spaces of their house, though she doesn't think about it much. *Gone* is all he said of her; where she went is hazy, but Cora realized soon enough that it doesn't matter whether you're bone-eaten in a dirt holler or living in an apartment next to the airport in Tucson—gone makes ghosts of us all.

Every so often Cora walks into a room to set the washing down, or put Abbie's doll away in its nook, and hears the floorboards creak—not where she stands, but on the other side of the wall. She does not allow herself to press her ear to the ancient plaster, but some deep instinct reckons if she did, she might catch the rustle of a crinoline skirt. These moments more than any, Cora remembers she is tracing the steps of a vanished person's life: the first wife's, or anyone's. Cora lives alongside so many vanished people.

She has also begun to notice, the last few months, that tufts of flesh and scales and fur more often pepper the riverbank. At night scrubbing dishes, she'll turn her back to the wide front window and smell a force field of rot inching closer to their doorstep.

Or perhaps it simply seemed that way. Perhaps, Cora thinks, as she walks home from Blue Tree and glimpses yet another tangle of bones in the grass, it was not that more death had arrived, only that she'd begun to take notice how gone things never stayed that way.

◆　◆　◆

Near afternoon, Cora hears the whinny of the screen door shutting and the plod of Samuel's boots behind her. She turns, and his eyebrow jumps like he didn't expect her.

"I'd doubt blackberries this summer," he reports of the bushes behind Blue Tree, where Cora and Abbie pick them when they ripen deep purple.

"Just about all of it's ailing."

"Oh. That's a disappointment," she says. Samuel sets a jar of ice water on the table, but doesn't sit.

"Strange, more like."

"Troubling," she agrees.

"What came of that bird?"

She thought first of the crow at Blue Tree, the sharp cork-screw.

"Whose bird?" she asks.

"What got stuck in the vents week before last."

That was how it was on this land: soon as the snow melts, the outside starts breaking in. Sometimes it was a bug or two, and Cora could handle that, even the buzzing ones. Although she intimately knew the seasonal clockwork of the house, she was never prepared for the creatures that clawed their way inside. Squirrels scraping in the walls. Mice nibbling the paper labels of cans in the pantry. Barn cats that drag their young below the porch and get trapped there—the eerie meows pulsing under the bedroom floor, and the eerier silence when they cease. Last year, a black rat snake, dark and thick as oxblood, came down through the chimney while Samuel was elsewhere, and Cora had to grab a shovel from the porch and sever its neck before it could slither past the hearth.

The house where Cora and Samuel live is old and needs tending same as the others: some lights simply no longer switch on, and there are spots no fire or radiator could keep warm. The small inheritance Samuel's kin left behind is all they had beyond what he could do with his own hands. Wires and fluffy pink fiberglass hang from the ceiling beams and poke through the oak-paneled walls, and Samuel tapes them back where they belong. That's how he fixes up the house. Fixing can be different than solving.

But in recent months, when the guts of the house spill out, they don't get taped. Cora reminds Samuel, but it's like he forgot, or he never heard her, or some other place in his mind needed him more. Some days Samuel didn't act right, and Cora never knew when those days were coming until she found herself in one of them.

He rinses his face in the sink, dries it with a dish towel, and lays a palm on Cora's lower back—almost jovial in a way that aches her—before stepping out the door and setting off across the yard again. Cora knows he is going to Down-to-Almost-Dirt today, and dreads it. She knows how hollow he will be when he comes home, how the ghosts there wring him out. How all his people are gone from this earth, but Samuel keeps them, close as bone.

Samuel is so many things beloved to Cora—bright in his smile, prickly by nature but holds himself careful with others—and he carves himself out to be a vessel for other people's memories. She has silently come to resent it, the way he devotes his life to refusing to let the past pass. There is so much vivid *now*, it has seemed to her since Abbie's first red screech into the world, and he lets it fall through his cracked hands like water.

There are parts of yourself you sign away when you choose someone else's life as your own. Cora had been ready to cut off all those fragments of selves for what she wanted more than anything: a choice, and the chance to use it. But the choice was never hers. She was looking to abandon herself to someone, and too late realized Samuel was doing the same.

Even in death, Samuel intends to cling to the land. Won't even let her grieve him with the finality of a well-tended stone. She wonders sometimes if he wishes, at the end of the dragging, for Cora to have no choice but to climb into the dark holler and rot alongside him.

She wonders if she would.

◆ ◆ ◆

It was hard to say when the disease had come upon Samuel, or when he'd known it himself, since he only got the doctor involved after Cora began to notice his color sliding away. Though it was never spoken aloud, she knew it was before her.

Of course, there was no money for the doctor to do anything with the disease but name it. The doctor himself was a video screen wheeled into a stark white room, a portable trailer plopped across the street from the local school, for people like Cora and Samuel who could barely afford to keep light in the bulbs. The man himself, the doctor, was sitting four counties away. Lag blurring his face like he was passing through time slow as water, he explained Samuel's body, what parts and pieces, how long till it goes.

The disease sickened his gut and distended his belly, so that his shirtless flank reminded Cora of the old men she'd glimpsed waddling around the garage and drinking from dirt-colored bottles when she was young and went to pick up her once-foster uncle from work. Samuel's blue eyes went gray and watery, like paper spilled over and dried out again. Cora discouraged him from going into town without saying it outright—gently nudging someone to do something like it was their own idea was a skill she'd mastered before puberty—and without him realizing it, it had been a month or more since he'd ventured beyond the thicket that bordered their slab of land.

The empty houses worsened his disease, but he refused to stop his work. He called himself tired when he came home with someone else's voice in his mouth, but she knew those houses carved holes in him where strange spirits could flood in. His silhouette went sheer as the specters that flitted in the corners.

Sometimes he didn't know her name, or his own hands. The ghosts of his father's people and the people before them and all the sunken stones of the weary sleeping under the ground for miles bled into the spaces where Samuel had gone missing from himself. Moonstung and holy. Throat of the world.

◆ ◆ ◆

When she doesn't sleep, Cora slips out the back screen door into the oil-slick night. The dark air thicker and more deadly quiet than she remembers from the last time she did this. The river swollen with melting snow and rain. She can feel it as if it were a flesh-thing, heat and dagger-cold at once, licking its way out of its own body.

Cora walks the riverbank, boots clinging to mud, and she practices the dragging route. She marches from the house to the trees, past Eda Jane's and Blue Tree, Samuel's handprints all over the once-wild hedges, Samuel's clippers gleaming on the broken front porch. From the trees to the river, and Down-to-Almost-Dirt where nobody goes, where nobody lives and still something survives, cracked open and seething and frighteningly alone. Cora imagines the weight of her husband's body, the stilling ocean of blood and impossible tendon, the metallic weight of memory much larger than one man, bigger than one patch of earth or sky or county, imagines the strain in her arms, the screaming pull in her back, and she practices, she prepares, she walks the dragging route and knows that if she makes it to the cave she will survive this and many other things, that she can be someone who holds duty and love in her throat like a terrible anchor, she can be someone who stays. To make yourself into someone's home or to accept them as yours is a choice. In this life we have choices.

Cora repeats this silently as she weaves through the woods, as withered leaves give way to the squelch of moss beneath her boots, as she approaches the ridge where she knows the mouth of the cave to be. The snaggle-toothed limestone layered around the opening, a hole where any creature could slip through. Once or twice, she imagines peeking inside to glimpse piles of bone, Samuel's ancestors soldered together into a cantankerous mass; or imagines the grave empty, the dirt floor littered with crinkled chip bags and spray-paint cans that rattle. Whatever was, vanished into the placeless expanse of the gone. Once or twice, she feels her foot drive forward to find out, but she does not follow it, and calls this, too, her choice.

She calls her footsteps *choice* as she retraces the river and makes her way back. When she slips out of her mud-caked boots and shuts the screen door so carefully behind her. When she washes her hands at the kitchen sink, holding them under for a moment longer after the water begins to burn. When she sees the pepper duck sitting solitary on the counter. The salt duck discarded on the floor again, its head tilted back in an almost-grimace, an almost-smile. One day this land, this home, will belong to someone else, someone to whom she is just another ghost, and she will be gone.

◆ ◆ ◆

When the sun has burned dew from the grass, Cora treks down the gravel path to fetch her daughter, thinking how many women in all of time have done the same—in deserts, across water, through mountains that pulped skin from their feet— carrying babies, chasing babies, saving babies, or trying and failing. To raise a child turns a person riverlike, rushing past yourself and corroding beneath layers of touch. To be a daughter is its own terrible duty, but to be a mother is something unbearable.

In her childhood, Cora couldn't conjure even an outline of whoever had birthed her. It was like trying to stick paint to the wind. But when she became a mother herself, she came to understand the heart of that woman; that woman who bled Cora into the world and said *Go*, and may have meant it as a gift. She gave Cora a life that was only her own, a life without the burden of being chained to a place that only reminds you of what is already in you, inescapable.

And yet, as Abbie's limbs lengthened and her round face grew the shadow of some new person—not part-Samuel and part-Cora, but some person all her own—Cora felt the claw of time snagging on her heart. When she watched Samuel, she understood why it would be easier to call a thing gone as if it never ached within you. Why it made him feel whole to press his hands to a place and feel someone reaching back, even if he had to spin that presence out of dust.

Cora follows the Cumberland till it parts from their land, but even when the river strays from her side, she can feel its presence: the desire to rise and demand a cleansing. An ending no one really gets.

Still, Cora thinks to herself in the quiet parts that are left and hers alone, each day is a choice—or rather, she hasn't known anyone whose choices weren't already made for them, and why should she be different?

She sees her daughter up ahead, descending the bus stairs. A blaze of red and freckle shuffling the dust. Cora walks toward her.

WATCHING BOYS DO THINGS

It was the summer of ant suicide. That's how I remember it. The ants showed up everywhere: in the shower drain, trying to work their way into the cap of the shampoo bottle, running chaotic lines from the cracks in the floorboards to the kitchen trash can. Each day in my first-floor apartment became another battle against a tiny army that was gaining ground every time I looked away.

I accidentally left a marshmallow-scented bar of soap on the counter, and the ants ate through it, their motionless bodies dotting the sink's ledge. They snuck through the vents of the old oven and gorged on charred bread crumbs and ash. I set out traps and they piled into those, too, climbing over their dead, swarming up from the floorboards, ravenous for a brief taste of what would soon cause them to limp away and die.

When I looked close, I noticed all the corpses were split down the belly, foam and shiny black guts spilling out their middles, sprawled as if comatose with pleasure.

I was twenty-four and poor and skilled at living with whatever I had to: the sink leaked, so I placed a plastic take-out container under the pipe, which I'd dump out every six hours. If I came home late or slept too long, there'd be an overflow soaking the cabinet and the floor below it, puddling up near an electrical socket I vaguely worried would fry me dead as I bent to sponge up the flood with dish towels. At times I was certain I felt a shock when I placed my hands under the faucet, but it could've been the water spraying my raw cuticles, which I compulsively gnawed when my hands had no other task to keep them busy. Eventually, I just turned off the water, twisting the rusted knob under the sink back on when I needed to wash dishes, and that seemed to solve it.

And there was the stench of mold in the bedroom, which I covered with patchouli body spray from the mall, and the cockroaches, of course, who for three seasons of the year inhabited the wall behind the bathroom mirror like a set of rowdy tenants. The landlord was a rosacea-faced old man with a syrupy drawl who would've immediately fixed the sink if I'd asked, but I was lazy, or anxious, or bristled at the thought of strangers lumbering in to inspect my dark spaces and tell me what I'd done wrong.

But the arrival of the ants struck the house like a dreaded omen. I made a rare attempt at cleaning the tub, and when I sprinkled the cylinder of powdered bleach, the ants were there, too: a thousand grotesque confetti pieces tumbling in a cloud of white.

I slept, and in the morning: the ants, the ants, the ants.

◆ ◆ ◆

I called Callie. "They're getting worse."

"Disgusting." I heard static as she took a drag of her clove cigarette and exhaled into the phone. "You should really just move out of there."

"I can't just *move*," I explained. "I'm still waiting to hear back about grad school. If I don't get in, I'll probably have to sign on for another year at the food pantry. I mean, what else am I going to do? Work at the single shitty coffee shop in town?"

"I thought that place closed."

"Exactly."

Callie and I'd met in AmeriCorps the previous summer, placed in Lake Charles, Louisiana, living on the government's thin dollar in student housing at the edge of the McNeese State campus. I was assigned to the university food pantry, and Callie was given the veteran's center nearby, but wherever we ended up didn't make much difference. The people we worked for barely learned our names, regarded us as we were: just the next iteration in a rotating stream of wandering, idealistic twenty-somethings who got stuffed into crumbling studio apartments and slotted into jobs none of the real people in town wanted.

I took a chance on AmeriCorps because, as it turned out, my bachelor's degree in anthropology qualified me for nothing but a bleak series of restaurant jobs. Three years out of college, I was working three part-time serving jobs to afford a student loan payment twice the size of my rent. The few moments I had to myself when I wasn't sleeping or driving are not ones I remember; they were dissociative, a washed-out, barely human way of occupying a body. After three years of eating lentils and potatoes with every possible spice combination in a desperate attempt to make them taste like something I'd choose on purpose, I would've abandoned any semblance of a life I had to defer my student loans for a year.

Callie's family was from Atlanta and had more money than I'd ever see in my life, probably more than I could conceptualize, but they refused to keep doling it out unless she found some appropriate way to fill her time, a tagline they could tack next to her name in the holiday card. So that's how we both ended up making nine thousand dollars a year to work in a Gulf town eternally recovering from natural disasters. We were each embarking on another of the transient one- or two-year-long lives to add to the pile we'd collected already; me because I had so few options, and Callie because she had so many.

"Cut your losses and get out of there," she said. "What could breaking the lease cost, a couple hundred dollars?" I imagined her twirling her wrist in the air the way she often did, flashing her perennially pink nails—painted a new shade every week—with the elegant fan of her fingers, as if everything could be done just by summoning the will to do it.

I recalled the exact figure in my bank account, every cent I had to get through the next two and a half months, and wished it could've been *a couple hundred dollars*. There was $189.46 in my checking, plus $26 on an otherwise maxed-out credit card, after I sold some of my clothes and a lamp last month to make the minimum payment.

The irony of choosing AmeriCorps to get a break on my student loans is that at the end, they offer you a big chunk of money to sink into those loans, or a little chunk in cash. I'd needed the cash, though, and now I was living on the last of it, watching the balance dwindle faster than seemed humanly possible. The grace period in my contract gave me a place to live for the summer, but come August, I'd have to either sign up for another year or move out and find something else. I'd flung myself into uncertainty, betting on a long shot that I'd get into the anthropology master's program at McNeese, with funding.

"Yeah, of course I want to, but I just can't. I literally don't have the money to leave."

She sighed. "Well, if you get bored of being fertilizer for the bugs, you know you can always drive down and chill at my place."

Since Callie moved to Lafayette, I hadn't gone to see her, though she invited me often. A part of me wondered if she was lonely—if these phone calls took the edge off for her like they did for me. But Callie and I were not the same. Our loneliness did not cast the same shadow.

Some days I woke up and hallucinated ant bites, every inch of my skin covered in red swells. It was becoming harder to discern what was hallucination and what was real; the itch stuck to me, even if I couldn't find the marks to prove it.

A sick flash forced its way into my mind: a corpse in the crawl space under my house, ants swarming out of the tear ducts, into the nostrils, the expression of resigned terror as they coated the collapsed throat in rivers of black. In the vision, the corpse's face looked like my own.

"No, it isn't a good time right now. Thanks for offering, though."

◆ ◆ ◆

Once, I allowed myself to want in such a split-bellied way.

I'm not going to tell you his name, but let's say it was a standard American name, like James. That I'd watched my mother burn through a series of gruff, one-syllable men, and told myself it wasn't the same; that James wasn't like those men because he was a PhD student at a university, his parents had been university professors, he drove a hybrid, voted progressive. James had a girlfriend, but we never talked about that. I didn't know what she looked like and I didn't want to, though she also worked for the university and I knew I could've found her online profile very easily, had I dared to try. The previous fall, he'd wandered into the campus food pantry where I worked, and the corners of my vision softened, in awe of this long-limbed man who'd been carried there by a force I mistook for empathy.

James would only kiss me after at least three beers, and I'd only allow myself to hope he would after four vodka Sprites, guzzling that moldy-tasting liquor until it crested my levees of restraint. If I saw him while crossing campus, I never knew if he'd flash his dimples in a knowing smile that blossomed through me like morphine, or walk by like I was part of the monotonous Louisiana brush. The terms of our relationship made it easy for James to deny we'd had any interaction at all, which meant our connection survived mostly inside my head, metastasizing in the dark. I fantasized that he'd wound me in some way that stayed: a visible bite mark or bruise left behind on my skin, something to prove he had been there, that it had been real.

When I was a child, growing up in the foothills of the Appalachians, my mother sliced a shovel through the neck of a copperhead who'd ventured onto our back patio. I watched the beheaded snake's jaws open and shut dumbly around emptiness and air, her eyes two dull pearls staring blankly at the darkening sky. The ribbons of her throat spilled onto the concrete, brown scales shining like dense sequins. A bundle of swallowed things protruded from her gut, severed from the gaping, hinged-forever maw.

When I recall living in that swamp town, in that infested apartment—the faint blur of sweat and sensation I can still grasp these many years after—I think of that snake: split open, defenseless, but even in death, the body prepared for attack. There are so many ways we are taught what it means to be a woman.

◆ ◆ ◆

The summer of the ants was the summer I started working for the boys.

One late weekend night, when James wasn't returning my texts, I drank Kroger-brand red wine from the bottle and combed the shadier pages of Craigslist, hoping to come across something with an acceptable income-to-dignity ratio. Among the calls for threesomes and offers to buy soiled yoga pants or pics of women's pubic hair, one post stood out: *Will pay you to watch us. Girls only, any shape fine*, the ad read. *No sorority, no theater majors.*

The next morning, the sun battered down on my scalp as I walked, hungover and unshowered, to the far side of campus, where the row of frat houses stood. I couldn't tell you what the letters on the building meant, in terms of social standing or Greek translation, but it seemed to have been built in the eighties and left to its own devices since: chipped brown brick with white columns, a wrought-iron balcony, and a red door collaged with tape and torn flyers. I didn't bother knocking.

Inside, dust motes settled on stained Oriental rugs, piles of clothing, and half-crushed Solo cups. A carpeted staircase swooped through the living room, the missing balusters leaving random gaps like punched-out teeth. The house wasn't very nice, but it was very big, which is easy to mistake for nice. I remember thinking only kids who'd grown up rich could live in a place like that comfortably, without feeling like a runaway squatting in a hotel. The smell was of French fries and cigarettes and weed, and a cloyingly sweet scent that was unmistakably bodily. Being there was almost peaceful.

The boys were expecting me. They paraded down the stairs, emerged from the kitchen, rose up from their slumbers on the floor. They rubbed crust from the corners of eyes and mouths and donned their most convincing smiles—the ones they used for class presentations, for internships, interviews, and later, news pundit appearances and rally speeches when they ran for office. They did not look me up and down, the way boys do when deciding how to take what they want from a girl without her noticing. If they looked at me at all, it was in a non-looking way, and their excitement was in seeing themselves reflected on the still surface of my vacancy.

A blond one stepped forward. He had protruding gums and ice-blue eyes that bugged and squinted at the same time. He was not un-handsome.

He walked over to the cluttered credenza at the entryway and pulled the head off a porcelain snowman, holding up the torso so I could see the roll of twenty-dollar bills inside. *This enough?* he might have asked. They already knew it would be.

It was deeply intimate and unusually lucrative, but it wasn't sex work, exactly. The boys didn't want sex—at least not in the way that has to do with bodies touching. They wanted to be watched.

I found I was good at keeping silent as I ghosted from room to room, listening dutifully as the boys grumbled out loud to themselves, cooked and devoured a pile of eggs, did dishes, masturbated quickly beneath the stiff tent of an old quilt, most likely gifted by a mother or aunt. I watched them plug cords into walls, pull their fists through a tangle of wet laundry like kneading rings of bread, watched them lie and stare at screens, and watched them fall asleep. I watched them go about their day, walking out doors and back in again, a silent presence that required nothing, gave no feedback, only reassured them that the mundane moments of their lives were accompanied. That their efforts at existing were being witnessed. So much of my life had been spent watching boys and men do things, being terrified or amazed at their doing. I was very skilled at cultivating the feeling that they were noticed, with no obligation to notice in return.

Occasionally, they wanted me to dress up like someone, a pop singer or a too-friendly neighbor from childhood, but the wigs didn't bother me much. Every story we tell about ourselves is a performance; it's all about knowing your audience.

◆ ◆ ◆

Back then, I had this fantasy I kept returning to when I masturbated: a bunch of women wearing long Victorian dresses lined up single file as a group of men led them, one by one, to a machine designed to make them climax. The woman sits on the machine and drapes her skirts around it so no one can see what's happening underneath. The machine's mystery is part of the fantasy; the men see the results but can't steal the methods for themselves.

The woman on the machine sits still and tries to survive the pleasure, shaking and sweating as the crowd watches her writhe. Despite her modest sensibilities, an animal cry cracks through her and she comes hard, publicly.

I fantasized James would be the one to chaperone me to the machine and look upon me proudly as I orgasmed. Or, in another fantasy, James and I would slide into a booth at the run-down tiki bar we frequented (because no one in his department went there and it was too townie for the undergrads), and hidden under the table there'd be another man—his identity was incidental, unimportant—and James would direct the man to place his head inside my skirt and lick me while James observed the shifting colors and twitches on my face, fascinated.

But in reality, I was nothing to marvel upon. I was his ugliest secret.

He was mine, too, in a way. Callie knew nothing of James, and vice versa. He believed I was alone in the swamp, and I let him, because he loved the idea of becoming a world and I loved the idea of being presented one to dissolve in. The world our secrecy created was self-contained, separate from any other part of our lives, making it easy to pretend we had no other lives— that we blipped into existence only when touching, like jumper cables that spark when their metal teeth clash. But I did go on existing after he left, and carrying our story alone turned me feral with grief. I wanted to claw under my hair to find the place where memory lived, pull it out of my skull as an object I could hold in my hands, to prove I hadn't just made it all up.

When I met James, I was still young enough to believe myself unspeakably lucky if a man wanted anything from me. Though the sight of my thighs no longer reminded me of uncooked Christmas hams, experience had taught me again and again: I was not in the bracket of what was considered acceptable to love in public. But I also learned most men would fuck anyone that let them, so this became my currency.

I kept my affair with James going by the same rationale that kept me from killing myself: there was an eternity to be dead, but only a brief flicker of time to be alive, so you might as well take whatever's there while you can. Every time he dropped me off at my apartment, looking over his shoulder before he leaned in to kiss me, I knew it might be the last. But I decided to let myself be happy, or some approximation of it, while I was still allowed to be.

Tell me what you're afraid of, James would demand, his hand inside me, hot breath vibrating in my ear.

I fear depletion, I replied, or sometimes, *I fear abundance.*

Yes, you do, James cooed, his voice slurred with lust.

When he was ready to come, I'd get on my knees and he'd spread me open, as if examining meat for quality, and reach down the underside of my body to fondle my dangling breasts. Sex with men has a particular way of making you feel like livestock. Afterward, we'd lie together like two wet leaves, his belly ballooning to fill the C-shaped space in my back with each exhale.

Before and after sex, he'd reach for the blue plastic inhaler on the nightstand and suck in the metallic-sounding air. His childhood asthma followed him into adulthood and was the only thing I'd ever seen him bashful about. It was not for this alone that I loved him, witnessing this tenderness his body demanded of him without his consent, but for this that I allowed myself to keep calling it love.

When I ached lonely and aflame, even years after James and I both abandoned that swamp, I'd hallucinate the click and woosh of his inhaler. But the point of my strongest fantasies then, as I coaxed myself to the edge of electric release, was always the women, their bodies kindling beneath stiff fabric, grasping at their ruffled dresses; in their greatest state of vulnerability, they're undeniably, unbearably seen.

◆ ◆ ◆

As June smoldered on, the ants continued to gain ground in my apartment. They streamed from the bathroom sink and seemed immune to water. If I had to use the bathroom, I ran quickly in and out and always wore socks, after one incident when I'd sleepily set my foot down and ended up with a school of ants darting between my toes. I began locking away my perishables in Tupperware stacked neatly above the stove, but within days they were splattered with brown dots where a militia of ants had crumpled their skulls trying to force their way in.

When I was away from the ants, with James or the boys or at the food pantry, I almost forgot about them. But come evening when I pulled into my apartment's lot, I was again soaked through with dread. A week or two into my new gig, I was spending most nights at the frat house, staring blankly at passed-out boys with half-open mouths or wandering up and down the halls waiting for one to come out of their room for a drink. Another week, and I'd stopped going home entirely.

The ants had started following me; they spread through the tree branches of the dogwood I parked my car under, and when I unlocked it, cities of them circled the latex tubes around my car doors. They writhed manically at the ghost of old bubblegum stuck to the floor, drowned themselves in a bottle of power steering fluid I kept in the trunk. I attacked every crevice with a can of Raid, enough to get inside and drive away, but I never stopped jolting at the phantom sensation of a crawl or itch. I

parked farther and farther and farther away from my apartment, until I was parking so close to the boys it didn't make
sense to leave them.

So I slept on a couch in the basement of the frat house, or in
my car parked outside the house, or sometimes in a hotel room
James paid for, in the cheapest section of a casino compound
overlooking the river. I lied and said we couldn't meet at my
place anymore because it was being renovated—I couldn't imagine anyone caring enough to renovate those apartments, but it
sounded like an excuse fancy people made. We couldn't meet at
his place for obvious reasons.

After the first time at the hotel, he asked me to give him half
the money for the room. I got a sly pleasure knowing the cash
he walked around with in his pocket that night, when he went
home with the smell of me on his skin, was the same I'd gotten
from the boys earlier that day.

◆ ◆ ◆

I tried charcuterie for the first time in Callie's apartment during
orientation week of AmeriCorps. I'd never heard the word before, which she pronounced *chartreuse-erie*, and it took me years
of saying it that way until someone finally told me I was wrong,
that I was pronouncing it like the color or the French liquor,
which I'd also never heard of.

She was horrified to learn there was no Trader Joe's within
a hundred miles. Instead, we bought Brie wheels and salami at
the Piggly Wiggly around the corner from campus. The total the
cashier rang up was more than what I spent on groceries in two
weeks, but to my relief, Callie handed her card to the cashier
and paid without discussion.

We sat on the floor of her living room, the graying carpet and flaking walls same as mine, same as those of every unit in the building. Hers was furnished sparingly: pictures taped to the walls, curling from humidity (the only one framed was a printed-out Instagram post of Callie posing with one of the Real Housewives of Atlanta), a huge flat-screen TV placed on the floor, and a red fainting couch she called by its French name. She explained it was a family heirloom, "older than the war." When I asked which war she meant, she looked at me like it was obvious and answered, *All of them.*"

Piled around us were empty take-out boxes, wrappers, trash crusted with red wine and days-old food. A swarm of fruit flies lingered until November, when the weather began to cool, but Callie didn't seem bothered, swatting them away with a coral-polished hand as she chatted on. We sat close enough that I could smell her deodorant, slightly floral and comforting.

"I love eating with my hands like this. So luxurious," Callie said, folding a ribbon of meat into her mouth. "It makes me feel like a Spaniard."

"What's this?" I asked tentatively, pointing to a shriveled brown ball.

"Dried figs wrapped in prosciutto." She motioned at me to try it.

"I've never had figs before. Dried or wet."

She tossed a champagne laugh into the room, as if I were being hilarious. I bit into it, and the buttery, delicate crunch of seeds made me also feel like someone who ate with their hands on Spanish verandas, someone whose sensory experiences I never imagined I'd have access to.

I waited to swallow, then said, "I remember learning some-where that there's a female wasp inside every fig. It crawls in there to pollinate it, and then the acid in the fig dissolves it as it matures. The fruit wouldn't exist without them."

"Super gross."

"I mean, you can't see it or taste it or anything."

"So you're telling me they're not vegan?" she asked, seemingly concerned as she folded another slice of salami between her teeth.

I was in awe of Callie. I never saw her switch masks in the middle of a conversation, afraid she'd said something small and unforgivable. I cowered in guilt if I tried to claim a nibble of self-worth, but she was unapologetically herself, even when that self proved inconvenient.

◆ ◆ ◆

Earlier that spring, before I made money watching boys do things, I watched college freshmen assembling shredded cheese on tortilla chips, walking their family's Pomeranian through a paved neighborhood, buying hair dye at Walmart after midnight with their friends. I didn't connect it then, but these videos weren't unlike the in-person watching I'd do a few months later: both the watcher and the watched seeking an intimacy they know is constructed, until the construction becomes the truest intimacy.

That spring, James had given his Intro to Anthropology students an assignment to film a series of short videos; something about the archival process extending to our own lives, and it being an easy thing to ask of nineteen-year-olds, who already record so much of themselves. He suggested I take over his grading for the semester, reasoning that it would be good practice for when I got in at McNeese and started teaching classes myself.

James had happily helped me with my application to the master's program. We were the same age, but our lives had resulted in very different skill sets, so he taught me the etiquette for emailing my old college professors to ask for rec letters, and how to apply for an assistantship. He told me what lines to cut from my statement of purpose, the ones that, according to him, made me sound too earnest, too desperate. For him, manipulating how you were perceived was an elective political art form; for me, it was second-nature survival.

No one in my family had finished college, and grad school was beyond what I'd been able to imagine for myself. From my federally subsidized housing at the edge of campus, I marveled at the grad students, these young, worldly hybrids of teacher and scholar. My AmeriCorps apartment was originally built for, and occasionally occupied by, postgraduates, and at times it was easy to imagine the shadow life I could live as one of them. If I got into the program, my real life would paste itself over the fantasy at last. I wouldn't even have to move out of my ant-infested apartment to do it—but I would, because I would have the choice to.

I watched grad students chatting with white-haired professors on their walks through the parking lot, watched them driving to class while swarms of lowly undergrads sweated beneath their backpacks. At the campus food pantry where I worked, grad students would sometimes stop in with their cohorts, giggling loudly as they took a bag of rice and cans of expired martini olives off the shelves, as if hunger were inconsequential, nothing to be ashamed of, a chore.

James once told me that as a child, he'd thought all adults were called "doctor," because every adult he knew happened to be one. The first night we had sex, we drank Chardonnay from glasses with the Stanford insignia, his alma mater, and he told me about fucking a sorority girl on the president's lawn the night of graduation. He wore steel-toe boots under his slacks because James, like many white men in academia at the time, worried that since people had begun acknowledging racism and sexism out loud, in order to go on getting the jobs they already had and publishing in the places they'd published before, they had to heighten the sense that their families had worked, and therefore, their lives had been hard too. Of course, James's parents were both literature professors at a small liberal arts school in a large midwestern city, but he grew up in a state that shared a border with Appalachia and could seamlessly affect the round speech of mountain dwellers. The boots helped with this performance.

James was a man not unlike my father or yours, or anyone's that gets memorialized as a footnote rather than spouted as a reason: not a bad man, or a guilty man, or a man so ectopic with grief it was pressed like coal and spilled over the bodies of his loved ones as embers of violence. Just a man: regular, frightened, and inheriting the world.

◆ ◆ ◆

I watched boys fail to do homework, marking up the pages of books with angry black spirals and stick figures set on fire. I watched them take bong hits, their eyes red and wonderous, laughing like doughy-faced babies at a joke that could only be shared with themselves. It was delicious to disappear, to be devoured in the swarm of boys. The house itself was an all-consuming extension of them: swirling with their smells and eyelashes and stubble, trapping in amber their last meals or movements through it.

Sometimes they brought girls home, or threw parties to draw girls to the house. The girls left things behind, too: flecks of mascara on pillows, smears of foundation on washrags, long dark hairs curling mosaiclike on shower walls. When the girls came over, they didn't know how to regard me. Even if the boys told her what I was for, the girl's noticing was obvious underneath the most convincing performance—but they'd always try, humoring the boys. Then, there'd be some moment in the night, both of them lost in pretending, that she'd stop seeing me too.

Occasionally, I'd catch an opposite shift in one of the boys; following close behind on the basement stairs, when he'd reach up to switch on the light, our bodies so close that a single breath would force our skin to brush, and he'd look not quite through me. When one rolled over in the dark, burritoed in puffy blankets up to the neck, and slanted his eyes at my spot on the wall while he sleepily touched himself. Something, every once in a while, like noticing. Like teasing. Like gratitude.

In time, I understood how their lives hinged on my daily offering of dutiful absence. Without me, their every minute felt purposeless, futile pawings at the foot of the grand human story. My nonexistence allowed them to exist so much more.

I was not so nonexistent to them that my gaze didn't curb their worst impulses—not so forgotten that if they tried to drug a girl or drag her to a room against her will, I wouldn't stop it. There were limits to our contract, and they were careful not to break it. Sometimes, when one of the boys brought a girl over for sex, I'd notice him touch her more carefully, be more patient in his fumbling attempts to earn her orgasm. And there was a pleasurable pain in never participating, in longing to be inside the bodies of both people and watching them long only for each other. When the boys pulled out with a wasted grunt, my own body grasped at the hollowness.

Sometimes, though, one of the boys would get rough with a girl in bed, and I knew it was because of my watching, like their anger was directed at me. At whatever I represented to them, not so dissimilar to what the girl naked in his clutches represented.

One night I was in the kitchen watching a brunette one with hairy arms and dainty hands as he half-ass scraped a burnt pizza pan before giving up. As he walked down the hall, a single ant crawled up the side of the sink.

When I'd last returned to my apartment a month ago, ants ran the length of the arch between the kitchen and living room. I ducked and shook out my hair when I passed under it, then went to my room to throw some clothes in a bag. I imagined they'd probably taken over the apartment in my absence, every surface black and pulsing, and I decided to let them. The ants could take the whole house if they wanted; that life had nothing to do with me anymore.

In the frat house, the lone ant pranced across the counter, wiggling its feelers. I stamped it out with a finger. Easy as that. Upstairs, the boys burst out laughing at something I'd never learn—even if I did, it wouldn't have made sense.

◆   ◆   ◆

Callie lasted all of six months at her appointment doing clerical work for the local VA, complaining every time she climbed the rickety metal stairs of our apartment building to hang out after work, mostly about the smell of the building and the old man who'd had a seizure in the waiting room during her first week. She vowed never to wipe up blood again, broke her contract with AmeriCorps, and moved to Lafayette "to get into the art scene." From what I could piece together from her stories over the phone, being "in the art scene" meant she attended elaborately costumed parties at bars, where large macramé projects were constructed in real time for drunken onlookers, and she'd taken up wearing glittery kitsch butterfly clips in her hair.

She met her boyfriend, Travis, at one of those parties. She was dressed that night as a Confederate-era widow, and he was costumed as himself, a shitbag yacht boy: one of a handful of lesser oil heirs raised on the Gulf Coast, and almost certainly a known rapist. Despite this, Callie said things worked out perfectly between them because he was dumb, his moneyed entitlement familiar, and she knew how to easily "handle him." She boasted that she'd even gotten him to clean up her apartment— though when I pressed her, she admitted he hired a maid service for her, claiming it basically amounted to the same thing.

When other women in their Lafayette circle whispered about things Travis had done—not just the gray-area too-drunk incidents, but degrading violences—she flicked her hibiscus-pink hand to the sky and called it gossip. She blamed the women for not being smart enough to *handle him* the way she'd learned to. This was her prize: she could have anything in the world, but she chose this mangled man who she alone could tame with the power of her gaze.

◆ ◆ ◆

During our once- or twice-a-week phone calls, I held back on telling Callie what I was doing with the boys. I knew the strangeness of the experience would lure her, and she'd want in. These boys, in this limited way, were mine, and I didn't want to share them. I wanted to be the only one they needed; the only one who could provide them this service, even if it had nothing to do with me beyond the ease of imagining my absence.

As I watched the boys boxing or building things, watched them eat and shower and shit, I could imagine myself ghosting in the shadows of James's days—watching as he stood in front of a classroom, typed in his cubicle office at the university, made a grilled cheese on the stovetop. In truth, I spent far more time in my head with James than I did with him in front of me.

I let myself wonder about his girlfriend, too, when I was bored and poked at the shame-bruise in the center of my chest just to feel something. I bet she was thinner than me, the kind of woman who looked older when she was nineteen and younger when she was thirty, the kind of woman who could wear sweats without looking sloppy. She was probably the kind of person who had no tattoos, or just one or two small ones: her maternal grandmother's birthday in Roman numerals across her wrist, or a delicate ankle dolphin she got on spring break with friends in college that now she'd tell you she was embarrassed of. I'd never felt anything like embarrassment about the tattoos painting my thighs, wrists, shoulders, and upper arms, until I imagined his girlfriend's miles of clean, untouched skin.

I watched boys pile sugar into their coffee and watched it dissolve like a swimmer beneath the surface of a lake. From a grime-streaked second-story window, I saw a blue chair and a red backpack on the side of the road, and I saw a boy take it like he'd taken things his entire life: because it was there. I watched them not check the back seats of their cars before they drove off, not look over their shoulders when someone cried out, not inhale sharply as they passed an open garage door in the cover of night. They were lonely, some of them, truly, poignantly lonely. But they were not afraid that they deserved to be.

◆　◆　◆

I had three weeks, till August, to decide whether to sign on to AmeriCorps for another year and stay in my apartment or move out, and I was supposed to hear back about grad school any day. As weeks went by without any news, my anxiety about the future grew sharper teeth. James and I had talked about serious things before, though never without some part of ourselves obscured. But when I shared my ambitions with him and he'd urged them along, it opened a window into my real, vulnerable self. He'd even offered to mention my name to the professors on the admissions committee, though of course later I'd realize he never did, never intended to.

Finally, he said, "You don't need to worry. You're going to get in."

I smiled a painfully large smile. There was a not-small part of me that openly sought his admiration, like a teen daughter with a distant father.

"You really think I'm smart enough?"

"Smart doesn't matter," he said. "You've got a good sob story, a whole 'phoenix from the ashes' thing going on. That's what's gonna sell them."

I was stunned quiet, so he continued. "This stuff is all decided by some rich old white people trying to fill a quota so they can feel good about themselves. You're a woman, *and* grew up poor in rural nowhere Kentucky. So, yeah, you're gonna get in."

"It was Tennessee," I muttered, my face stuffed red with embarrassment.

"Same thing."

James sighed—frustrated, then pitying. "None of this is about being good or trying hard. You of all people must know that, right?"

I might've nodded, but he had already looked away.

I kept our conversation close the following days, like tending a festering wound, until Callie and I spoke. I told her it was one of the AmeriCorps supervisors who'd said it, bringing it up with a false chuckle, like, *Can you believe someone would be so silly, so rude?*

Her response shouldn't have surprised me. "They're not wrong. Even nothing-colleges like McNeese have all kinds of hierarchy, weird fucked-up backwoods politics," she said. "My uncle is on the board at Emory and it's, like, a whole thing. The stuff he tells us about is pretty gross if you think about it, like the unfairness or whatever. But it's super normal."

I muttered something in reply and heard myself echo— the familiar tell that she'd switched me to speakerphone so she could scroll through her notifications while we talked.

"Don't worry," Callie said. "Things always turn out how they're supposed to, you know? You've just gotta trust the universe."

I'd always known Callie and James were alike, and it was one of many reasons I kept them separate, tension poles balanced on either side of my life. If they met, the version of myself I got to inhabit with them would combust, revealing the unformed self I believed was lying dormant underneath, like a gown stitching itself closer to brilliance until it was ready for me to step into. Or he would think she was prettier than me. I couldn't decide which was worse.

James and Callie both moved through the world freely, seen or unseen whenever they chose. For once, I wanted the privilege to exist to others, to disappear for myself.

But even if they were right, and my only hope for a better future was how destitute my past had been, I could take it. If I got what I wanted out of pity, I still got it. I couldn't become real to the world in the way James and Callie were, but maybe I could become happy.

I began to focus on *trusting the universe*, visualizing good things coming down the pipeline, grad school springing forth a shiny new life as attainable as I hoped it would be. It had been days since I'd seen an ant, even on the sidewalk, and that seemed like a good sign. It felt almost inevitable, the way it played out in my head, almost like it was already happening to me. It is dangerous to confuse belief and hope. But I started to believe.

◆ ◆ ◆

When I started believing in the future, I stopped watching boys do things for money. Enough money was never enough, really, but come September, I'd be able to move out of the AmeriCorps apartments and get a cheap place somewhere else in town. I had enough money to survive the rest of the summer, and as long as I got into McNeese, with an assistantship, I'd be fine for the foreseeable future.

Some of the boys were sullen when I told them. Some shrugged. One built me a cherry-varnished chair by hand that sits now in the corner of my husband's home office. A few asked me for recommendations, other women I might know who could take my place, but I didn't mention Callie. She wouldn't have been good at it. She didn't know how to make herself invisible—and even if she could, I realized, she wouldn't have wanted to.

I went back to my apartment for the first time in almost two months, and soon as I arrived, I saw the brigade of ants trailing onto the doorstep. I shook a mass of them loose from a pile of mail that had overflown onto the concrete stoop, and the future was there, sandwiched between coupons and credit card spam: a flat, form rejection reminding me how limited the spots were, how rigorous their selection process, encouraging me to throw another sixty dollars in application fees their way next year, printed on plain computer paper, sagging with humidity.

In the months that followed, I remembered a story Callie told me once, in our AmeriCorps days, about an Italian performance artist who let people do anything they wanted to her. She stood in a plain room in front of an audience, and people ripped her clothes, cut her hair, sucked blood from her neck, threw garbage on her, so that anytime a person chose an act of kindness it was almost shocking to witness. And I thought about how an experience like that makes neutrality, or indifference—anything other than explicit harm—begin to look like tenderness. And I thought: Is that what happens when you give your body over to people, they will always be tempted to respond with cruelty because they know they can get away with it?

In the years after, I left and carried out my own small cruelties and still never knew the answer. I just knew what Callie told me: when the performance was over and the woman stepped toward the audience, they all ran from her.

◆ ◆ ◆

At the end of that summer, as I signed another year of my life to the food pantry and August returned the hive of students to campus, Callie went missing. Her glowy, round face was plastered on telephone poles and national news. Her parents took out a billboard on the stretch of I-10 between Lafayette and New Orleans, and another in Atlanta near the airport, an 800 number pasted below a selfie she'd taken earlier that summer in her ivy-covered backyard, taffy-pink nail polish and glittery butterfly clips in her hair, glancing downward, frowning sultrily at the cars and cargo trucks that passed by.

Three weeks had passed without a call from Callie, but I'd thought she was ignoring me. I assumed she was vacationing at Travis's parents' condo in Biloxi, or doing Instagram lives to try to get brand deals, or just rejecting the outside world to sit in her apartment eating Thai noodles and bingeing *Vanderpump Rules.* She got like that sometimes, disappearing for however long, and I think she thought I was a good friend for not caring. But I was resentful of how she existed only how and when she wanted to, how other people's expectations didn't even cross her mind. Ironically, the qualities I hated most about myself made me most appealing to her: I always existed, and would be there waiting whenever she was ready to return.

I wasn't a very good friend. I'd sent her a message—after the rejection letter but before I knew she was missing, of course—with as much sharpness as I could muster back then. About how she dealt with Travis, how she didn't believe the other women, or did believe them but didn't think their pain mattered. Or said something about how she called us friends, but you can't be friends with someone who needs your life to be limited in order for theirs to be expansive. I don't remember the words now. Looking back, I doubt what I said was really about her at all.

Travis was questioned, of course, as was her landlord, and some boy she dated in high school who'd since racked up a collection of domestic violence charges; all were released the same day, tossed free into the sticky afternoon heat. I don't think anyone in Callie's life knew I existed, just as no one in mine knew about her. Wherever she was, the history of our friendship was a room only I could enter now. A room that echoed.

Across the southeastern seaboard, a cable TV spot played every night for a year: Callie twirling, colorful and carefree, at ages five, twelve, sixteen, eighteen, twenty-two. Home videos her parents must've paid some producer to splice together and throw a sweeping musical score behind, inspirational and heart-breaking at the same time. After blowing out the candles on her birthday cake, she flutters her eyelashes up at the camera, blond at the root where the mascara had worn away, and says in a teen-beauty-pageant voice, *The most exciting thing about growing older is that the future is all yours to discover.*

I envied her and I didn't. Leave it to Callie to disappear while becoming more visible, more *real*, than ever. She would've loved it, being crystallized this way for us to behold, filtered in the pastel light of tragic beauty. But she would've rather been real. I knew it. I know it. Despite the privileges that made her life seem infinite, she didn't get to choose whether she got to keep it.

Every night, she smiled at me from the screen and talked about the sweet fog of the future, her perfectly contoured face protruding from the darkness, only to dissolve again.

◆ ◆ ◆

In the end, I did finally take Callie up on her offer. I drove to Lafayette and parked my car in the gravel lot next to her apartment. She'd been missing for three weeks, and her apartment had been sitting empty all that time. I approached the gray house, split on the inside, I knew, by a wall of ceiling-to-floor bookshelves that separated Callie's apartment from the old man's next door, his occasional muffled footsteps the only proof of his existence. A cluttered vigil spilled off the front porch into the yard, votive candles with Callie's face pasted over a busty saint, posters with Callie's name in pink glitter glue, teddy bears soggy with fleas and festering rain. Her doorway was roped off with yellow caution tape.

I peered through the front window and saw that her things were still there, untouched, and all around them, the familiar piles of trash. It was like looking into a diorama of Callie's life. I kept waiting for her to step out of the darkness in a crown of tawny blond braids and one of her ridiculous vintage nightdresses, like the ghost of a Nordic princess who refused to let history forget her.

In a different story, Callie goes on existing like that, a faint silhouette on the other side of the tape, drifting from empty take-out box to empty take-out box. In a different story, her body was found floating in the Gulf, or buried on the far side of an orchard; her family got closure, the police released her possessions, and some divorced woman who worked at the bank moved into Callie's apartment and had a happy life there, never knowing any of it. In a different story, I moved to a city, any random city, and met a man soaked all the way through with kindness, and we sat on a park bench talking until our sorrow watered the garden of our lust, until we grew together like twisted shrubs. In another story, James locks me in a wooden house and I bear his standard American sons, I cook his standard American meals thick with weaker creatures' flesh, swallow thick pills for my standard American grief, he calls me his little wife, and I become her. In another, I learned something from this loss, made friends with hunger's clawing need and started naming my basic desires out loud, as if it were that simple and always had been.

In another, you crack this story open and find a million eyes swarming in the sweet gelatin meat, like the multiplicitous seeds of a fig.

I went back to my car and watched whispers of electronic light dance in the window of the old man's apartment. I sat in that position for a very long time, until dull blue was leaking across the dashboard, and I had the strange feeling that I must have slept, although I didn't remember closing my eyes. I knew when I went home the ants would be there, and I would have to deal with them. I would have to keep dealing with them all summer until the winter came and froze them to death, but then next year's cantankerous sun would thaw them, and they would return. Even when there was nothing to fight against I would be listening for them, hiding in the walls with their dormant colonies, ready to wake and flood in, to destroy themselves for a morsel of what they were never meant to have.

◆ ◆ ◆

In the fall, a few months after Callie went missing, I saw James and his girlfriend getting into his car outside of an upscale Cajun restaurant. It was October, still too hot for the cardigan I wore, and I was on a date with a man who would not be cruel or violent, a man I would never mention in the following years when a therapist asked me to catalog my traumas. A man who, one night in the safety of my living room, I would get too drunk with and prod him to tell me which parts of my body he hated most, and when he did and I turned away from him, feeling shame sizzle through my body in a sharp line to my clit, it was he who would howl and sob until the neighbors turned their porch lights on. Then he would rub his palms and grasping fingers over the parts of my body he had proclaimed disgust for, and I would retreat into the long dark tunnel of myself while he had sex with me and for the first time—with this man or any—he would tell me that he loved me. The next morning he would leave, and I would cut five inches off my hair with a kitchen knife. When we later saw each other at a coffee shop in town, we would not mention any of it, not the love or the ragged sounds we made. He would smile and I would smile, and out of politeness, he would not comment on the parts of me that were missing.

I watched James open the car door for his girlfriend and walk around to the driver's side. I watched her tuck her long blond hair over one shoulder as she reached to tighten the strap on her bra, white skin and a thin shock of blue under her blouse, then gone again. I watched him lean over to kiss her before he started the engine, then turn his eyes to the overpass and pause, as if there were something he'd forgotten. A tingle of breath on the back of his neck, a crawling feeling. A phantom itch that stuck. Then I watched them drive away.

II

A MANUAL FOR HOW
TO LOVE US

ELECTRICITY

Before there was light, there was a surge that swallowed all of what was formerly known to be light. The People stumbled around their Houses, tapping on the glass, not sure how to lure the glow back into the cages they made to hold it. It was a bounty that had always just *been* there, like sudden bursts of laughter behind locked doors, or water pouring from a faucet. The colored panes of windows, void of the sun's warmth, atrophied and shattered in their frames. Able to see the guts of light bulbs for the first time, fashioned from friction and simple wire, The People grew panicked. They had lived so long in illumination they'd never considered the properties of darkness.

At first, they felt the absence physically, like every yellow pigment had been licked away, leaving shapeless cavities, unexplored territories of flesh and vein and wishing. In those days, The People lived as one synchronized Body, and when a Person was racked with emptiness, The People communally felt that emptiness as their own.

In an attempt to trap the fled light, The People split from each other into new, separate cages of meat and bone, and they no longer recognized one another as they had in the old world. They learned for the first time to migrate by blind noise, to recognize the edges of their own shadows. They touched without speaking, came to relearn friends by the unique funneling of breath through nostrils, and lovers by the particular lack they nursed. They mimed fingers the shape of candles, made lanterns of their hollows. They sometimes took comfort in the blanket of night and allowed themselves to be lonely, knowing that in the dark there is always someone you can't see watching. They sometimes did not try their best to be kind to one another.

Sometimes they tried very hard, and when it seemed they had succeeded, The People might, for a moment, hallucinate a spark—might imagine the lamplit flicker of a face come into view. They realized if they visualized the light clearly enough, it could be so again: the wires of their bulbs electrified, the neon of a supermarket's smile, the orange glow of a childhood kitchen in the humid middle of night. This is how they were by the time you were born, The People, stumbling through a blackness they believed could turn inverse by the power of crude hope. The lightness of memory more brilliant than it had been in reality:

This is the world you were born into.

TONGUE

Before those futile ladders called limbs, this wet, writhing appendage was your first way to reach into the world. After the light left and The People confined themselves to the empty cages of themselves, the Tongue was the last part of the Body that remembered the old way, when The People belonged to each other. It carried pieces of the world back, so that you could inspect them and decide which pieces you would reject as Not You, and which pieces you would absorb as Part of You. Mouth-knowing is the perfect symbiosis of the desire to experience and be experienced.

However, once a Body grows to a certain height and weight, The People no longer approve of Tongues, preferring use of the more obvious (if less sophisticated) human limbs; the loss of the reciprocal relationship of mouth-knowing is our first trauma. Each Person will try to re-create it years later, in a struggle known as Intimacy, but find sadly that the punished Tongue has atrophied, incapable of its familiar ecstatic knots.

THE HERO

The People say you are The Hero of this Story, but you are not so sure. You have never owned a cape, you fear fire and sharp objects, could never jump from a building and land safely. They tell you that you were brought here for a reason, and that reason is to learn how to be very, very good at all this living.

Once you are proven, they say, you will get a star. They're not clear if the star will be a thing you can hold in your palms like a morsel of food, or a thing that burns bright and untouched on a wooden shelf in your room, or if, when you are proven, you'll leave your flesh and zoom up to greet your star where it lives. You stare up at the night sky in wonderment at all the freckles on the face of this universe, awed and frightened. You catalog the stars obsessively in the pages of your mind, wonder which one will be yours, how long you have left to prove yourself, who will get to choose.

MOTHER

Before she was yours, she was Someone. She belonged only to herself and to the bite marks like rose petals lovers left on her skin. When she was Someone looking for Someone else, she was terrified in the aimless way of all People, and all she wanted was to tell a Person about it out loud, face-to-face. The Story goes like this: When she met your Father, or Someone before your Father, she said to him: *I'm terrified.* He asked her why, and she tried to form new words that meant *I'm afraid you're going to give me everything I've ever wanted and then you're going to take it away and afterward I will still have to go on being alive* (for this is what all People are afraid of). Eventually she said something that was not exactly that, and when he responded, his words were stone—not mausoleum walls scrubbed white by rain, but something for a pocket.

Twice in her life she felt it: the bright-hot flood of fear that comes when you know that you are about to love something. The first time was then, with him. The second time came into the world with you, and never ceased.

When you are born, the doctor, once a child himself, will make note of the smell of salted fruit. Your Mother's human fear will remain, but time will mangle it into a different monster; she will by then have seen joyless babies at dawn, their milky eyes serene and pensive, and become disturbed to realize they're able to see something she'd missed. Her voice will become as faded and indistinct as her partner's, though her hair will always have its own swirling mobile of planetary light. She will look at her family and think, *How does anyone survive such violent beauty?*

FATHER

A ship, a shape, a shift in temperature, a slab of wool, a suit of feathers, a captured serpent, a caution, a potion, a phone call, a bird's jaw, a bramble, a bottle, a congress, a forest, a fondness, a fortress, a fevering, a fly, a fishhook, a flight of stairs, a flock of freckles, a northbound train that's finished boarding, an error, erasure, the drum of boots pounding, a doctoring, a denial, a damaged umbrella, a disturbing metal shine, a hallway with lamps on only one side, a House with windows only in the floor, a pixel glow, a pane with torn-off shutters, a pair of hands red and shuddering, a shattering, a stolen sweatshirt, a lifeboat with only one bench, and on deck the band playing loud their lunatic sorrow, a harbinger, a hope, a hole in the dirt, a bath in holy oil, a broken fence, a bear's chest, an accident, an absence.

SISTER (ITCH)

Perhaps you have a Sister. Perhaps she is a cherry-scented gust of smoke, or her smile is the steely rind of a lime. Like a fork in a flower's stem, she can bloom at any moment into friend or

Stranger. A Sister is a thing that burrows just beneath the flesh and can't be burned away by any fire The People have created. She itches and itches, like a loose tooth you can't bear to pull.

BROTHER (THUD)

Perhaps a Brother is your lot. And a Brother is, as you will learn, a lot. If you catch him while he is sleeping and press your ear to his chest cavity, you'll hear the scrape of talons and hammer of horses' hooves pounding beneath his skin. Remember the sudden music of him, and pray the horses don't find their way into his hands—The People refer to this as a stampede, and fear it to the point of bloodshed. If your Brother has a name, wait until it is fluttering around the room and try to catch it in your mouth. Swallow it fast, so if his Body goes to the grave, a part of him can remain on land, moth-winged and carelessly gentle.

GUILT

One unremarkable afternoon, it blooms plum-violet and lovely as a bruise, its source a mystery: Did you breathe it in unknowingly, a virus loitering on the sidewalk? Swallow it in cherry tomatoes from the garden? Invite it between canyons of skin like a rotten accident? Like a shadow-limb or a phantom sibling, it follows you everywhere you go. When you grow legs and wheels and engines to slingshot yourself across the land, it still knows where to find you. In hotel rooms, in deserts, and tucked under mountains, it slips into your sheets and lies silent beside you, an always warm bedfellow.

It's smarter than you are, and ancient, and if you try to drown it with poison or cut it out with a pocketknife, it simply moves to another part of your Body. *Stupid child*, it says, *don't you see that you're only cutting away pieces of yourself?* As soon as you think you've caught hold of it, it slithers away. You can hear it humming all night, a faint song swimming in your bloodstream. You are not anymore a child, you try to argue, but you have grown tired, you are so, so tired.

At least, it reminds you, *you will never be truly alone.*

HOUSE

Houses are structures infused with a magic only the inhabitants can see. When you are asleep and you dream of a building, or a forest with the warm tunnels of a building, that building will always be your House. When The People read Stories about humans who live in rooms, they lack the imagination to picture any House that is not their own. A House can be a single room, or can be the silent space between rooms, or can be the skin that covers a collection of many rooms (also referred to as cells).

Sometimes a House will trick you, hide its door, and disguise itself as a Body; when this happens, its inhabitants tunnel secret pathways behind the walls and give the paths names like Destruction or Survival. Sometimes a Person will lose their sense of direction and show up inside another Person, mistaking them for a different kind of structure. A House should not be confused with the heart, which also has rooms, but whose rooms are deafening, nailed shut from the inside, and smell incessantly of burgundy.

HOME

Home is most often experienced as a city of brilliance carried on the echo of an old lullaby you can almost, just barely, remember the words to. Home can sometimes appear as the ghost of a House that has been abandoned by its magic, but often, it cannot be seen with eyes. A symptom of nearing Home is violent, musical trembling and a fever that reddens the chest—while distance from Home manifests as pain in the throat and the sensation of a wire being slowly removed. It's been known to appear as a shadow of lamplight at the end of a dark hallway, so gorgeous it coaxes you out of your Body. Of course, this is mostly speculation; very few People have ever found a genuine Home in the limited span of their lives.

SOMEONE

See: Home.

STRANGER

The game is this: each time you meet one, try to figure out if they are Someone, or simply a collection of bones with intention. Test them with your voice, your mouth, your hands. Watch to see if your words bounce off them like raindrops, if they circle like gnats, if the Stranger shakes them off like a wet dog or eats them one by one like jelly beans. Examine all edges and angles of their smile for potential foundational problems, leaks, cracking, or faulty construction. Bite into a randomly chosen part; take a chunk of them away and watch what grows back in its place.

If tree bark, or any hardened substance: they are not Someone.

If fur, or bone, or any fragment of creature: hold them gently, then lock them in a quiet room, and swallow the key for safekeeping.

If a buzzing with no source: this Stranger may require further interrogation, but check first to make sure what you're hearing isn't just the wind eavesdropping through an open window.

If a hive, stillborn: run, cut your hair with any knife in reach, and take immediate cover.

If fresh leaves, or any variety of budling: it is possible they are Someone. Before you celebrate, though, look away and turn back quickly. Watch how their foliage behaves when you leave the room, whether the petals begin to dance or rot.

THORN

A Thorn is rarely seen coming, except if you live on a tall mountain and make a habit of cloaking your body in weapons. It can be an interruption in the Story, or can become the Story itself. If you find a Stranger who you believe could be Someone, you must brace yourself for their Thorn, which always strikes when their floral aroma has distracted you from your own Body. Some People seek out the Thorn itself, uninterested in whatever wilting bloom crowns it; those People are lucky to know what they're getting, and luckier to get out alive.

A Thorn takes many forms, but the symptoms are the same: anxiety :: House-sickness :: the sensation of being dismembered wing by wing under a microscope :: irrational levels of nostalgia :: impulse to declare war that lasts four hours or longer :: nausea :: a silver sheen to the skin :: voiceburial :: paleness of the Tongue :: leakiness in the orifices of the face :: an air-filled grief that cannot be held without gloves :: excessive thirst :: the tops of hands stained as if by thunder :: sudden nighttime visions of a Stranger's face, usually in the shape of a Father or a Person you've never met :: motion sickness :: inability to view street signs :: hallucinations of feathers :: a Body filled with arrows :: strong odor of maple syrup.

Occasionally, a Stranger will go around flashing their Thorns when they want something from you, usually: permission to be ruined. If a Person invites another Person to identify their Thorns, this is a standoff known as Compassion. It means they remember the way of the old world, when we shared the same light.

There is no known cure for a Thorn but to rip it out and hope it doesn't take too much of you with it. If there is bleeding, as is often the case, you can dam the wound with your Tongue. If Someone nearby is willing to lend you their Tongue, that will also suffice, although this method is generally unreliable.

BODY

See: Guilt.

STORY

Story is the name People give to their regrets. The things we do not regret do not become Stories; they dissolve, while regrets, indigestible, linger within the Body. When The People find a Story particularly troublesome, they might try to trick it into leaving their Body by drawing its various names on pieces of parchment and hoping it will show up. Every Story trapped in writing is an apology, a declaration, and a record of unchecked shame.

There is only one Story, but many ways of arranging its words, so it can appear to have multiplied:

The Story that is every Story is that you have swallowed something ugly and now you need to convince Someone to dig it out of you, Someone with a shovel and the right type of map. The Story that is every Story is that there is a wolf's eye beneath each Person's Tongue and it grows hungrier with every passing year. The Story that is every Story is that there is something, sometimes many somethings, that you will spend most of your time on this planet longing rough and messy for, and once you get that thing it will feel almost like it didn't happen at all.

A secret The People won't tell you is that it barely matters how good you are at living if you are able to accomplish love. When The People discovered love as a shortcut, they grew ravenous for it, constructed monuments in its honor, painted their faces in its favorite colors, and made their days long ritual parades in sacrifice to it. Love is the name we give to the precise moment when we recognize Someone as a protagonist, because what People love even more than being in love is feeling like part of a Story. We want to be a narrative with purpose, structure, referenceable blueprints, a definite ending. When we tell each other our Stories, we are attempting to construct A Manual for How to Love Us.

WELL

A Well is a sigh in the ground where we return to ourselves. What goes down into it is a secret, and what gets brought up is the surprise of what we didn't know we needed.

If the Well could speak, it would tell a Story like this: some Person existed for a while. The Person's Mother and Father walked in and out of rooms, breathing quietly. The Person's Sisters and Brothers floated clumsily in the yard. They might have been imagined. They were all very small in comparison to the landscape.

Some Person might remember opening a door into a long wooden hallway and walking down that hallway to a room with a roaring hearth, where their Mother was weaving her pale-gold hair in the loom and spiders were weaving blankets for the sun-lit corners. Someone, somewhere might remember this as Home.

A Well is a mouth that replenishes, a revolving bucket of give and take, of being regifted what you've given.

A Person who once believed they were The Hero of this Story stares into the dark reservoir and glimpses a bright flicker, slight as fireflies stuttering between cupped hands. It might have been imagined, but imagining magic into the world is one way of finding it there; grasping for what shines, holding rever-ent whatever starlight is shed when our Bodies briefly close the distance between us.

To be proven, The Hero now understands, is to leave behind a Story: toss it into the sweet, deep void, and hope Someone, someday, will draw up its ember in their bucket—which is one way of loving the world, which is one way of loving The People who make it our Home.

In this bottomless throat of dark and stone, a brightness festers.

III

BURROWING

I

Sometimes there are houses and sometimes houses have attics. Attics are made with splintered wood, and the splinters get stuck in the sleeves of sweaters, burrowing in like thin bugs. Attics can have stained-glass windows that splash color onto the wooden floor. Sunlight moving through them illuminates the air, like a church burning.

In the South, attics are rarely spoken of. This is because the South rips people up from the ground, washes them into mudslide; in the South, people burrow into darkness, into slick red earth, into steel storm shelters, and by the time the white sky settles in, it is already too late.

But sometimes in the South, there are attics. There are attics with stained-glass windows because women make them. Women sit in the attic sketching shapes: sometimes roses, sometimes birds. Sometimes the roses are blood and the birds are sky. A woman scores the glass, cuts it with copper, grinds the edges. Stained glass is always art, but the woman is not always an artist; she is a mother, a wife, a neighbor. She foils the glass, solders, frames. This is also how she raises children, refining them, grounding them in place. Her daughters are like windows that sit still and let the light pass through them. The woman is someone's daughter, too, unless she is free.

II

There were people who lived inside of walls. This happened a long time ago. They lived in houses, but *in* the houses, in the piping and bones. In the South and the North and elsewhere, they carved their own paths, and in this way, there was another, secret world inside of each house, a world that had nothing to do with rooms. Insulation made the wall-people feel safe. It was lovely, pink and furry, and sometimes they slept in it, or listened through it. Small portals of light filtered through, casting shapes and colors into their darkness, and they used them to tell stories. They had secret doors to where food was, and when the people who lived in rooms were sleeping, they took what they needed and burrowed back into the walls. They heard the people who lived in rooms arguing over where the food had gone, blaming each other. This did not make the wall-people happy.

They survived like this for a long time. Generations of wall-people were born and died without notice. They learned to silence themselves; their vocal cords sealed. When they gave birth, even the infants did not scream. They congregated close and synchronized their movements, so each limb raised in the dark became five limbs, or thirty. Their many lungs sounded like wind through a forest, muffled behind the panels.

Eventually, the people who lived in rooms decided to expand, and when they wrecked through paint and plaster, they found the wall-people.

Or sometimes an almost-man found a wall-person exposed in the night, searching for food. This was a story the wall-people knew well, a warning. Sometimes the almost-man was good and he promised not to tell, and sometimes the almost-man was bad and he made the wall-person promise not to tell. The wall-people had been silent for too long by then, and even if the people who lived in rooms had understood them, they would not be kind.

It went on like this, pathways wrecked, groups of wall-people pulled into the open, the walls sealed up behind them. The wall-people began to speak and the people who lived in rooms were not always kind. This is how attics came to be.

III

A room of any kind is a place to hide. Sometimes rooms can be walls and sometimes rooms can be bodies.

When there is an attic with stained-glass windows, the woman who sits in it does not speak, except to herself. She works in the glow of the oil lamp, humming church hymns and dated dance ballads under her breath. There's a phonograph in the attic, but it has been broken for a long time.

The woman in the South slices glass and wipes salt from her face with a hand towel. When her fingertips slice, she blots the blood. If she looks out from the attic, she can see green kudzu vines, like snakes frozen in place, creeping out of the patchy yard to devour the house. But she does not often look.

Sometimes she speaks to herself and sometimes she speaks to the glass. When she speaks to the glass it is not with her voice, but with her hands. She is saying, *I hope I am making things better for you.*

IV

Emily Dickinson was a woman who knew about attics. She looked out her bedroom window in Amherst, across the crooked-stone graveyard, and she wrote poems. She thought about death, in the kind of way everyone thinks about death if they are honest with themselves. Most people are not honest with themselves. A coffin is a kind of room, if you let it be.

Before she was born, Emily's family fell on hard times, and a man from town took over their house. The man did not care for the attic, with its precise, slanted corners, its simple containment. He wrecked through the walls, expanded the room, and raised its corners to the North and South. He ripped away the hip roof that sloped like petals over the top and adorned the roof with a gable. It is not said what happened to the wall-people of that house, whether they were exposed and gouged from the walls, or were crushed in the wreckage, or sensed the man's occupancy as a warning and burrowed pathways to elsewhere. They were not the first or last of their kind to disappear without notice. When the Dickinsons reclaimed the house, the attic was not spoken of.

She was not born to the South, never set a delicate boot inside its borders, but Emily knew about dangerous heat, strange wind. She knew what fire lived wet and lively behind her teeth, or inside that tender strip of flesh, pawed at by the heel of a hand through layers of fabric. That power, that shame.

Emily Dickinson wore white. She had black eyes and a long neck. She smiled very quiet. She burrowed into rooms, but her punctuation jutted furiously into the world, pointing toward what lies off the edge of the page. Her life was her writing, but she was not always a writer; she was a daughter, a neighbor, a woman. When she died, they found her writing collected in scraps, bound and sewn. A box to hold her words.

Now the attic in her house is a recording studio. People speak there and are heard, even after their mouths are shut. To remember her, scraps of paper are painted in green, blue, gray, poppy-red, and suspended from the wooden beams. When light falls into the window, the colors press through the glass like remnants of strange flames.

V

Somewhere in the North, a man lives in a very nice house. The house is in a nice neighborhood, and because that is what his family knows of human living, he has succeeded. The carpet is new and harvest-gold, the walls flocked with bronze, and late at night, the fringed pendant light above the entry casts shadows like millions of small fingers. The curtains hanging from the windows are red embroidered silk, which the man's wife bought from a market in the city—quite inexpensively, she would add if you asked. She smiles loud, like some thick board behind her teeth has come loose. He is a nice man, a doctor or a dentist.

He keeps assorted snakes in assorted glass jars on the fireplace mantel. The snakes stumble legless and slide themselves jagged, green scales like lake-drowned emeralds pressing into the glass. The snakes snarl and slither because that is what they know of reptile embodiment, and this means they are successful. For fun or out of boredom, the man drops furry white mice into the jars and watches as the snakes devour them. The mice are themselves until they are food; to the man and his snakes, this means they have succeeded. The mice are busy being mice until they are busy being food and they do not have time to learn how to be a thing with choices. The man's wife sits in a different room in the same house, but not because it's what she chooses. A talent for rot is not a choice.

Feeding time! the man announces in the evening after dinner, and his three small children shriek with excitement.

VI

In the South, a woman sits in the wooden attic and makes stained glass, and sometimes the glass shatters. Sometimes the shattering is an accident, and sometimes it is by force. The woman lives with a man, her husband, and he does not come into the attic, except when the white sky has settled in and it is already too late. He calls her Emily. They used to love each other with bodies and more than bodies, but they no longer do. He does not say this. What he says is about salvation, damnation, burning, and when he talks this way he is not being honest with himself.

The woman had three daughters but now she has two. She calls them Samantha and Susanna, names that sulk and slither.

There were three of them and now there are two. No one says the dead girl's name.

The woman and the man used to love each other until the man drove home after too many glasses of whiskey and crashed their car. One of the three girls died on impact. The impact was with a telephone pole, which, like the attic, was splintered wood. There were beautiful electric sparks raining down from the too-dark sky, and then a fire.

Susanna was a baby and she lost part of her skull and now when she speaks her words tumble out like dead flies. A part of her was burned in the fire and now she only grows hair on one half of her head. She has trouble moving. Her arms jerk at her sides. Susanna can't go to school and she can't speak with noises that other people understand, so she stays at home with the woman. Samantha can speak, but she no longer wants to.

The woman sits awake in the attic, and rings grow under the dark knots of her eyes. The woman's daughters sit still and let the light pass through them. Their father wears a jacket the color of swamp, embroidered with unraveling stars, and he drinks. Sometimes he drinks soda or beer from an aluminum can, and sometimes he drinks whiskey. When he drinks whiskey, things get shattered.

VII

In the North, a woman sits in a very nice house, and any room she sits in is nothing but a very nice box: a room is a thing with walls, doors, a way in, and a way out. A body can be a kind of room, if its door stays hidden.

Her husband stands at the fireplace and stares at his snakes. The snakes cocoon themselves in blankets of themselves and stare back from their jars lazily. He wears a tie printed with stars, their white limbs spread like insects pinned for dissection. Their three children dart from room to room like beams of light.

For fun or out of boredom, when there are no mice, the man taps the glass to make the snakes snarl. When his snakes refuse to unfurl for him, he shakes the jars hard, testing how long until their diamond skulls droop toward limpness and their scales leave bright splinters on the glass. When he's succeeded, he sets the jar back down carefully on the mantel.

The woman gardens the front lawn and listens to the neighborhood chirp alive with birds and bike bells. The doors of each house release snips of noise when they open and shut, like faint hums of music boxes.

The woman likes to garden, likes to listen to the exhales of other houses as the earth slices open beneath her hands. The blade of her silver hand trowel reflects beads of light as she plunges it to break ground. When she doesn't garden for many days, she almost craves that cool, wormy darkness hidden beneath the grass. She shovels enough space to dip her fingers inside and presses to the knuckle. Sometimes, she almost wishes to keep going, slide her whole body through and burrow in the pitch-black womb of loam. But if she dared to try, she knows, the rough pink fabric of her gardening gloves would stop her. She scoops the shallow hole clean and plants a small rosebush.

The woman used to touch the earth, until she learned to protect herself. Loose rocks would scrape away her flesh, and wood chips snuck splinters in her palms. Sometimes the rose thorns sliced her, but now she wears gloves. Even so, she often returns to the house and finds herself blotting blood from her fingertips.

If she glances over from the rose bed, she can see the stained-glass window, half burrowed in the ground, that leads to the basement. The stained glass is a design also called *rosebush*, mirroring her garden as if through a kaleidoscope.

A basement is a room, but she has little use for it. A basement is a shut-away place to hide acts and objects, or to hide during storms. In the North, the sky is blue when it's meant to be blue; there hasn't been a storm in so long, she can't remember the smell of it.

She does not see the window and think, *Who might have made it* or *What did it take*. When the man bought them the house, the real estate agent told some story about the stained glass, how it came to be there, but the woman doesn't remember it now—only the blue crayon circled thick around the real estate agent's eyes. Sometimes, if she looks, the stained glass spreads its red glow onto the grass, like fire frozen in place. But she does not often look.

She bends down to pluck a fistful of gangly weeds and hollows out the holes, so new spindles can't grow. The earth in her hand is grainy and dark.

When the woman in the North gardens, she does not speak. Gardening is a language of touch, but when she lays hands on the plants, she is not saying anything. She waters or uproots them and she is not changed. She touches the plants, touches anything, and remains only herself.

Inside, the man loosens his tie and pours a glass of whiskey. The woman fears for the snakes. Just one careless turn, she knows, and things can get shattered.

VIII

The woman in the attic must go to sleep eventually. She cannot keep her eyes open all the time. This is a fact. The woman keeps

Susanna in the attic with her while she is awake. She makes stained glass and Susanna sits on the floor and colors the pages of books not meant for coloring. Some attics are for hiding, and some attics are for being hidden.

Sometimes the woman grows tired and forgets to be careful, and the glass she is making shatters. When the glass shatters, Susanna makes a harmed noise, but it does not slice; the woman's hardened fingers clink against it, the sound of wind through a forest. There is no blood. Curls of wrought iron push through her nail beds, littering her desk with discarded fingernails. She cups her palms and collects them into a pile, and uses the hand towel to wipe salt from her face, and from the damp underside of Susanna's neck.

A body can be a room and a room is a place to hide. Sometimes a person can burrow into their own body, stay safe there, but sometimes another person can split a body open, carve a raw path, burrow into what isn't theirs.

The woman cannot keep her eyes open all the time. When she is asleep, the man takes Susanna into a closet below the stairwell. The man is bad and makes her promise not to tell. He says that even if people could understand her, they would not be kind. Sometimes he cries afterward, but not often. When he is crying, he is thinking the dead girl's name and not saying it.

IX

This is another story the wall-people tell: sometimes a wall-person is exposed in the night, searching for food, and it is not an almost-man—who have by now become plainly men—who finds them, but the gaping stomach of the house. The stomach of the house is no good place for a wall-person to be. Expelled into that emptiness, a wall-person gets lost, left to be only themselves.

A house is a body that hides its rooms, and the existence of rooms can turn people cruel; all that space to fill, empty air stinging like a threat. To own rooms and fill them with yourself is how a person knows they have succeeded. Still, people who live in rooms must find warmth, and when the cold chills them out of their burrows, only the stomach of the house provides enough heat.

The woman in the North has heard stories of the South, how houses there splinter wood and smell of burning. It is a warning, a story she has escaped becoming.

When a woman in the North passes through her rooms, she listens for shifts behind the walls. She listens for the bones of the house to croak and sigh as they merge with some other body. In a rare trip to the basement to retrieve the broken radio, sifting through dusty boxes, she presses a hand to the wall in front of her and hears breath muffled behind the wooden panels. Then decides she doesn't.

This is what they tell about the North: the woman and her roses calling themselves free, and when they tell the story, it is a warning.

When a woman in the South senses shifting behind the wall, she knows that other bodies follow in the dark, merging with her steps. Her torso is streaked with orange, pink, green, poppy-red, her shoulders opalescent. Her face is shirred crystal, like an ice pond rippled by wind. She is a story the wall-people know well. She raises an arm and becomes five limbs, or hundreds.

X

In the attic, the too-pale sky filters through stained-glass windows. Sometimes stained glass is a rose and sometimes it is a bird, and sometimes it is a sharp piece of fire-worn hope in your coat pocket. Sometimes hope is found, and sometimes it is forged.

When there is an attic window made of stained glass, the woman inside it is watching. Her daughters sit still and let light bleed into their rooms. Sometimes rooms can be walls and sometimes rooms can be bodies. People who live in rooms are not always kind.

This is how—as we, the wall-people, tell it—stained-glass windows came to be.

She is splintered into story, and the wall-people remember her. A woman can survive like this for a long time. Generations of them, suspended in beauty, burning in the spaces between the walls and the world.

When there is slicing, it will not shatter her. Sunlight moves through her, like a cathedral illuminated. When she speaks it is not with her voice or her hands, but with the house and the bones of the house and the sealed voices that live within.

They are saying, *I hope we are making things better for you.*

At the bottom of the stairs, the man is stumbling and calling her name. The attic burrows in and we wait for the storm to come.

NEST

My sister, Kate, had been huffing around the house since our dad died, and now she was convinced our dead dad was inhabiting a fly she found buzzing between her bedroom blinds the morning of the funeral. Also, she had begun to starve, because she decided it was immoral to kill anything, even a vegetable. I didn't really believe her about the fly, to tell the truth; I was pretty sure our dad's ghost wasn't hanging out inside a bug, but I didn't say that, and I didn't say anything to her about my knot. I had a hunch she might get jealous, and I didn't feel like dealing with all of that.

Kate had always reveled in any morsel of suffering, as if showing off how deeply she felt, how much she couldn't help it. When she was a little kid, she walked around boo-hooing when a TV show ended, boo-hooing when the mailman left us nothing in the box, boo-hooing when she found out the Loch Ness Monster wasn't real. She didn't always have a handle on empathy, though, until she started boo-hooing about cheeseburgers and baby carrots. People think sadness and empathy are the same, or are at least some kind of shortcut to each other, but that's not true. Sadness can be as selfish as anything, if you use it the right way.

Two months ago—a week before my sixteenth birthday, down to the day—our dad went fishing and drowned in Patman Lake. The funeral was the last week of school, so Kate and I began our summer early. That was that, I thought. I have a dead dad now, that's fine, that's manageable. But then, a couple weeks later, his ghost started inhabiting a knot in my hair.

I first noticed it one morning when I was getting ready to go to the movies with Tom. Tom used to be called Tommy, but started calling himself Tom when he took over his dad's vacuum store and became a Marxist. Tom was my boyfriend of seven months, though we never officially decided to be boyfriend/girlfriend; neither of us had ever had a boyfriend/girlfriend before, so when people said we were each other's, we assumed they must be right.

I was brushing my hair when I noticed the knot. When I took the bristles to it, I got tingly and feverish, like I might pass out. In summer, the Texas heat crept into the cheap plaster of our walls, chasing the bite out of our AC, and I feared I was succumbing to heatstroke. I sat down on the toilet, and each time I touched the tangle—the size of a small wad of gum near the baby-hairs at my neck—the walls began to swell and pulse, and it felt like a big rubber band was tightening around my ribs. I worried I might puke, which meant I would ruin my makeup and have to rush to do it all over again. But when I wasn't touching the knot, I felt nothing, like normal. So I simply braided my hair, tucking the knot carefully in the center of the braid, and drove to meet Tom.

After the movie, we walked to the arcade across the hall to catch plastic pigs in the claw machine. I guess he noticed I was fiddling with my braid, or took my silent focus on deploying the claw over the pigs' shining rubber bellies as something more.

"Are you mad that I'm becoming a Marxist?" he asked. He often asked this when he sensed we were getting into an argument. "You know, it just means that capitalism is against human nature, and people should get to have control over their lives. It's not evil, like they teach you in school," he said. "You'll understand when you're part of the workforce."

I told him no, it wasn't about the Marxism at all, I was just frustrated.

"Okay. Are you frustrated that I'm becoming a Marxist?"

And I told him no, though truthfully I wasn't sure, I didn't know much about the whole enterprise, and the only -ists I knew about were people who treated other people badly. Anyway, I didn't get around to telling Tom about the knot, and since he never tried to touch me in a close-up intimate way, it hadn't come up.

The knot didn't seem to have much to say about the afterlife, but it liked to whisper nouns in my ear. *Cow, cork, river*, it said. *Window, window. Countertop. Rabies*. Its first noises were weak and staticky, so it took me a full day to figure out it must be my dad trying to communicate; his human voice was different in the knot, like he was calling out through a plastic radio played from the far end of a sewer tunnel. I'd been expecting a haunting of some kind, to tell the truth, though I didn't expect it to be so straightforward. It all felt a little too anticlimactic otherwise, the way he was my dad when I went to school in the morning, and by the afternoon when I got off the bus, he was nothing. I wasn't sure if he could hear me speaking back, but it had become comforting, just having the knot there. A little reminder of un-aloneness weighing at the nape of my neck.

When I asked it what being dead was like, it just responded, *Pictureframe.* When I asked if it missed being with us, or just generally being alive—things like pancakes, weather, etc.—it didn't say anything. The knot could be distracting sometimes, but if I focused, I'd learned to pretty much tune it out. I could even fall asleep with it pressed against the soft conched back of my ear and listen to the knot dictate the course of my dreams as I floated away from consciousness. *Wrench. Iris. Clown. Utah, Utah. Albatross. Cantaloupe.*

I considered mentioning it to my mom, but she worked all day in the front office of the paper mill and had bigger things to worry about. She was starving herself for different reasons than Kate, like not getting a lunch break because some rich plant manager had something he wanted her to do, or because my grandma was already getting on her about fixing up her "shape" so she could start dating again. If I saw her eat anything, it was a handful of those fancy grapes that've been genetically modified to taste like cotton candy, and the bag usually went bad in the fridge before she could get through it.

Our mom had always spun through the world easily frazzled, but my dad interrupted her orbit, made her laugh to throw off the track of her worries. Now, there was no one to stop the spiraling, and she had even better reasons to worry, so I tried to stay out of her path and give her one less person to be concerned about. She went to work earlier and stayed later now, trying to sneak in overtime hours to pay the bills by herself. When she came home, she sat on the couch with her old wicker basket of nail polish and spent hours painting her fingernails and toenails. In the evenings, the paper mill exhaled and the smell of dying jellyfish descended on Texarkana. When the streetlights came on, you were supposed to lock your windows so the chemicals didn't suffocate your family in the night.

◆ ◆ ◆

I'd been living with the knot for ten days when Rachel called. I was on the couch eating a quesadilla and startled when her name vibrated across the screen.

"Hold on a sec," I answered. "I'm eating a quesadilla."

"I bet you already spilled it all over yourself," she said, and I had. I held the phone in the crook of my neck as I scrubbed cheese and red goo out of my shorts with a kitchen rag.

Rachel and I had been friends since the third grade. Her mom had pictures of us together going back years, prepuberty, with bad department-store highlights and middle parts in our hair, and one at a birthday party where my training bra is showing through my shirt because I insisted it was "the style," and Rachel was wearing reindeer-printed pajama bottoms because she hoped it would make her seem quirky, which was also "the style." Rachel's mom liked to trot out that particular photo every couple of years when I spent the night, insisting we were *so precocious*—though I was never sure if she meant *precious*—sloshing her glass of rosé onto the laminated corners of her photo book and smiling big.

We'd stayed friends as middle school bled into high school, the summer Rachel convinced her mom to let her wax and tint her ice-blond eyebrows to a soft brown, which made more of a difference than you might think ("The eyebrows are the curtains of the soul," she liked to say). By junior year, she'd become the kind of pretty that usually made girls popular, except Rachel was too self-conscious and too concerned with seeming nice to realize it.

So, Rachel knew basically everything about me, even how messy I was, historically, at eating Mexican food. A civilized person might eat at the table instead of the couch, for a start, but it was summer break, and my mom was at work, and there was a ton of extra food in the house now that Kate had stopped eating. Rachel knew all of that too.

"Sorry, I didn't expect a call," I said, excusing vague guilt I couldn't locate a reason for.

"Yeah, it was annoying trying to text it all, so I figured it would be faster just to tell you the old-timey way."

"So, how are things?"

"Things could be better, actually," she said. "Not to complain."

I knew her well enough to know that meant she wanted to complain. At sixteen, I knew everybody wanted two things: to be happy, and to have someone to complain to about being prevented from happiness. Most people didn't want their dad, ghost or actual, to live inside their hair. But that was a consideration I had shelved for the moment, to allow myself a more flexible definition of happiness.

"Go on," I urged her.

Rachel started telling me a story about how she went to the neighborhood pool with her mom to sunbathe and glare at the children splashing around—I made an affirmative noise, understanding that it was decidedly uncool to swim at our age, unless at night—and she saw some boys from school, David and Brandon and Clark Katz, hanging around by the dressing rooms. So she went over to them, she said, and she might have been flirting a little with Brandon, it was hard to tell how reliable her version of events was in that area, but when she looked back, her mom had untied her bikini top and was sunbathing half naked, boobs-down on the slatted lounge chair. And apparently the boys had been looking over her shoulder to ogle her mom the whole time. I kept making sympathetic noises even though I didn't hear the rest of the story, because Kate came downstairs and asked when Mom was getting home, and when I mouthed that I didn't know, go away, she started huffing around and scratching at the carpet with her big toe. I made a point of walking into the musty, hot garage and shutting the door behind me.

When Rachel was done telling me about her mom and the boys at the pool, she asked, "So, what's new with you?" Not because she was dying to know, but because she wanted to think of herself as a good friend, and this is the exchange friends make: listening to someone else's burdens as insurance that your own burdens will be listened to.

When my dad died, Rachel's mom drove her over to give us condolences and macaroni. Up in my room, we sat on my bed and she made a face that conveyed the perfect amount of sadness, her eyes watery with empathy—but holding back from going into a fit of over-the-top crying, which even she understood would be stealing my moment for herself. In a voice she'd likely practiced in front of the mirror, she asked how I was coping with "this great loss," or if I wanted to talk about it. I said no, which was the truth.

With the phone to my ear, I paced around the garage, stepping around mysterious stains on the concrete, though I knew the bottoms of my feet would be blackened when I went back inside anyway. "Well, my mom is going out of town to visit my grandma, and Tom thinks me and Kate should have a party."

"That's a good idea," she affirmed. Affirmation is one responsibility of friendship.

"Also, I have this knot in the left side of my hair, sort of behind my ear, because my dad lives in my hair now," I told her. "Not my whole dad, just his ghost. My dad's ghost is currently inhabiting a knot in my hair," I clarified.

"Oh," she said. She didn't sound surprised, though I knew that, too, was likely on purpose. I'd considered telling her sooner, but there was no good emoji that encapsulated it.

"How's that experience going?"

"It's fine," I said. "Nothing too dramatic." I told her about the nouns, but not the voice the knot says them in.

"Well, that seems manageable," she admitted. "What happens when you brush your hair?"

"I don't think that particular ritual is going to be part of my life anymore," I said, trying to sound nonchalant about the whole thing. And because I was worried Rachel might feel compelled to provide me with Tough Realizations, another obligation of maintaining a healthy friendship, I added: "For a little while, at least."

"I understand where you're coming from, and I support you," she said. "Anyway, if you curl your hair for the party, probably no one will notice."

"That's a good idea," I told her. "I think I'll do that."

◆ ◆ ◆

When I went back inside, Kate was on the couch in the next room, scrolling her phone as the TV droned on. I instinctively opened the fridge and stared at the shelves of browning lettuce, Tupperware stacks of casseroles that had gone bad, a package of store-brand tortillas, crusty-capped condiment bottles, and sliced yellow cheese. I sighed, and opened the pantry: canned green beans, a Ziploc baggie of chocolate chips, and mix-in lemonade powder clumped up like cat litter. I took a fistful of chocolate chips, then went back to the fridge for a slice of cheese, then another.

I'd eaten the last traces of my dad within a week of the funeral, while my mom was at work and Kate was spending the night with a friend; all he'd left behind was a half-eaten bag of corn chips, which in a fit of boredom I'd dipped in a swirl of mustard and ketchup, and three of the frozen microwave burritos he took to work for lunch. I kept waiting for my mom to notice the burritos were gone, thinking she'd be angry, but she never noticed—or maybe she was relieved she didn't have to make a decision about what to do with them herself.

The kitchen counter was cluttered with hair accessories, unopened mail, and last year's textbooks, and Kate's swimsuit was drying over the bar chair. The stairs were layered with clothes my mom had washed and folded weeks ago; we were meant to take them up to our rooms, but instead, we usually just picked them off the pile and dressed at the foot of the stairwell. Now that it was just us, a feminine chaos claimed every room, like weeds overgrowing untended yards.

I stood around in the kitchen opening and closing cabinets, waiting until Kate was absorbed in the TV, and then I snuck upstairs. I locked the bathroom door, took off my clothes, then reached to the back of the cabinet under the sink until I felt the crinkle of the plastic wipes.

Admittedly, the knot had caused some issues when it came to showering; mainly, that I couldn't do it without my skull pulsing till I got dizzy and had to throw up orange bile into the drain. If the knot got wet, it started whirring in my ear like a busted dryer and yelling creepy nouns, like, *Gurgle! Rot! Intestine! Noose! Feces! Banshee!*

So, I'd been avoiding washing my hair, and instead, sprayed a layer of dry shampoo over my roots every morning. And because sitting in the bath also felt dangerous, in terms of how the knot would react, I cleaned my creases with a package of baby wipes. I'd read in a teen magazine that women did the same thing when they stayed overnight at their boyfriends' houses and had to go straight to work the next day—some women even kept wipes handy in their purse for that very purpose. So really, I was just learning a skill that would become useful to me later in life.

If I tried to untangle pieces of the knot or clean it with the wipes I felt sick, so the way I groomed my hair was like this: after the dry shampoo, I'd spit in my hand and use my spit to flatten down the hairs under the knot, then comb the longer hairs backward to cover it. Keeping it hidden was the most important part. Anyone who found out about it would have some opinion on what to do—or they'd think I was lying for attention, inviting pity like Kate with her boo-hooing. Then, they'd only see me as a lump of sadness to feel bad for. I wouldn't just get to be a person.

◆ ◆ ◆

I never got to have a "sweet sixteen" like most people, since my birthday was at the beginning of summer break, my mom was stressed about money, and my dad being dead was all anyone cared about. So, when my mom announced she was going away to visit my grandma, I took Tom's advice and planned a party.

Rachel had been right: curling my hair hid the knot decently well. I tried untangling the ringlets with my fingers, but the knot had swollen to the size of a moon pie in the last couple days, and there wasn't much I could untangle. I smudged eyeliner into my shimmery bronze eyeshadow, and hoped I looked like a model who was still pretty even though she'd just woken up in a stranger's bed after a big night of partying in the city, and not like a regular person who'd just woken up in her own bed after a big night of nothing. I was having trouble figuring out what to wear, since only three outfits still fit me comfortably without squeezing or pinching or overflowing flesh in all the wrong spots.

Since summer started, I'd been eating more to fill up the extra time. Eating helped me zone out of myself, into a mind-less state of enjoyment, where what I wanted was in reach and I could take it easily. I folded food inside my body and folded my body inside rooms and felt calm. Everyone has to get outside of themselves for a little while, I thought. Nobody can be fully aware of every ticking minute in the day, or they'd go insane. How would a person fill up all that empty time? How was any-one supposed to fill the whole monstrous void of a life?

My mom had left that morning with her nail polish basket bubble-wrapped in her bag and six clean pairs of my dad's old socks for two days away. Since he died, she had exclusively been wearing them, even though the loose fabric came up to her calves and made her look like she was playing dress-up as a Victorian paperboy. On her way out the door, she rattled off her litany of "remembers": "Remember to lock the door before you go to sleep, remember to close the windows so the smell doesn't get in, remember Kathy June Sparks is down the street if there's an emergency, remember pizza is fine but don't go crazy on the toppings, remember have fun but don't spend all our gee-dee money, remember to call Grandma's house phone if you need me."

Before she left, she looked back at me, as if actually noticing me for the first time in a while, and added: "Erma, you need to go brush your hair. You're going to get a rat's nest."

She reached for the knot, but I pulled away and said I would, then rushed her out the door before she could get a better look. We nodded away her remembers, kissed her powdery cheek, and when the garage door shut, barreled upstairs to get ready for the party.

◆ ◆ ◆

When I came downstairs, Kate was sitting on the couch wearing a baggy zip-up hoodie with a low-cut, pink tank top peeking through. Gobs of lip gloss made her mouth the color of a melted tangerine.

She said, "Make sure nobody goes in my room. I don't want the fly to get out."

I thought that was ironic, since she'd spent the week after the funeral tramping all her little friends over to come see the fly like some kind of carnival barker. She'd always come down boo-hooing with a friend patting her awkwardly on the shoulder, that crusty look in their eyes like they were just dying for the moment they could bolt.

"If the fly is actually Dad, wouldn't you want him to get out? Like, he wouldn't want to spend his whole time as a fly being stuck in your room."

"That's not the point," Kate said. "I don't want any of your dumb friends to see the fly, or touch the fly, or to know about the fly. Or doing anything weird with my stuff."

"No one's allowed upstairs anyway," I told her. There was a knock on the door, and before I answered it, I checked in the hall mirror to make sure the knot was hidden.

Tom wore a blue shirt with black palm trees and held plastic grocery bags at his sides. He unloaded them onto the counter, revealing plain, store-brand tortilla chips, a plastic gallon of vodka with a shiny red label, and two cartons of from-concentrate orange juice.

"Hope this'll be enough," he said. "Who all's coming?"

"Oh, just some people from school," I answered. "Rachel, a couple drama club people, and the Clarks and them."

He didn't really respond, just stood there in my kitchen shifting from one foot to the other.

"Anyway, thanks for bringing the stuff, Tom," I said, putting a little more sweetness in my voice than usual. "I really appreciate it."

"No worries. Happy to redistribute my paycheck so everybody gets to have a good time." He looked over at Kate, who, to my knowledge, he'd never spoken to before. "I'm a Marxist," he explained.

"Cool. I'm basically a Socialist," Kate replied, raking her hair out from the bunched neck of her jacket, though I knew she didn't even know what being a Socialist meant and had probably just heard it somewhere.

"He's taking over his dad's vacuum store," I explained, willing my hand over Tom's in a way that appeared casual. He tensed up but didn't move away. "Taking over the family business, as they say." I laughed the fake dry laugh of a socialite in a passionless but respectable marriage. I was rattling on now, but I needed to get into the hostess mood, and talking seemed to be working out my nerves a little.

"Yeah, I know that already," Kate said, like I was the most foolish oaf she'd ever laid eyes on. Tom just laughed with his head tilted down and started mixing himself a drink as people trailed in.

Rachel had invited David and Brandon and Clark Katz, and even the other Clark, Clark Johnson, to the party. The boys made parentheses around her, chugging their vodka juice. Brandon said something and Rachel threw her head back in an exaggerated laugh, a near guffaw, and clamped a manicured hand on his arm. The whole time, her belly button gravitated back at David. I knew from the teen magazine that the belly button was a sure-fire traitor, a compass pointing in the direction of whoever you cared about most, whether or not you wanted people to know it.

It turned out that Rachel actually liked David and not Brandon, but was pretending to flirt with Brandon because David had sort of fucked-up teeth, and she was fearful that if David didn't like her back, she would always have to live with the knowledge that she was rejected by someone with sort of fucked-up teeth. Then she would probably be too embarrassed to lose her virginity, if she ever found someone who wanted to.

"It's a quality-of-life issue," she said.

After Brandon left to go throw up in the bushes outside, I stood with Rachel in the corner of my living room, nodding supportively while I watched Kate out of the corner of my eye.

Mulberry, the knot whispered, muffled under a layer of music. *Virus, pencil.*

◆ ◆ ◆

At the funeral, an old woman from my grandma's church gave Kate and me each a framed picture of our dad. I don't know why she did it; it was nothing we'd asked for, and as far as I knew my family had never met that woman before. Maybe the woman came from a time where you forgot what people looked like after they died because only two or three pictures existed of them, total, from their entire lives. They were in cheap dollar-store frames, plastic and Easter white, and in the photo, his face was blown up slightly too big and the contour turned up too high, so he looked unnaturally red and bloated. I recognized the picture from a fishing trip he took to Corpus Christi a few years ago, but someone had cropped out the ocean and photoshopped him into a suit and tie.

I threw my copy of the picture on my top closet shelf, sandwiched between some clothes that didn't fit and my dad's sweatshirt, which I'd snuck to my room while my mom was at work. Everyone at the funeral talked in whispers and wouldn't look my mom in the eye, because my grandma had told them all how my dad wasn't "saved," which meant his soul was getting incinerated in the down-below as we stood on earth eating lukewarm ham rolls, and nobody knew quite what to say about that.

Kate kept the photo next to her bedside, my dad's unnaturally big face looking over her while she slept. I bet she did something embarrassing with it, too, like saying good night to the picture before she rolled over. In the days between his dying and the funeral, I could hear her sharp cries pierce the wall between our bedrooms, like she was making sure everyone in the house knew she was definitely crying herself to sleep. I'd had to lie with a pillow over my head and felt like I might suffocate.

But since the knot showed up, I could drown out Kate's dramatics by listening to my dad's distorted ghost-voice through my hair. The words bloomed into pictures in my mind, then melted away to reveal new images, which dissolved into dreams. A petunia bloomed into a baby's bottle. A wolf bled upward until it was a ladder. It was a type of hypnotism.

Sometimes, as I lay in bed in the dark, I'd reach up and squeeze the knot, dig the tip of my finger into its tangle, just to make myself feel bad. If I tugged on it to induce that woozy feeling, like my ribs were about to snap and slice me in half, I could make tears start to flow. I figured if I got myself crying and heaving in private, where I could drain the bad feeling out like a pus-filled blister and muffle myself with my pillow, then it wouldn't leak out accidentally around other people.

But mostly, I just tried to ignore it.

At first, my head was just a little itchy where the knot rested, but now I was always scratching, trying to hide my hands so no one noticed the brown crescents of scalp blood dried under my fingernails. When the knot grew to the size of a broccoli floret, I had to give up on wearing earrings. I started layering cover-up on the sweaty side of my neck underneath the knot, where I'd broken out in a bumpy rash, the hair growing rougher and more gnarled against my tender skin.

◆ ◆ ◆

The party built and multiplied, more people trailing in with their parents' half-full whiskey bottles, and I tried not to itch at the rash on my neck. The alcohol dulled the pain, but with each drink I found it harder to control my hands from floating up to touch my head. When Tom went outside in search of new people to talk to, and Rachel was whisked away to hold back Lucy Vang's hair while she puked, I walked up to Kate.

"Potatoes died to make that drink in your hand," I said.

"Whatever." She rolled her heavily lined eyes. "Just let me have fun. I need this."

"You always think you need something."

Admittedly, I was being mean, but it bothered me how she could make such a big hoopla about starving herself and then give up whenever she felt like it.

Clark Johnson walked up to refill his drink.

"What's up, ladies?"

"Hey Clark. Having fun?" I plastered a big dumb sparkling smile on my face. Despite everything, I was committed to being a good hostess.

"Yeah, thanks for putting this together," he said. He was standing between us, but his belly button was pointed right at Kate.

"Who's this?" he asked, as if Kate were an interesting statue he was commenting on, instead of a person who was standing right in front of him.

Kate said her name and I said, "My sister." I added, "She's in eighth grade." I knew telling him this fact would embarrass Kate, even if it didn't embarrass Clark, which I felt it should have.

Clark said, "You're drinking too? Want me to fill your cup?"

"Sure," she said. We both stood there, silent, while Clark poured the jug of vodka, then splashed in some orange juice, and handed the cup to Kate.

"Thanks," she said. She took a sip and her face screwed up, but at the last second she made it look like a pouty smile.

Clark looked in my direction and remarked, "You must've been getting pretty wild on the dance floor, huh?"

"What do you mean?"

"You know, your hair? Looks like you've been doing some serious headbanging."

My face reddened, and my hand instinctively shot up to the back of my head. I knew whatever look was caught on my face was a stupid one, and desperately hoped Kate wouldn't try to mention it.

"Thanks for your help, Clark," I said coolly. "See you later."

"I'll be around," he proclaimed.

"He seems nice. Cute eyes too," Kate said.

I'd never stopped to consider if Clark Johnson's eyes were cute, but I didn't like Kate thinking they were, or telling me out loud she thought so. It spelled out something ominous.

"He's just being nice to you because you're my kid sister," I said. "He's a nice person. He's nice to everyone."

"I'm not a kid, Erma. I've done all kinds of things you don't know about."

"Like what?"

"Like, all kinds of things," Kate said. "I've kissed people, I've done stuff, I've lived a life." She was slurring a little, but I couldn't tell if it was real or for dramatic effect.

"Plus," she said, "I had to get mature for my age. Most fourteen-year-olds don't have to deal with seeing their dad's drowned dead body. It's not fair. It's not normal."

She clutched her plastic cup in both hands, and I wondered if it would break open and spill all over her. I sort of wished it would, so she'd disappear for a while.

"Not that you care, you've never even cried about Dad dying."

The knot was telling me something, but I pulled my hair behind my ear so I wouldn't have to pay attention to it, and in the process, snagged my finger on the knot. My head was shot through with a bright jolt of pain that made my stomach wretch. I winced, then flooded with anger.

"Whatever. My feelings aren't your business, Kate. Anyway, I'm only letting you stay because Mom would figure things out otherwise, but don't try to talk to my friends. Nobody wants to hang out with a slutty middle schooler."

Kate welled with hot tears, her eyes red already from the slow ascension of booze, and in a show of great spite, she unzipped her hoodie and tossed it over the banister.

"Fuck you," she said. "I'll talk to who I please. And if you try to stop me, I'll tell Mom you had people over drinking."

She walked away, her small boobs poking through her pink tank top like dried figs. For the first time, I noticed how Kate's bones pressed insistently through her skin, her neck taut and hollowed, her ribs like claws lurching outward under her shirt. My sister drifted through the room, a husk with a vaguely Kate-shaped aura.

The less space she takes up, the more people are going to want her, I thought, sickened by the truth of it. Clark Johnson had never bothered talking to me in all the years we'd been in school together, even before I started swallowing the surplus groceries Kate refused. Maybe all boys wanted was a girl they could fold up and fit in their pocket, to carry around discreetly as they went about their lives and take them out only when they were bored or horny or needed entertainment to help burn up a few hours. But even though Kate's body was shrinking, she wasn't clearing space for anybody else. Her sadness was so big no one could walk into a room without being sucked inside its orbit.

I understood then that no one would ever love Kate, not really. She walked around shedding pieces of her grief everywhere she went, and no boy would tolerate such a thing if they didn't have to. Nobody wanted to fuck you if your grief was always watching. That made me feel sort of sad for Kate, but at the same time, better about myself. Any grief I had was translucent, unobtrusive—I was careful not to let it touch my real life. Unlike Kate, I was responsible with sadness, I kept it to myself, safely tied away from everything and everyone outside of it. Actually, I was an easy person to love. I kept myself so empty, anything could fill me.

I caught myself suddenly surging with fondness for Tom. Who cared if he had aberrant social views? I decided then that I would absolutely learn about Marxism, I would buy books on it and I would read them, I would even start recycling and stop eating meat if that was part of it. I wasn't sure if that was part of it, but I was willing to try. I thought about the way he tipped his head when he laughed his gentle laugh and all I wanted in the whole bright and gushing world was to make Tom happy, to be worthy of being his girlfriend.

I hurried outside to find Tom, pressing past classmates and strangers who clogged the steps by the porch, smoking cigarettes with a false sway of sophistication and one neurotic eye darting to check for any adult who might be lurking, waiting to punish them. In drunkenness I had separated from my body enough to convince myself nothing I did now could hurt. Nothing good or bad could graze the parts of me that mattered. The world was mine, if I only reached out and took it.

I spotted Tom by the bushes with Brandon. Brandon sipped a bottle of water, swished it around his mouth, and spit it out on the ground. There was a splash, and the smell of the paper mill wafting on the breeze like a sea creature that just wouldn't rot right. Beyond the border of the neighborhood, East Texas pines loomed like giants in lumpy trench coats. There was a bush length between them, but Tom's belly button was pointed so unmistakably in Brandon's direction, as if he were being dragged by an invisible rope at his center. Anyone who saw them standing together among the bushes could see that even before the belly button's existence, if the umbilicus at the center of Tom had been able to speak it would have said: *Yes, this is the direction the hole I will become was meant for.* Tom reached for the water bottle, his fingers lingering over Brandon's, and my face grew prickly, not understanding exactly what I'd seen, but that I shouldn't have seen it. I turned around and rushed back inside before my breath could be heard.

◆ ◆ ◆

I looked around for Rachel in the swirl of sweat and noise, but couldn't find her. I texted: *Where are you?* Within seconds she responded: *Don't judge me.* And next, a picture of David's gaudy state football ring around her middle finger, her hand posed on David's bare, acne-scarred chest like a shitty engagement photo.

I didn't know how to make words from what I couldn't unlearn about Tom and the whole sham of my supposed desirability, so I wrote back: *Cute!* A friend whose despair comes at the expense of snatching away her friend's happiness was not a good friend, I feared, and I still wanted to be good at something in this life. She responded with a kissy-face emoji, a sparkler emoji, and a lady-salsa-dancing emoji.

A crash came from my parents' bedroom, then three rough-housing boys in neon tank tops were spat from the doorway and rushed outside through the garage, giggling. In the living room, some other boys were watching a movie where a man clutched another man's blood-streaked body and howled into the empty, blinding white as snow melted around them. Under my dad's plaid throw blanket, one of the boys reached between the legs of a girl I didn't recognize, who munched her bubble gum and pretended to pay attention to the death on-screen. There was a smell in the room, but it wasn't the paper mill smell.

"Do you smell that?" I said out loud. One of the boys on the couch looked up but didn't respond, and to the rest, I was a dimly lit ghost in the shadows surrounding the TV screen.

I realized after a few moments, embarrassed, that the smell might be coming from me. The knot, whose voice I'd blurred out for most of the night, had begun to emit an odor like moss and wet pennies. The smell of tinny lake water.

Because I couldn't help it, I pulled out my phone and texted Rachel again: *I feel a little insane.* Minutes went by and she didn't respond, so I sent another message: *Some boys are watching a war movie while they finger this girl on the couch.* And then: *How do we know her? She has brown hair. Thoughts?* And then: *I'm so drunk haha. Also, what if people can see the knot?* And then: *Everything is fine. Race car emoji. Sushi emoji.*

I knew her well enough to know that she'd seen my name flaring across her phone, flashing in the dark of David's car, or a neighbor's backyard, or wherever they were—but if she could pretend she hadn't, she would. With plausible deniability, she could maintain that she was, in fact, a very supportive friend, that it's not like she chose not to respond or to abandon me so she could lose her virginity to someone with bad teeth, which seemed worse to me than being rejected by someone with bad teeth, since we forget all the time about the people who don't like us, but virginity is a story you have to keep telling for your entire life, over and over, until it's like an urban legend that happened to someone else whose name you couldn't remember if you tried, and years from now when Rachel was the wife of a state senator giving an interview for a well-respected lifestyle magazine, or a college dropout who'd developed a heroin addiction then gotten clean and made gobs of money writing a sitcom pilot about it, when she'd lived a whole life fleshed out with disappointments and ecstasies, sexually and otherwise, if someone asked how she lost her virginity she'd still have to tell them the story about this party and David's sort of fucked-up teeth, and when she did, she'd undoubtedly leave out the part where I stood invisibly in my own house while some future car-wash employee fingered a stranger in front of everyone beneath my dead dad's favorite blanket. That wouldn't be part of Rachel's story at all.

◆ ◆ ◆

I went upstairs and found Kate in her bedroom, crouched by the windowsill, black eyeliner smeared on the tip of her nose.

"Get out," she said, but I didn't.

"Sorry I said that stuff to you. I was just nervous about the party," I said, though each sentence contained only a morsel of the truth.

"Whatever," she said. "Your friends are lame anyway."

"I know."

"A person was in here smoking drugs. They could've let the fly out. They could have smushed it with their druggy hands."

"I don't think anyone was doing drugs," I said. "It was probably just a cigarette."

"Tobacco is a kind of drug," she said.

"Okay, sure, I guess."

I sat down next to her. Her carpet was abnormally clean, and I wondered if she'd vacuumed it in secret.

"Where's the fly now?"

"Here." She pointed to a spot on the window.

"I don't see it."

"It's right there."

"I don't see it," I said, and then, "Oh, there it is."

There it was, perched on the glass, rubbing its stick legs together. The fly looked like any regular fly. In fact, how regular it looked made me wonder for a second if it wasn't a real fly at all—it looked too perfect, like a computer-generated model of the culturally idealized fly. But even then, I didn't think it was harboring the spirit of anyone dead.

"Flies puke every time they land," I told Kate. "It's the only fact I know about them."

"Gross."

"Yeah. Why do you think it's Dad's ghost, anyway?"

"Don't say *ghost*," she said.

"Okay, why do you think Dad is inside the fly?"

"You'll say it's dumb."

"I still want to know."

"I had this dream, the night before the funeral. We were ice-skating on this big pond outside the good mall in Shreveport."

"We've never been ice-skating," I said.

"That's how I knew it was a dream. We were ice-skating, and then we had to get off the ice because it was cracking. And then, the mall authorities or whoever said they needed us to make it become water again, so I was hammering at the ice with the metal part of my skates. And then, finally, the ice cracked open and the water got set free through the cracks. But then I realized the water was flies.

"Anyway," she said, "the next morning this little guy was stuck in my window, buzzing around. I figured Dad must've sent me the dream so I'd know to pay attention."

"The water isn't Dad, though," I said. "It's what killed Dad."

As if she hadn't heard me, she continued, "Plus, if he could stay, why wouldn't he?"

Kate opened her mouth to say something else, but the knot started talking over her. *Jukebox, liver, blouse. Meteor. Arugula.* My eardrums started to flutter, lightly at first, then thrumming and painful. I feared a moth had gotten in somehow and was trapped, thrashing its wings furiously inside my brain. Or maybe it was the fly. Maybe he'd swum inside me and was vomiting all over my ear canals. *Blister! Maggots! Gremlin!* The knot began to shout louder than it had before, my ears ringing, a stinging behind my face like the worst spell of brain freeze. The smell of worms and overripe loam was overpowering.

"Do you smell that?" I asked Kate, but she scrunched her eyebrows and I could tell she didn't know what I was talking about. I bolted to the bathroom.

◆ ◆ ◆

Before I understood water as a sinister element, rather than something that swam silent inside ourselves, an ingredient of our daily motions, I stood on the porch and cut Kate's long hair to her shoulders.

It was an afternoon project in rare trust between us, the springtime weekends making us pollen-lazy and bored, and it turned out blunter than I meant for it to, but she said, "No, I like it," and smiled as she swished her hands through it in the mirror.

Then my dad came home from fishing. He dropped his metal box, containing brightly colored baubles whose uses I couldn't fathom, so foreign were they to my understanding of the slick, eyeless flanks he portioned onto our dinner plates, and said, "Why not, I could use a trim."

I carefully cut the lines around his neck, his ears, took the kitchen scissors to the thick hair at the crown, his temples, careful not to disturb the ecosystem of swirls and thinning patches. When I finished, he glanced quickly in the handheld mirror and said, "Nice job, darlin'," before taking the broom and sweeping everything I'd cut away from him and Kate down the steps and into our front yard. Kate's hair lay in the grass like strands of stretched golden taffy mixed with our dad's black tufts, the texture of wool sheared from an animal.

"It'll make good homes for birds," he said. And he was right, within days it was all gone but a few glimmering strands caught between the blades of sod.

No—

That isn't how it happened.

I was cutting Kate's hair, animated by that springtime prickle that's half heat and half chill, when my mom ventured onto the porch. "What are you two doing?" she exclaimed, and we braced for her anger, but she laughed and said, "It doesn't look bad, actually. Maybe you're a natural." Then my mom surprised us, sitting cautiously in Kate's place so I could trim the splits from her ends, which were blond like Kate's but wavier, with the slightest silver tint.

We were like that when my dad came home from fishing, sunburned and ornery as he walked up the driveway.

"What the hell did y'all do?" he said, and Kate and I chuckled, because we thought he would sigh and smile like my mom had.

"Y'all have gone and ruined your hair," he shouted. He'd been fishing with Glen and Ron from work, I could tell, from the hostile twang he absorbed when he drank with them.

"Oh, come on," my mom teased, "it's fine, it's just a little haircut. Erma did a pretty good job, I'd say."

"It looks ridiculous."

"I like it," Kate offered.

"You're a kid, you don't get to decide what you like. Sweep up that mess, now. We'll figure out what to do about y'all later."

He lumbered inside, and my mom went after him, and when Kate went to her room, too, I was glad she couldn't see tears falling in the spots where I swept.

Later, I watched my mom gut and scale the fish in the sink while my dad napped. The bluegill's black eye pointed at the ceiling, looking away from what was being done to it. I saw the fish, so small and useless in my mother's hands, and wished my dad knew what it was to feel like that—to be trapped in someone's grip, your joy sliced away just because someone decided they could do it.

Now my dad was only this ugly sadness, he was nowhere and everywhere, and those pieces of my mom and Kate were out there, too, forming the tenderest nest for a robin or a shrike, and I wanted it all back.

I stood in front of the bathroom mirror, truly looking for the first time at the knot in all its gnarled splendor, a nest for nothing. The back of my head was consumed by the knot, protruding like a thick fist holding me by the hair. Whether it grew during the party or I just hadn't noticed its size before, I wasn't sure. I rolled open the drawer and glanced down at the scissors, struck with a wave of harsh noise and dread. I did not move to touch them.

The knot was speaking again, not just nouns but broken noises, words sliced and sutured together: *Bonegulf. Shineaway. Wake, shut, knifedive.* It was ugly, a pulsing, repulsive tangle of what was once mine, what was once me. But I did not look away.

Bitterstar. Fieldswell. Oilaloud, oilaround, slice. Dive.

It felt important to hear what it had to say.

Clumsily, quickly, I stripped down to my bra and underwear. I pulled back the shower curtain and sat on the cold floor of the tub, and before I could think too much about it, turned on the faucet.

Water sprayed down from the showerhead like droplets of ice, the cold flooding me with shock, entering my nose and making me gag. I pressed my face into my knees and I could hear the knot screaming into my ear, intimately close, slobbering with demonic-voiced rage: *Stranglecarcass! Fleshooze! Corpsemeat! Fishwound!*

I squinted my eyes open and saw long black hairs, too dark and wiry to be my own, clamoring at the drain—not washing away, but climbing up the tub toward me. I gasped, coughing up water, then scrunched my face shut and held my breath while the ghostly hairs dragged like wet seaweed across my naked skin.

Snakejawsinksoakbeetleswarmfloatbloatgutterruinruinchoke-chokechoke—

"Dad," I spat back at it, *Dad*, as if testing the word for the first time, water pouring over my face, my voice interweaving with the knot's in a monstrous kind of music. I knew I was not speaking to my actual or past-tense father or to whoever was inside the knot, but that the word was only itself, guttural, a fractured cry like any other word. *Dad*, I said. Feeling the word slip through my mouth and away like lakeslime. *In this way I will know you.*

The tendrils of dark hair filled the bathtub, braiding into my own hair, nesting around my body until I was cradled, cocooned in place. Between the webbing of the hair-nest, my eye caught a glint of the scissors on the counter. But I had no need for them.

The knot writhed, language swelled and crashed, the words all sliding now to the unreachable bottom of some familiar, ethereal place. I broke through to my lungs. *I will collect the pieces*, I said. *Swallowhowl. Wailblessing.* I can get it back.

THE FORGOTTEN COAST

Not two days after Luke and I'd finally drug the months-rotten Christmas spruce out to the ravine, Piper got riled up into one of her great tizzies. I came home from my shift at the Donut Kingdom and Piper was rampaging through the house, flinging all manner of laundry onto floors and door handles and over lamps, Cap going red on her hip as she bounced around in her furious machinations.

"We need to get a nanny for Cap," she said. "Now."

Her wheaten hair was awry, sprouting from her high bun in wisps that fell around her face, and there was spittle down the neck of her old gray T-shirt.

"Is it necessary?" I asked her. She huffed and I turned to Luke, who was leaning his whole broad body into the corner of the kitchen wall. "Is it needed?"

Luke nodded, sighed. "Cap's been going red all the livelong. It's too much for her to handle alone."

"But she's not alone." I told Piper, "You're not alone. You're the opposite of alone."

"Easy for you to say," she sniffed.

It *was* easy for me to say; I'd been picking up more shifts at the Donut Kingdom and hadn't been the one in care of Cap for a full day in a while. But my being gone was meant to be good for all of us. Cap went through formula like a healthy mongoose suckling the guts from its prey, and all that powdered milk cost something outlandish. We oftentimes had to mix his bottles with a whole mess of sink water just to get it to last.

I work and Luke works. Piper calls the shots. Luke listens to Piper and I listen to Luke. It'd been like that between us a long time. It was Piper who wanted a baby, so we got Cap—a round, jovial fellow, except when he went red—and now Piper wanted a nanny, so I reckoned that meant we were getting one.

I'd known Luke the longest, since we shacked up together in his van one winter outside Tampa. Piper came in later, after her parents cut off her cash flow when they found out her pro-clivities. She slept in a cramped loft with failed artists and fishermen then, and worked in the downstairs café. Luke and I'd go there to charge our shared prepaid phone and drink the blackberry lemonades Piper snuck us when the van got too hot. It was summer in Ybor City, the wild chickens flocked back to roost in palms and roam the cobblestone streets lined with ocher-lit bars and vape shops. It had been the three of us since then.

Now the three of us had a nice little house in Wakulla with two thick wood doors on the inside—real crystal doorknobs—tucked away far back on Harms Road. Beautiful vines grew through the split boards around the windows, and when pal-mettos and little lizards climbed in through the chimney, we'd open our door and let one of the ferals in the yard take care of it. We had an electric stove and a velvet couch and a big, good bed for tossing each other around and contorting in pleasure's wild shapes, me feeling Luke's love through Piper and Piper feeling my love through Luke and Luke feeling Piper's love through me and all of us in the great heaving immortal beast of our together-love in the bed, where we twined and sunk together into sleep when it was done. It had always been like that between us.

It had been a good many days since love heaved through us, but sometimes we'd touch and bloom in a gentler way before sleep untethered us, me buoyed around Luke buoyed around Piper buoyed around Cap. When we got Cap, we built an extension to the bed from a pile of quilts and old clothes that we called The Pile. More and more lately it was me who had gotten to sleeping on The Pile. We agreed Piper and Cap needed the bed, for now at least, and Luke was so kind he would have granted us anything and slept on The Pile himself, but he was chopping lumber out in Panacea three days a week and his back cricked something awful if he didn't get the mattress.

"Okay," I told them. "I can do it."

I kissed Cap's greasy head and went to go get changed. The evening light plowed into the bedroom and stuck in the air, lingering even close to dark, so I was sweating as I shucked off my Donut Kingdom polo and pulled one of Piper's thin spring dresses over my head. I was fixing to leave when Luke pulled me aside.

"Get a good nanny for Cap, but don't feel you have to pull a trickery for it. You know we can't afford any more doom hanging over us."

I nodded. Luke got that solemn look behind his big dark eyes, and I melted a little for it. We were on the same page, in terms of what needed done and how to do it, and in that way I felt we were in cahoots. With Piper, you sometimes had to be in cahoots to keep life turning. At her best, she was a big fun blaze to behold, like a hydrogen star plunked into a riverbed, her lithe limbs flailing around her. But when she wanted something to be different than it was, she pummeled all her energy at it, and nobody could say a thing to make her think it through.

Piper had done a shameful trickery getting Cap in the first place, and though my heart still lived with her, it had begun inch-worming away after I'd learned fully what she was capable of. Luke forgave her trickery outright, like he was bound to, being Luke, but I think it made him feel a little humbled to her, maybe even a little fearsome. There were times I feared Piper's unpredictable ways, too; nowadays when I crept into her orbit, I was measuring the air around her like a thermometer for chaos, hoping to halt one of her storms before it did damage. I believed Luke's heart still lived with her—and with Cap certainly, who none of us less than flat-out adored—but if he'd begun to ponder his slow escape, he didn't let it show.

"Trust is all we got," I said.

Luke nodded and plopped a big sweet kiss on my forehead. Though I'd just gotten home, it was almost a relief to have reason to leave again. I called out that I'd pick up a bag of ice from the gas station on my way home so he didn't have to go out later, and I knew that would be a welcome help. The fridge had been broken a couple weeks and we didn't have the cash for a new one by a long shot, so Luke had been getting ice from the Circle K to fill up the bin where we kept our perishables. But hot as it was, the ice melted in an hour, and the cost was racking up—no help from the hole in the roof that leaked black sludge down the wall like mascara tears, or the draft that rendered the AC pointless even on cooler days. The house sometimes felt like a pressure cooker trying to spit me out.

When I gathered my keys, Cap was sitting on Piper's lap on the couch, looking up at her with big happy eyes like he'd never known another way to feel. Piper grinned up at me with the same kind of look and my heart threw itself over my rib in guilt.

I hollered bye to them and walked out the front door.

◆ ◆ ◆

I drove down to Carrabelle to find a nanny for Cap, reckoning it to be the closest shot at hard-up tourists who'd booked a few cheap nights on the Forgotten Coast. On the way, I pulled into a truck stop in Medart to buy a stick of elk jerky and a canned margarita for the drive. Gas station treats were a small glory to me, and I needed sustenance after standing behind that donut shop counter all the livelong.

It would've been a tussle, I knew, if I bought frivolities with our shared fund, so I paid with the money I snagged from the tip jar at the Donut Kingdom. Taking a few bucks might have been tricky, but it didn't count as a *trickery*, per se—the jar said TIPS on it, but every night the boss came in after fishing all day and poured it into the register rather than give it to us who ran the store. So in rightness, the money was mine to begin with.

I walked out of the gas station to the truck and peered back at the hoard of vines crawling across the building. Put your hand over one eye, and you can convince yourself you're walking through the earth during dinosaur times.

Over the years, I'd noticed how people raised in Florida tended to forget the glorious cruel beauty of it. All that greenery fades into regular life until a tangling of caladium and magenta blooms may as well be a standard sidewalk, like it's nothing to go out and pluck fruits from wild brush during a day's stroll and chomp into the sweet gritty juice right where you stood. But I hadn't forgotten. As I drove, I still liked to marvel at those big oaks, with trunks like a mangled fist and mossy tentacles all afoot of it. It felt sacred to know the intimacies of Spanish moss, how up close its barbed chains drape the sky like the split hairs of a giantess peering down at you. From time to time, I still got flooded all through my body while gazing at this land, at the ferns and weeds wilding themselves silly as if working out some deep-rooted, tenacious sorrow. I hoped I'd never come to find it usual as long as I breathed on earth.

When we first moved up to the Panhandle, I would come through Carrabelle in the off-season and stop at the cash-only diner to get a root beer float and drink it in the parking lot of the nearby beach, across the street from the RV park. Before we got Cap, I'd sometimes pull a small trickery and tell Piper and Luke I was going to work, and instead, drive down here and do the same, just sit in the parking lot and listen to the radio with my windows cracked while the ice cream melted in my cup. Truthfully, I'd kept this trickery up even after Cap, though each time felt more and more like pulling off a heist. But having secrets wasn't the worst thing for a relationship. It kept us hanging on to a piece of ourselves, so that we could return again and again to the collective. We'd all started off with only one self to worry about, and you can't just up and dissolve that way of survival so easy. But I was learning how to hide the feral squirm, the way an embrace could still look like a chokehold coming in my direction. I suspected Luke and Piper each had their small secrets, and I didn't guess at what the big ones might be. Trickeries or not, I believed I would always return to them.

I passed the skinny rows of slash pines, some snapped and flopping broken-necked from their trunks. I passed the dark-windowed series of vacation cabins propped up on stilts by the water. When I pulled into the parking lot of Fathom's, the sky was getting the way it was bound to get before a storm, that red and greenish hue, like a false Christmas.

I posted up at the sticky bar and ordered a double gin and tonic while some local band clattered in the corner. Before too long, a pretty brunette came in from the smoking porch. She wobbled up to the bar and a shine caught in her long hair, glowing under the weak lights like rubies in a dark cave.

I told her my name and the thing about her hair being like rubies, and she giggled and thanked me. She said her name was Jaqueline and she was down from Valdosta. Jaqueline told me she'd planned to come down for a bachelorette weekend, but it got canceled due to the bride contracting a suspicious illness and the groom taking off with their honeymoon vouchers. So she'd decided to keep the hotel reservation and come alone. We got to talking, and she asked me where I'd come from, and I told her about the house in Wakulla and even about the crystal doorknobs. We got to ordering more drinks, and then she leaned in closer so her arm was resting lengthwise against my arm. I noticed dark hairs sprouting on her flesh, hairs most girls plucked or waxed, and seeing them felt like something private and special. Before I'd even finished my one drink she was ordering me another, and so on, throwing around cash like it burned her to hold on to.

A few drinks in, I asked her what she did for work, and she just giggled and giggled. When she stopped giggling, she started up again, and I grew impatient of keeping that expectant look on my face, like you do when you're trying to make someone think they're so fascinating that your world's hinging on whatever comes out of their mouth next. When she finally got it together, she sucked in a slurry of air and announced she was in between endeavors. So I explained to Jaqueline the way it was between Luke and Piper and me. I explained to her Cap's needs. "Does that sound like something you'd be up for?" I asked.

"Sure," she responded. "That sounds like a job I could do."

I told her that was great news, and if she closed out her bar tab we could go now, though admittedly neither of us was in any kind of shape for driving. But I was feeling the exhaustion of the day start to settle in my bones, and I longed to get the task done and get back to the house, where I could lie across any surface that would have me.

But then Jaqueline said there was a catch, and I got the feeling that I wouldn't be getting home easy or soon.

She said, "I would want to be part of things. I would want to have a home with y'all."

I told her she could have a home with us, that it would be her home as much as ours, but I didn't know if it could be with her like it was with the three of us.

But she said no, she wouldn't accept anything less than equal and undying love. "I know my worth," she said, with the air of a person who had to convince themselves they meant it.

"What is it y'all have that I can't be part of? What is it you have that I can't have?" she asked.

I thought about that a minute. "Trust," I said, calling forth through the liquor haze what I'd told Luke not hours before. "We have a certain understanding."

There's this way only a handful of people in your whole life will have of seeing you so deeply that it reminds you who you are, all the good and the bad, all that you're capable of. I had that with Luke and Piper, and we had it with each other.

"I think we have an understanding," Jaqueline said. She said, "I could come to know you in such a way."

After she said it, I wasn't sure that we *didn't* have understanding between us, so I sipped my drink and pondered until my drink was done, then I poked at the wasted lime dregs at the bottom of my glass and pondered some more. I didn't blame her for wanting to be part of what I had with Piper and Luke. I'd only wanted the same, to live with others in the harmonies of love and truth. All I'd done was want it and want it and now that I had it, it didn't seem fair to deny it to someone else. It seemed shameful, to gatekeep belonging that way. To offer someone your home and care of your child and your friendship but keep them from knowing you in the full way a body can be known seemed, on reflection, a kind of cruelty.

◆ ◆ ◆

In honesty, things hadn't felt quite right between the three of us since we got Cap. It wasn't Cap's fault, how he was got, but sometimes, when Luke's and Piper's slumber gets going in the dark bedroom, I turn over on The Pile and think back through that first night, making sure I keep every detail lined up right in my head.

Piper had always been bouncy in her near-dangerous way, and that was part of the fun of her: the way she cared hard and loud and never got bored of being alive, as long as there was some new idea to strike out on. But in the month before Cap, she got a wild flicker in her eye and neither me nor Luke could look straight at it without a queasy sinking coming over us. It was like staring into bramble, tangled and festering and endless.

But we went on with how things were, trying to ignore that Piper'd given up bathing herself and gained a sick shimmer to her skin, that she spent afternoons walking up and down the back roads, digging in abandoned yards and trailer lots, and we'd come home to see a bunch of dirt-streaked aluminum and plastic bits piled up in trash pyramids on the mantel, or a bouquet of weeds leaking its insects all over the kitchen table. Then, one day she took Luke's truck to the store for groceries and didn't show up again for four days.

Those days seemed like minutes looking back, but at the time, they felt like they stretched the length of mine and Luke's entire lives. We talked that first night about what to do, but short of roaming the streets hollering out her name, there wasn't much to be done—due to some technicalities in our way of living, we couldn't alert the police, and we were the kind that even if we'd been pure with the law, they'd find some reason to believe we weren't. My stomach was rotten over Piper's well-being, but I also felt the slight gnawing of jealousy at how much of Luke's focus it took. As if without anybody saying it, it had been my job to build the structures that kept Piper tethered, and I'd failed.

Though the nail-chewing days stretched blank and gray around us, I think we both expected Piper's absence to be overwhelming, like a crazed animal filling her place in the house. But in truth her absence was a polite shadow-being, easier to live with in some ways than Piper herself, and we felt a bit of sad relief, though guilt kept either of us from admitting it. Almost out of respect, me and Luke didn't touch each other in those gone days, only floated through the house like solitary meteors—till the night before Piper's return, as if we somehow knew, we turned over in the big bed and smashed our bodies into one another desperate.

◆ ◆ ◆

"I can't speak for Piper and Luke," I told Jaqueline. "I can't speak to what they'll do."

"We'll just have to see how it goes," she said. I got the feeling from the way she flashed her teeth that she imagined us in cahoots, and the thrill of power and dread dancing in my gut made me a little sickly, like I'd eaten something too sweet too fast.

We cashed out at Fathom's, and as we traversed the parking lot, I had to admit myself too wobbly to drive. I asked Jaqueline if we could go to her hotel room, so I could find something amenable for lying on. She just walked past and motioned at me to come on, so I followed her onto the side of the road, where we walked for a good while, front to back like a mother and her duckling. Her shiny brown hair sucked up the sparse light from a waning moon, and I got dizzy watching truck headlights zigzag across her back and bolt away like phantom doe.

I couldn't pinpoint when I'd lost grip on what I came for, but the boozy numbness put me on autopilot, like the clearest thing was to follow Jaqueline wherever she decided. It was meditative, almost spiritual, for wanting to be so simple—to give up on considerations and circumstances and let myself be drug along by desire. It began to rain hard, and we came across some shelter to linger under.

We looked at each other in the hidden dark, and wetness pooled in fleeting rivers on our skin. That sharp wrong hunger spread rapid in my gut, my hot neck and stunned fingertips. I almost said *Wait* or thought it—though there was nothing to say it for, she was just standing there—but as if dangling above the scene I now saw the crossed threshold between the road and leaving the road. She pressed her mouth on me and my mouth accepted her. In the half-drugged panther of night, there was no guilty flicker of remembrance, and I was only myself. My body and what I did with it was only my own to decide. We broke into one of those stilted beach houses and got our sweat all over each other. We gasped and writhed in all the ancient ways. I was approaching a thick wave of slumber when her voice pulled me to the surface and I sat up in the dark, wrapped in someone else's blankets. She said it was time to go and led me to climb out through a window I didn't remember shattering.

◆ ◆ ◆

Four days after Piper went out for groceries, we came home to the truck in the driveway and a baby, plump and cooing, stark naked on the couch.

Luke said something like, "Who the hell's this?"

I always think back on it like I walked in and said, *Oh, Piper, the misery you bring on us,* or, *Is this a new one of the yard ferals, ha ha ha?* But in the real version of events I said nothing anybody could hear.

Piper was loath to admit her trickery, but Luke finally wrangled out a version of events: Piper was meant to go to the Winn-Dixie in town, but she claimed to be craving adventure and had driven the truck up to the one in Tallahassee instead. She was minding her own when she saw a ragged woman shopping for nursing bras in the aisle with the discount makeup and packaged pairs of socks and pantyhose. The woman saw Piper coming and asked her to watch her sleeping baby while she ran to try on some stuff in the bathroom, and without waiting for an answer, left to do just that.

Piper took one look at the child in the stroller and felt the ache of her own emptiness slice through her. She felt a duty to take Cap as her own, and figured it wouldn't hurt to relieve the woman of her burden, ragged as she seemed. She figured she was actually doing the woman something of a favor. By the end of her telling, Piper'd wrung the neck of her dirt-stained blouse loose from her shoulders with nervous energy, and the baby had flopped off the couch to go investigate the fire poker.

I asked her how come if she was driving all the way up to Tallahassee she didn't just go to Publix instead, but she looked at me with that rough wildness in her eye and said to leave her alone about it. She wouldn't say what she'd done with the other three days, and I could tell by looking at her it was because she probably didn't know either.

Luke said, "Come on now, if you wanted a baby we can whip up our own from scratch," managing through the horror to get his voice soft and low, to put on that look in Piper's direction like a lusty hound, flicking his eyes over at me to try to get me in cahoots.

But Piper said no, it had to be this baby. She said it might be that Cap was somebody she had known before, some kid she went to school with, or one of her dad's normal-looking business friends. Somebody who might've died years ago but she didn't even know about it. And now here was that person again, smack in an infant's body, reaching out to her in the light-bleached aisles of the Tallahassee Winn-Dixie.

Then Piper stomped off to the bedroom and Luke followed her, and I stayed behind to keep tabs on the baby. He'd gotten into all manner of dirt and soot from the fire poker, and now was sitting there in his nakedness, smearing black grime all over his face. So I scooped him up, careful to evade his naked parts, and took him to the sink to wipe him down. Then, I tiptoed to the bedroom and pulled one of Luke's old T-shirts from the drawer and put it over the baby, and pulled one of my old winter scarves from the closet and wove it around the baby's fat, kicking legs to make pants. All this time, Piper had her face slammed into the bedcovers, and Luke was there, rubbing her back. I forged a little worried smile in Luke's direction, and he returned it. When I went to leave and turned around in the doorway, though, Luke's focus was all back on Piper's wilting.

◆ ◆ ◆

Jaqueline and I walked through the dark, stepping over roots and sticks until we reached the beach. There were some old Y-shaped pavilions and a big rock with a faucet for washing sand off your feet. I recognized the parking lot, and a spot where I'd once sat and watched a young boy chase gulls into the briny surf; the freedom in watching his body speed along the coastline, mixed with nervousness when he'd dip too close to the saw-toothed waves. I tried to tell Jaqueline about the boy, but she didn't seem to hear me right.

"Your boy?" she asked.

"No, not mine. A strange boy."

I'd never quite figured Cap to be *my boy* but I reckoned he was mine as much as anybody's. The fact I was out here wasted on a weeknight trying to wrangle him a nanny just as much proved it.

Truth was, a part of me wished I got more credit for how Cap was mine too. But under the right light I understood Piper only took Cap because pouring all your care into someone else makes it easier to escape yourself. We were all, everybody, try-ing to drown ourselves in other people, and at the same time, wanting to hold the truest piece of ourselves hostage, where nobody could get to it. It wasn't that the three of us cared for each other less now, just that we were always swinging between claiming a self and sacrificing one, and Piper's swinging got so un-ignorable it frightened us into realizing we were the same.

In the end, Luke had chosen Piper, and I'd chosen to hang on to Cap, which meant that I'd roundabout chosen Piper, too, and such choices require a deathless devotion to keep them go-ing. To choose to be alone or to be among—to be made more of a self by putting the pieces of your life into something else—that was what made it deathless.

A slow guilt leaked into my blood then, remembering the ways I'd used my body with Jaqueline. How quick I'd been to forget who my heart lived with, that I had an allegiance to a fuller life than one self could build alone.

"We should go," I said. "I can drive us back to the house now. You can meet everybody in the morning. They'll love you, they'll all love you."

I didn't know if any of what I was saying was the truth, and it had gotten increasingly hard to imagine morning ever arriving. The whole endeavor had grown burdensome, but I couldn't leave now, with Jaqueline knowing about Cap and the way things were. Wind hissed over the waves like a pit of vipers and the humidity from the rain was making me woozy. In the dark, the roiling sea looked oily, bloodied.

"We'll go now and we'll sleep, and in the morning we'll all come together and drape you in the sunlight of our love," I promised. "We'll come to know one another as few of history's creatures have," I begged.

Jaqueline looked at me under the half-moon and smiled a too-wide smile. I glanced down, and the keys I'd been digging in my pocket for were gleaming in her hand. She giggled and tossed them at the water.

I scurried out into the Gulf and lunged for the keys as my feet sunk in the sand. I was crouched down, searching for that gleam of silver freedom, when the riptide tugged at my ankles and swept me into deeper waters. Plowed by waves, I tried to keep paddling, but each time I was able to pull myself to the surface it put me in a heavy delirium. I reckoned it was the same gravity I must've felt upon waking from my own birth.

On shore, I saw Jaqueline raise a glint of metal to the black sky: the keys still twined in her hand. Between bobs and static gulps, I heard her call out something about, *Trust is whatever people want to believe it is.*

Salt sloshing into my lungs, I remembered this folk legend about a pair of teenage lovers who drowned near Apalachicola, their bodies still clinging to each other when they were pulled up from the river, fish-feasted limbs ensnared for all eternity. But as I flailed and sliced at the unrelenting water, I was hit with the gladness of being just one body. The ocean opened around me to make space, and it was like spreading out atop a California king that stretched for hundreds of cool dark miles.

I thought of the fiery glint in Piper's smile. I thought of Luke's kind brown eyes. I thought of Cap, round and red and screaming with so much aliveness. I could see them all nestled up in bed, and the way the light from the hall would fall in hard shapes across their faces when I opened the door and climbed to rest in The Pile. I could see Jaqueline standing on the shore and the whole savage expanse of the future raging out in front. I filled up with the sweet weight of belonging and let it take me under.

CRESCENDO

When I can no longer hide that I haven't been sleeping, I work up the courage to tell my husband what I'm afraid of.

He looks up. *What? That noise? It's just a plane. A car with a busted exhaust pipe.*

But I'm not so sure.

He turns back to his computer screen or his cell phone screen or his video-game screen, and I turn away, too, as if having said the thing is enough—as if I understand that saying the thing is not a path to opening some new door inside me, where fear can finally tumble out like so many mountains of dirty laundry stuffed in a child's closet.

I tell my therapist how I cower in the grated corner by the air vent, wrapped in the blanket my grandmother crocheted for my thirtieth birthday a handful of weeks before she died, trembling in wait as the sound rises and rises, rattling the walls, shaking leaf-clung branches loose from the trees, until the noise is sucked back into the void it emerged from. Sometimes, I get so nervous with anticipation when the crescendo starts that

I crawl, blanket draped over my back like a lioness carrying the limp corpse of her cub, to the bathroom across the hall and vomit.

The therapist prescribes me Ativan, noting, *Women seem to have more luck with it.*

I'd lost my job, but it was probably for the best that I got fired when I did. I'd caught myself gripping my desk when the heater switched on, the clanging growing louder in the vents overhead, like the hot breath of a beast drawing its mouth ever closer. I had to replace my aluminum water bottle with a plastic one because the crescendo showed up at the cooler, and I feared it an omen of devastations to come. Each evening, I bolted to the parking lot and drove straight home, my hands on the steering wheel trembling along with the radio music, a horror-stone heavy in my stomach like something big was about to happen. Whatever the name for it was, it was the opposite of hope.

The thing is, I spent half a lifetime alongside the crescendo without realizing it was there. There used to be jets trailing their sonic screams overhead, clouds bellowing into cul-de-sacs, fireworks and shotgun mufflers punctuating nights I slept through soundly, immune to their sharp patter. There used to be birthday parties with kazoos and the crinkled silver trunks of party horns. The familiar music of living came and passed, some barely registered tinkering in the background.

◆ ◆ ◆

It introduced itself like faint tinnitus: a barely perceptible high-pitched buzz, like a power strip with too many electronics plugged in. My husband rarely raised his eyes from his screens, so I'd started doing the same. Absorbed in the world of screen-light, with other people's thoughts bouncing around my head, I could tune out the noise. It was slight enough to ignore, except when I found myself completely alone.

It was already becoming the kind of life where I woke up and began looking forward to the next time I could sleep. Turning on the news was like strapping into a dread machine. We could usually predict what flavor of badness the world would invite upon itself next, or otherwise ignore the whining ache of it until it dissolved at the back of our skulls. But lately, big things we'd never predicted kept crashing down, and just when the dust began to settle, we were bowled over by another unexpected wave of terror. In every video, in the shootings and collapses and burnings, I recognize it: the thing you can hear coming but can't save yourself from, because by the time you hear it, it's already too late.

◆ ◆ ◆

I don't remember exactly when the hum became more than an irritant, how it built up decibel by decibel to a full-blown roar, but I remember the elevator. Before I was fired, I worked on the fourteenth floor, and after lingering at my desk until everyone else left the office, I packed my laptop and Tupperware from lunch into my tote bag and took the elevator down.

As the elevator picked up speed, the woosh of cables dropping the box through a tunnel of so many stories grew too loud to be normal; concerning, then terrifying. I gripped the metal rail and tried to recall an infographic I'd seen online—was it locking or not locking your knees that would shatter your legs on impact? The metal walls screamed and vibrated and I envisioned my little nothing of a body, the not-at-all-durable bag of flesh that was the entirety of me, splattering when the elevator plummeted through to the foundation. The crescendo ceased with a sickly, grinding shriek as the doors pinged and opened gently into the parking garage.

So I started taking the stairs. I preferred to spend as much time as possible in the stairwell anyway, because I knew it was the safest place in the building to be during a natural disaster. But my coworkers noticed when I emerged into the office sheened with sweat, failing to control the embarrassingly loud hunger of my lungs.

I didn't tell anyone about the crescendo, but soon I was on alert for it every moment of the day, flinching at any creak or moan of the building, a cell phone chiming, a distant motorcycle, a sudden burst of laughter in the hallway. I could not bring myself to ask if anyone else heard it for what it was—though I wished to abandon myself so fully to my need that it transcended the restraint of shame. Every time someone passed my desk, a desperation rose to call them over and plead for reassurance that whatever was coming wouldn't destroy us, at least not this time; or if it would, to know that they were scared, too, and we could sit in our fear together as we waited for that final, painful note to land. When the impulse crawled up my throat, I swallowed hard and stuffed it back down.

Once, at the office, I found myself in the middle of a thunderstorm. It seemed to me nothing short of perversion, the way everyone complained lightheartedly about traffic and how long it would take to get home for dinner, when there was no guarantee of food or home again, nowhere to escape to, I thought, wincing as the wind split pines outside the window. I snuck away to the bathroom to call my husband. He tried, halfheartedly, to comfort me, assuming I was only nervous about the weather. But my voice went anemic and I had to hang up. He, who doesn't fear untimely disease or turbulence on planes, has no idea what it means to be constantly clawing for survival.

These days, when my husband and I have sex, I don't let myself come. I pull back and let him work on my body until he feels useful. Crouched like an animal, I clasp my hands in front of me till he jolts, and ends, and slithers away. When he begins to snore, I take my blanket to the corner and hide in wait for the crescendo. It's rare that I sleep, but when I do, I dream of a faceless person clinging to a thick braided rope, climbing higher and higher.

On my therapist's recommendation, I try massaging the scowl out of my face, sticking my fingers in a secret notch between my jaw and cheekbone. But then the crescendo comes once more, and again I'm scraping and biting and crawling. My therapist says, *You have to learn how to protect yourself without maiming yourself to do it.* If anyone alive has learned such a skill, I don't trust them.

◆ ◆ ◆

My husband discovers me one night in the dark corner, the hollows of my face carved out by the dim screen-light of the phone in my lap. His eyes snap from the hallway to my hunched form, and he startles.

What are you doing? he says, not a question inviting an answer.

This is the safest place in the house. I add, *You can come down here, too, if you want.* I don't care if he joins me, but I reason that the offer makes it seem like I'm not withholding something.

He retrieves a glass of water from the sink and sets it down on the ground beside me on his way back to bed. I pull my grandmother's blanket tighter around my shoulders. I didn't speak to her much when she was alive, but I knew all the stories about her, which is how any of us come to feel we know people. The noise, perhaps, was fainter during her time, in its infancy: a little mewl you'd occasionally pause to hear, then shrug before switching off the lamp and tucking into bed.

When I shuffle through the dark to the bedroom, my husband is breathing rhythmically into his pillow. I open the FEMA app on my phone and set it faceup on the nightstand, and stare up at the orange rectangle it burns into the ceiling.

◆　◆　◆

Since I'd gotten fired (my boss claimed I slipped out early too many days, though anyone could guess some version of the real reason), no one from work had reached out. The only person other than my husband that I've spoken to in a month is the neighbor, Helen. Her husband recently left her, so she got two big dogs, a Great Dane and a bluetick hound, to help her forget the extra space. But she can't afford the townhouse on her own, so she'd be moving away soon, too, at forty-three and with a master's degree in engineering, to stay with her mother.

We sit on her porch drinking the last cans of her gone husband's beer, and I ask her about the crescendo, if she'd ever noticed it. She shakes her head, then describes a dream she had while feverish as a child, in the months after her father wilted from cancer: everything was dark, but she felt the hot shadow of something monstrous shifting around her, huge and pelted, with gooey, wet fangs, and the noises it made. She says she can still remember the noise so clearly, that even now it sometimes comes back to her in the seconds before waking, like breaking through to the surface of the ocean from a deep place.

I ask her to do the noise. Helen puts her beer down and stares into the damp, chirping night. When the sound starts, it takes me a second to understand it's coming from within her. From between her lips, she exhales a creepy whine, soft at first, growing louder and louder until it sounds like a wailing siren, a harsh and helpless thing made of meat and absolute failure, the end of the world.

Yes, I say, *that's it*.

She nods and gulps from the can.

Past the oily light cast over our street, the whistling begins again.

INSTRUCTIONS FOR ASSEMBLY

1

My grandma had smoke in her heart. All up in her heart. Sometimes she bled a little of it when outside got cold, and her mouth opened up dragonlike into the gray winter air. She bled out her smoke-breath and/or coughed, and/or laughed: and if laughter, it came out sounding like a cackle. Her skin looked to be sliding off her face-bones. It was funny, until it wasn't.

I'd say, "Granny, your skin's falling off right down onto the floor!" And touch her wrinkled cheek. And she'd hack up some laugh noises and boil noodles for dinner.

That was when it was funny, when even Mama, who's always been hawk-sharp with brown-eyed concern, thought the game amusing. Then my grandma started peeling away from herself, caving in like a rotten peach.

That's when she told me about the smoke in her heart, and said, "You have it, too, you know. All us women do."

Not a warning, just bestowing facts. There are holes in a body where only smoke can survive.

Granny died and Mama's brown eyes got sharper, her nose-to-brow ratio more hawklike. Now the Big House was all our own, even though it was still coated in Granny's wallpaper, her white kitchen towels strewn dirty-damp all over the place. When Mama and I had the Big House to ourselves, she let me draw on the walls, as long as I promised to draw nice things. I drew boats, flowers, and swimming pools, juice boxes and pocket change. I drew clouds that were secretly brains. I drew raindrops falling from the actually brain clouds that was actually brain goo. I wanted to draw people or animals, but had no way to know for sure whether or not they'd be nice.

Mama tore down the wallpaper when Howard came to live with us. When the wallpaper came down, the Big House started to smell like metal. It started to smell like a nosebleed. I told Mama I didn't want Howard to live with us in the Big House, that it was big enough for just the two of us and no one else. I told her I wanted the wallpaper back, and Granny.

Mama's eyes got deep, like the muddy sky too long past bedtime. She spoke low and quiet. Behind her tongue I saw a flicker of brilliant red, a red so pure-bright it made my chest ache. She had a cardinal wet and strangling in her throat, and when she talked, I could hear it trying to flap its way out. She mentioned milk and eggs, how there hadn't been any since Granny got rotten and went into the ground.

She said, "This is how you scrape together a life."

2

Howard's eyes were sand-colored somehow, even though I know that when he came to us, they looked blue. Mama says she knew them to be blue. Howard was the first bad man I knew, mostly because he was the first man I had ever known, and he wasn't all that bad, really, just reckless with his hands. So he took to shaking things, like Mama, who had gone all bones and feathers. Her rib cage more cage than rib, more sky than nest.

When Howard came to us, the bird inside him was already missing. On days when the sun melted away and there hadn't yet been any shouts or shakings, Mama would claim to have heard Howard's bird shake off dust and flap its spotted wings as she stood tiptoed and smacked her lips on his. But we both knew she was only telling a wish: something nice, like the drawings I used to make on the walls. Neither of us had ever seen or heard Howard's bird. It was death-quiet, buried deep down under a dense mountain of sand.

There were things Mama didn't talk about, except to say not to talk about them. Our smoke-heart was one of those. When she started to go gray in the skin, and her brown hair fell like clumps of plumage, I got scared she would slide away from herself like Granny. I came to her troubled, and she explained:

"Us women are special. We can't let too much of what's inside out, or else it'll burn up everything. It's what you have to live with."

As she was saying it, she seemed half in the room and half not.

I asked, "Did Granny die because her smoke got too big?" But Mama shook her head and said, "No, her body was just old."

I asked her, did Howard know about our smoke-heart? She got real serious then, her mouth puckered in a sharp point, and said no, it had to be secret. The secret was part of the smoke-heart.

"If you know what you are deep down, you shouldn't talk about it," she said. "And if it's all gonna have to burn up anyway, it's better not to know."

What she meant was: if you're not aware of what's being strangled inside you, you can survive anything.

I realized with a fright that the cardinal inside her was choking in her own heart's soot, and I wanted her to let it come out. I wanted to scream at her to rescue her bird before it fell dead from fumes, but Mama didn't see it so urgent. I didn't understand why anyone would let a creature of such beauty breathe in poison, but maybe Mama didn't think her bird was as beautiful as I did. There wasn't much of a choice; we were not the kind whose birds were safe flying on the outside, where anyone could pluck them from the air.

I was always getting scared for people's birds, which seemed a little ironic, since I hadn't met my own yet. I never said it out loud, but I think Mama must have known. It was another thing we didn't talk about. When I was little, I worried I was born without a bird, but when I thought deep down into my body, I didn't feel empty. Sometimes when I yawned, I hallucinated a flash of blue bolt across my vision. When I sat still at my desk in school, I could almost convince myself of spiny feet perched on my rib.

Most of the time, though, I worried the reason I'd never seen my bird was because the smoke inside me had already come and killed it. Sometimes I figured that might be for the best, to help me survive, like Mama said. But when I paused to think about my bird truly being gone, I felt a deep-rumbling ache stretch from my toes out the top of my head, and my eyes went wet and blurry.

So Mama's trapped bird was another secret we kept, a sad, hopeful understanding between us. I didn't know of anyone else with a half-inside bird, but I sensed it meant something had gone wrong. I almost got to thinking sometimes that Mama was too hungry with that cardinal blocking her throat, and if the cardinal could get free, she wouldn't need Howard around. But sometimes it seemed like she was keeping the secret of the bird even from herself—like because Howard's bird was gone, she started believing hers was too. Sometimes after Howard put his hands on her, she'd cough up a red feather, then wash it down the sink like ash.

Howard didn't seem to miss his buried bird, so it was like he'd just been walking around empty the whole time. But with Mama, it was like she was falling in love with her own pretended emptiness, willing it there until it started feeling real. When I'd be sitting Upstairs with my door open, she'd float down the hallway without noticing she had even been there. Hawk eyes dim and ruin-dark, staring straight ahead, her shadow vapor thin.

Upstairs was the better place to be in the Big House, and I always got a falling feeling in my gut when Mama left it. From Upstairs, I could hear everyone's noises shifting beneath and know their mood by the space between creaks. I could look out over the small, tangled garden where cherry tomatoes grew since before I could talk. When Howard was away at work, Mama and I went Downstairs and picked them, talons scraping through to the black loam, popping those sun-bright orbs straight into our mouths before we even got in the door to wash them. Like we all belonged to the same earth. Even when Howard walked in after those garden days, his red knuckles didn't shudder when he held them toward Mama to scrub the oil grime from, and his eyes almost looked like they could've once shone with lake colors.

But more often Downstairs with Howard the walls would rock, some noise shattering on the tile. And the front door flown, gaping out at the whole beaming wound of the world. Later, I'd find Mama kneeling in a prayer of broom and dustpan, scrape-scrape-scraping slivers of fractured light from the floor, gathering up the sharp stray pieces of our life.

3

Goose lived on the far side of the long dirt driveway, through the thicket, third in a row of Little Houses. How he became my friend was on the school bus, and why is because we shared the same early-route bus stop. Our bus was early because we were what the bus driver called Rule Kids, which meant that we had to follow different rules since we lived in the Country, far away from school and everybody else.

Nobody told us what the rules were, but we knew them anyway. One rule was: you fend for yourself. Afterschool with Goose was always spent at his Little House. His dad drove a truck and was sometimes there, sometimes not. Sometimes neighbors checked on Goose and brought food, like the old lady next door, Mrs. Temple, who had eight parrots and no husband. Therefore: Goose's refrigerator was an adventure, weird casseroles and pork steaks we ate with our hands, cold. After food, we'd dig in the backyard, looking for the treasure Goose's dad promised him was buried out there. Or otherwise sit on the floor in Goose's room with loose sheets of notebook paper and draw maps: of our houses (current and/or dream), our town or others (real and/or imagined), interplanetary highways, lost underwater cities, etc.

Goose told me he was born with his bird on the outside, an orange-bellied robin that nested on top of his hair. But when he got older, he had to put his bird on the inside. To prove it, he stuck his fingers through his parted, crooked teeth and pulled out a slick brown feather, orange at the edges like leaves getting ready for the cold. I carried it around in the pocket of my summer shorts, until they got washed and the feather disappeared.

We stood together on foggy mornings between the fence of the Big House and the start of the thicket. Goose liked bugs, collecting them and bringing them onto the bus for Evan, who also liked bugs. Their favorite kind of bugs were the winged kind, because they could take turns plucking them like flowers and watching the bodies writhe in the palm of Goose's hand. Evan always looked a little sickly when Goose plucked bugs, especially the fleshy arms and legs, which sometimes bled. But he laughed anyway because Goose laughed.

I secretly knew that the roly polys were Evan's favorite, how they wiggled free until you poked them and they'd fold into themselves, go circular, roll-roll-rolling as the bus jostled over road bumps. Evan's hazel eyes sparkled dark and pretty when the roly polys went circular. So I kept his secret, all the little sparklings Goose wasn't gentle enough to notice. I had gotten very good at holding other people's secrets inside of me, keeping them safe in the passages of my smoke-heart.

If Evan came over Afterschool, it most likely meant we'd be drawing maps; he didn't believe in Goose's dad's treasure and said we were wasting our time, that the treasure was just a lie to keep us busy. Goose used to argue that he was a moron and the treasure was real, but after about a year of Afterschool digging and the backyard all scarred up, he just went strange if Evan mentioned it. A few minutes of coloring maps usually worked out Goose's silence, and in no time he was flopping around on the carpet with open-mouthed, crinkly eyed giggle-snorts leaping out of him once again.

Me and Goose figured pretty easily that Evan was the kind who got to keep his bird on the outside, even though we'd never seen what it looked like. We assumed Evan carried it in his backpack, like most other kids. School wasn't the safest place to go showing off your bird, even if you weren't a Rule Kid.

Goose told us his dad used to have a bird, a big brown one like an eagle, but it got lost around the time his mom left. Goose's dad didn't say his mom took the bird with her, his dad just acted like it never existed, but that's what Goose thought. Then he understood better when his dad was gone, and/or came back mean. If somebody took your bird away, it was easy to forget who you used to be when you had it.

Evan said he heard about a kid at his old school whose parents didn't have money for food, and one day the kid was so hungry he had to eat his own bird. Goose said, "I had a couple cousins who did that," and Evan gasped. I nodded calmly, but I was just as surprised as Evan. Goose had never told me that story before, or that he had cousins.

Evan wasn't a Rule Kid like me and Goose, but his parents didn't mind if he got off the bus at the Little House some days. He didn't know about the rules, so there were certain things we had to teach him. When he first came over and figured out no grown-ups were around, he got twitchy, looking over his shoulder at every noise. He didn't get why Goose's dad's bedroom smelled like weird ashes, and/or why we didn't have to wear shoes in the yard, and/or how we knew to start a burn bin out back when the trash piled up. When Evan's mom and dad came to pick him up, they drove up to the edge of the road and waited, hidden behind the windows of a shiny black car.

Evan was our friend, but there were worlds inside of me and Goose that only we could understand about each other, and Evan had a whole world outside the Country that wasn't ours. Another rule of being a Rule Kid was: there are parts of people you can't reach if you don't have to follow the same rules.

4

I grew up slow, then fast all at once, and around the time I couldn't fit my old summer shorts over my hips, Mama started pecking at my habits. She said I was becoming something other than I was, something like what she was, and now I had to act different. That meant I couldn't walk around in shorts anymore, and I had to cover up my shoulders when Howard was in the Big House. She got onto me if I sat spread-out on the ground to watch TV like I always had before. She showed me how to sit so my body was all folded up, scrunched and small like hers. Then, she hinted how it would be time for me to stop going Afterschool with Goose in a year or two, and I nodded while thinking up frantic plans to sneak to the Little House. When she said it, I was surprised how her voice sounded more scared than scolding.

As I got older and Mama told me all the ways not to be, shaving pieces of my child-life away, I waited to get the smoke-heart. I waited to get gray in the skin and feel a drowning smog take over. Sometimes I got scared waiting, and sometimes I was convinced I already felt it there: a blister at the back of my throat, the scent of smoldering wood sticking in my nose no matter where I went. In my fear I even started seeing Mama's sickness on me, a grimy tint on my skin and the amber streaks snuffed out of my eyes 'til they were just plain brown. I washed my face raw, afraid everybody else would see it on me too.

When I was alone in the Big House, I unlatched my jaw wide at the ceiling and waited for something to emerge: a measly string of smoke, or a chirp from way down. I didn't yet know what kind of bird lived inside me, but it seemed cruel to get to know it if I would have to let it suffocate later. Secretly, I hoped to open my mouth in the mirror one day and see a pretty blue wing flicker at the back of it—but at the same time, I hoped my bird stayed away if it couldn't be safe with me. It seemed better never to let anything good get inside you, if you knew holding it close would only destroy it.

When I was in the Big House but not alone, I sat in my room Upstairs and listened for the noises of Mama's and Howard's moods underneath. I recognized the passively ornery sound of Howard's footsteps as he came Upstairs, walked down the hall to the bathroom, paused, flushed, then I heard his steps pick up to annoyed and turn the corner toward me.

He pushed the door aside and moved his body in to fill up the frame, saying, "Why're there all those hairs coating the bathroom floor?" I knew by the way his snaggletooth came forward through his lip that he wasn't so much asking as blaming. He said the hairs were so many and so bad that they stuck to the sweaty soles of his feet. For proof, he leaned down and pulled off a thin swirl of dust and grime, dangling with gray strands, and let it float to the carpet.

I knew the hairs were Mama's, left behind by her smoke-sickness. But for a second I did wonder if they were mine—if the furnace of my smoke-heart had roared to life and I hadn't noticed my hairs collecting in a death-nest around me. Just like how Mama seemed not to notice the tiny brown claws that occasionally hung from the bristles after she brushed her teeth.

Howard got reckless with his hands then, gouging me from the bed by my arm and pulling me to the bathroom, swinging me inside so my spine caught the towel rack with a metallic burst of pain. Howard hollered to get on my knees and sweep it all up in the dustpan, so that's what I did, my palms growing itchy with the filth. But then Howard burped out some more words and I got reckless with my voice, too, asking him, had he ever noticed how Mama's skin smoldered to the touch, or the parts on her head that looked plucked in patches? I was getting around to the point of: Have you even noticed your own wife is swallowing down sickness to survive you? but I didn't spit that part out in time before Mama came flying up the stairs to see me crouched there, yelled to finish up, and shut the bathroom door fast.

I heard their feet leave and stayed there a minute longer than I had to, down on the gritty linoleum, sweep-sweep-sweeping the smallest parts that fell away without our noticing.

When I opened the door to the hallway, Mama was standing right there, lurching over me with near-black eyes. They were so piercing and animal-wide that her eyelids seemed to vanish behind them. She looked winged and witchy in the shadows, the day sucked from the windows while I'd been contained in the starched bulb-light of the bathroom.

"You don't realize what you almost did," she said, her voice full of terrible wind.

She said, "It wouldn't be a secret if letting it go didn't cost something."

Then she told me:

5

In olden times there was a girl—plain as day around your size— the father of the girl was a minister—the mother was blind—they lived in a Big House like this land all around it—farmland gone barren where the river flooded—scraping together what they could same as us—

One torrid night a fortune-teller walked up to the farm—a young man in yellow linen—the family shared their measly supper—as thanks the fortune-teller pulled cards and told them what it meant—the minister a man of God was wary but respectful—the mother was curious—you see she felt there was much else under the surface of the world—more than God and books and getting pruned by the sun to live at the brink of starving—the mother of course knew the girl was changing going strange—a new smell about her—but her sightless eyes shielded how the girl blushed and burned when the fortune-teller noticed her—he handed the girl a card picturing a dark-haired gentlewoman a falcon perched atop her hand—and she mashed it to her chest—the fortune-teller said he'd been a farmhand in Oregon—he predicted pentacles knew how to pull up potatoes honeycomb squash again—the family thought it odd but needed the help desperate—

That night the girl in her room was disarmed—she was ignored usually—plain with scratchy round cheeks—and in her sleep dreamed of the fortune-teller approaching in a field—handing her a falcon—and in sleep her smoke-heart kindled to flame—singed her bedclothes crawled up the curtains spread like bathwater across the floors—the fire ate up her parents in their marriage bed and her siblings who woke screaming to the melt of their flesh—too late the girl climbed from the window into the festering wet night—ran to the fortune-teller in the stable—together they watched the house burn to cinder and she howled into his chest—

Then it was over and he was all she had in the world—she told him about her smoke-heart and he promised to marry her—they rode horseback to the courthouse the next day—the girl in her ash-stained bedclothes—ripped strips of her dress to weave into the horseblanket for wedding bows—the fortune-teller went first and when she followed—guards seized her at the altar—the man told her secret of course a pouch of gold coins for her capture—she arsoned her family to bones after all confessed to it—no matter how she gasped "accident"—you see when a person controls her power she's a danger to be managed when others manage her power she's a weapon to control—

They shackled the girl and took her North where it's cold forever and ever—you don't know this but it's worse for people like us in the North—our home is a burning place but it's our own and we are made for it—we are not made to freeze in the gallows of a Massachusetts basement—do you see what I mean—it's foolish to trust to burn down your life for a little glint of attention—so you can never tell not Goose Howard anyone—there is no safety only surviving what the world won't allow dumb hope to solve.

6

Because of Mama's warning, I never told anyone about my smoke-heart. I told Goose about Howard, and what I remembered from when Granny was alive, like the noodles, and the cigarettes in the pocket of her blue church dress. She'd never wear blue otherwise, said it reminded her too much of sadness. I hadn't known what she meant by that, if there was a particular sadness swirling around her own heart-passages that I never saw. All Granny's smiles bloomed full-up to her eyes, the sunny wings of her canary flitting happily at their wrinkled corners.

I'd always thought that yellow bird must've been happy inside Granny, but now I wondered if maybe the flapping was it trying to climb out. All the way 'til her body caved in, what if Granny's bird was trying to escape the smoke, to signal for help, while there was still time?

I dreaded what getting the smoke-heart would do to my bird, or to whatever else might fly around the hidden parts of me. After Mama's story, I dreaded what it might do to everyone outside of me too. If I did have the smoke-heart already, I must have been good at hiding it, because Goose never noticed. Neither did Howard, or my teachers, whose heads rotated quick to see every little thing happening in the room. But the anxiety of waiting took on its own noxious presence, until it felt like the anticipation would burn me alive before anything else had the chance to.

One afternoon we were at the Little House, coloring maps on the floor. Goose kept getting distracted, jumping up and saying dumb stuff to be funny, like, *Oh my gosh did you hear all the lions escaped the zoo,* or *Tell me mister president where did you get that haircut?* Me and Evan glanced at each other secret-like to grin or roll our eyes. Soon Goose stopped and went back to coloring, but after a while he sat up and said, "I think the kitchen is on fire." We ignored it, thinking it another of his funny blurtings, but he said, "No, for real, I smell smoke."

He got up and went to check, and I was glad he left because my face was shock-pink and I didn't want him to see. When Evan looked over at me, I kept my eyeballs down on the paper.

Goose came back in the room and said, "There's nothing there but I still smell it."

"Maybe someone's doing a burn bin?" I offered.

He said no, it smelled different, and asked Evan if he smelled it too.

Evan shrugged and said, "I guess, when you mention it."

My skin started prickling with sweaty fear, and I worried my bones would splinter from trying to sit as straight and still as I could. I couldn't believe I'd gotten the smoke-heart right then at the Little House. Since I didn't know how to control it yet, I was even more scared of Mama's story—what if my insides lit on fire and melted the walls and Goose and Evan and everything?

"I don't smell anything at all," I said. I could tell by Goose's face that my words sounded real weird, so I got up and walked fast to the bathroom and locked the door.

I sat on the floor with my side pressed to the neck of the porcelain sink, dirty with scum that left a white mark on my shirt sleeve, but I didn't care. I felt wobbly and trapped in my skin, realizing the truth of how I could never again control what my body did without me. Worse, I could never tell anybody ever about how scared I was or how bad I felt or ask for help. I just had to keep going along like nothing was wrong. I sat in the bathroom breathing hard and fast for some lost stretch of time, until I got weary and my breathing slowed down.

I came out, and Evan was alone on the ground, coloring new maps over his old maps from earlier. He said Goose had gone over to Mrs. Temple's. And that was when, I don't know exactly why, my face crumpled up and I couldn't help it, my stomach felt kicked in half and I melted to the floor crying. I was crying so hard it felt like blood was coming out of my face, but it was just so much snot and salty water.

Between heaves I told Evan about my smoke-heart, how Granny had smoke all up in her heart and I did too. How there were burning places inside of me that I or nobody else could ever be allowed to reach. I admitted I hadn't seen my bird and was scared I accidentally killed it with the smoke-heart, or that without it I'd get so twisted up inside like the other people who forgot who they were supposed to be. But even if it was alive, I'd have to let it choke dead on smoke because Mama said it was the way us women survive.

I made Evan promise five or six times out loud that he would never tell anyone my secret, not Goose or his parents, or friends at his old school, or friends he would meet when he grew up, and I had him promise doubly that he wouldn't make me go to Massachusetts.

He listened quietly until I was done, then took my guilty, trembling hand with his and walked us both outside, past the street of Little Houses, into the edge of the thicket. And when we were covered over in dense green, he showed me: a fledgling tree with a twiggy nest at the center of it, housing three gentle swallows. Tiny and delicately chirping, I wanted to reach out and touch the blue of them, but I knew how birds worked, that they'd never survive it—being tender-held by a human and then abandoned.

I understood these were Evan's birds, but not why he had to hide them. It was rare to have more than one bird, and I guessed some people weren't okay with it if they found out. Evan's life seemed on the outside like a place where the birds would be safe, but maybe there were dangers he battled inside that I didn't know about.

He said, "These are secret too. Now neither of us has to go to Massachusetts."

And I knew what he meant.

Above the thicket, our small heads, the bouquet of swallows: a starling was circling, making itself quietly known. I glanced up from the nest and saw it hovering there, its blackish feathers cosmic in the sunlight. White speckles spread across the purples and greens like flecks of stardust. It was brief, a few seconds' glimpse anyone could've missed, but I got a warm feeling from seeing the bird. It draped me in the coziest haze, like the rightness that fills up your muscles in the seconds before drifting to sleep.

The starling floated away from the tree line, and me and Evan walked back to the Little House, both different and not. But when I turned back to shut the door, I saw the bird watching from a distance, waiting for the right spot to perch. Waiting to land when it knew it would be safe to stay.

7

After the swallows, I came to see the rules of being Rule Kids differently. I noticed how when me and Evan left the Little House, Goose's chin went wobbly watching us leave. Then, his eyes hardened over with a glimmer of beige, and he shut the door hard. I noticed how Evan's face brightened when he saw us coming down the bus aisle, and how he sucked his light back in when Goose stretched his hand out over Evan's, full with whatever creature they were expected to dismember that day. While Goose and Evan pried the skins from beetles or pulled apart a daddy longlegs, it was like they didn't remember I was there. Like their shared bloodthirst was a pleasure I could never wedge myself inside of.

The rules of being a Rule Kid meant you fend for yourself, I came to realize, but the boys were fending against the world, and the girls were like those bugs, fending against the dismembering.

By the time high school came rambling, Evan's parents had long ago gotten better jobs and moved to the City. Goose's eyes turned sand-colored once he sprung tall and rough-voiced, and the robin behind his tongue went silent, and soon after, his dad took him away to Montana.

Me and Mama and Howard stayed in the Big House, until we didn't. Howard went to rot like Granny, and Mama made ashes of him. I went away from there when I realized that Mama's cardinal had long since suffocated and fluttered dead in her hollow stomach. I went away and watched the sun orange itself delirious over Cities/Towns/Desert Nowheres, watched May lie down and die for June, June decay into July, revolution of months spinning out over again.

It was longer before I understood what Granny and Mama knew: sometimes you have to incinerate what sings within you so other parts of you can survive. I took my cinder and scraped those old fires into a new kind of light.

ELSEWHERE

Like you and I, Elaine is the kind of person who is always keen-
ing for another way. She drives up and down the world's peaks
and crevices as if this were not the case, she burns chemicals
into her hair to contrive unnatural colors, she takes unironic
thrill in gas station taffy, and she'd worked hard to become
casual about smoking a few puffs of cannabis from a galactic-
swirled glass pipe, then replacing it casually in the trick bottom
of her teenage jewelry box and walking her midsize city's
sidewalks in the sprawling daylight. On her walks, she passes a
large white house on a hill and longing snags in her chest when
she imagines floating barefoot down its molded halls. She thinks
to herself that nothing bad could happen in a place so large and
lovely, with so much history to guard itself against the world.

When she was young, sixteen or so, she used to prowl the
streets of her cardboard suburb in the dark. She liked to look
through the lit windows of strangers' houses into their rooms,
at their dressers and draperies and old cats perched on the sills,
like dollhouses in a toy village blown up to scale for her perusing.

She hasn't walked at night in years, unless cloaked in the mirage of indestructible freedom that accompanies coming back from the bar with friends. Now, the stillness of the dark makes her squirrelly; even when she ventures out after nightfall to wrangle the trash bin from the curb, she finds herself jerking, jolting at each noise, like a feral thing who would rend its own fur to escape into the false safety of underbrush. In the dark, there is always someone you can't see watching.

This night, Elaine is tidying her apartment, repositioning and removing select objects from her shelves, and lights a vanilla-scented candle for the man who is coming over to fuck her. She lines her lips with a color like the sliver of sky behind her kitchen window at dusk, just before the light snaps from it. She has to look up the man's profile on her phone again to remember his name, and then again, to make sure she doesn't embarrass herself by getting it wrong. Ryan is twenty-eight and wears glasses, which makes him good enough. In his profile picture, he's standing next to a Christmas tree and grinning blandly, wearing a sweater with that image of a woman's severed leg fashioned into a lampshade—a reference Elaine has never understood and feels that, at twenty-five, she's made it too far into her adult life to bother learning.

These moments before she invites a stranger over and into her body always feel a little like preparing to host someone from out of town, only to find when they arrive that her guest's interests have nothing to do with the owl figurines on her mantel or the slices of Gouda in her fridge. She doesn't bother trying to anticipate what Ryan might be interested in, or what kind of person he'll turn out to be—only what he might imagine, correctly or incorrectly, about her. The best sex makes her feel like someone else, which is almost as good as feeling like no one, feeling nothing, disembarking from the burden of a self altogether. She spends most waking moments lost in complex, radiant sexual fantasies, but when it comes down to actually being naked with a human being, surrounded by their unwieldy motions and slippery skins and unpredictable bodily scents, it doesn't feel like anything important is happening to her at all.

So she makes up stories in her head. Sometimes, she imagines the guy is forged from smelt metal and is going to literally crush her to pieces. She envisions what it would look like as he thrusts into her until her legs come loose from her sockets and her limbs start flying off like a wrecked Barbie. She could sit back and let it happen, comforted in knowing that no matter what level of physical or spiritual dissolution she's experiencing, the metal man would keep plowing onward, an insatiable machine. Or once, when a bartender was calmly fingering her in her bed, she imagined they were both teenage girls at a slumber party discovering masturbation for the first time, and she came almost immediately. But afterward, when she opened her eyes to the bartender's slightly damp beard and smarmy smile, she felt a little disgusted, and has never been able to replicate the fantasy since.

When she hears shuffling at her front door, Elaine suddenly feels gassy and wishes she'd thought to dedicate some time to burping earlier in the day.

She would say it's just a matter of convenience, having dates over to her place instead of going to theirs, but when she summons these men and they arrive, she gets a little thrill of power at knowing what they don't; the horror of what *could* happen to them, and that the only reason it wouldn't is because she's chosen to let them be safe. She believes a subconscious part of them feels grateful, even if they don't understand why.

The year she turned seventeen, Elaine was driving home from her part-time job at the movie theater when her car broke down in heavy rain in a neighborhood she didn't know well. Tornado sirens started whining ominously in the distance and blaring through the radio, so she put her coat over her head, abandoned her car, and ran up the steps of the brick townhouse across the street. The man who answered the door invited her inside to wait out the storm, then kept her in his basement for seven months. It was simple enough when she explained it. It had been years, though, since she'd brought it up to anyone; once she was able to recognize the frozen looks on people's faces as a polite strain of absolute fear, she figured it might be best to stop telling that part of her story. If she felt rage about swallowing this fact as if it had never happened, as if she'd never survived anything worth telling—and accept, too, that she'd never be allowed to let any person know her fully—she quelched it.

The man on the other side of the door knocks. She retucks her low-cut T-shirt into her high-waisted skirt, un-wedgies her black satin underwear, shakes some volume into the roots of her hair, and takes a breath large enough to survive on, as if it's the last one she'll get. Then, she unlocks the double dead bolt and opens the door.

"Hey," he says. His voice is deep with a hint of a crackle, his glasses fogged like it's raining, though it isn't. In the place they live, the air often goes soupy like that.

Ryan's sneakers trail wet brown leaves onto the carpet when he walks in, and they lie in the entryway like flecks of animal shit. Elaine immediately worries she'll be looking back at them all night, embarrassed, though she isn't in any way responsible for their presence.

"Hey," she echoes. "Want a drink or anything?"

Ryan finds her prettier in person than he expected. The nearly faded pink tips at the ends of her short, wavy brown hair remind him of the girls in high school who used to stain their hair with Kool-Aid in the summers and travel en masse around town arm in arm, a conglomerate of giggling bronze limbs. Ryan asks for a beer, and Elaine says she doesn't have any, so he tells her whatever she has would be nice. When she hands him a greenish mixed drink, her lips part in a grin, and he notices a small gap between her front teeth. He remembers hearing somewhere that people with tooth gaps are more sexual, but never understood how the two correlate.

They sit on the stiff blue futon in her living room, where he balances the drink on his knee and she sips brown liquid from a mason jar. They sit far enough apart not to enter the bubble of each other's body heat, but close enough that the distance doesn't feel intentional.

Elaine initiates the requisite small talk, asks what Ryan does for work, and he tells her he's a car mechanic, which is a lie. He looks down reflexively when he says it and sees a fleck of yellow vomit on his jeans from work that day. He scrapes it off with his fingernail onto her carpet.

Ryan works as a caretaker at a hospice but doesn't like to tell people because of the look they give him afterward, like he's a bird who's mangled itself falling from a tree; a being more worthy than some, certainly, but nothing anybody wants to touch. He's noticed, in particular, that the women who come to learn about his job expect a certain innate empathy of him, and after spending most of his waking hours displaying steel-force gentleness to patients who holler and hit him, who piss themselves and don't know their own names a lot of the time, the thought of being expected to offer that level of care in his regular life feels like an immense burden.

When Ryan tells her he's a mechanic, a shock of tenderness runs through Elaine, and she begins to feel that maybe they are meant for each other, that this interaction is more meaningful than the loose premise of the night suggests. She begins to spin sketches of a whole possible future in the corners of her mind, one where Ryan turns out to be her long-awaited soulmate, where they travel Europe and settle in a Scottish cottage and laugh as they watch each other's faces slide into old age. Elaine muses that if she'd had a mechanic boyfriend all those years ago when her car broke down in the rain, maybe she would've driven home that afternoon unscathed, she'd have gone on with her life and been devastatingly normal, and this simple, errone-ous fact makes her begin to think of Ryan as safe. But no one is safe. There are no truly safe people, no soulmates: only people you would die for and people you wouldn't.

And perhaps because she now clocks him as someone she could share herself with without repercussion, she decides that's who she'll be tonight: a person who can say anything, every-thing, as if there's nothing she could do that he would not accept. And perhaps that is why when the small talk peters out and Ryan edges toward the last sip of his drink, she asks if she can tell him a story.

"It's not my story, actually. But it was told to me, and I haven't been able to stop thinking about it since."

"All right," he says, assuming this is her long-winded attempt at telling him what she wants him to do to her when they get to the bedroom, or the floor, or wherever they end up moving against each other—he isn't picky about the setting.

Elaine takes a breath and begins:

"Like you and I, Z was the kind of person who always felt there was a chunk of her life missing. When she was a child, she believed she was a twin separated at birth, that she was the one who'd gotten adopted or left on a stoop, that she had been unknowingly ripped from the elsewhere she belonged and that was all the source of her loneliness, wrongness—"

"I didn't feel that way growing up," Ryan interrupts. "I mostly get along with my parents. I had a brother." Elaine notes the past tense, but doesn't point it out.

"But you know what I mean, that feeling like there's something people aren't telling you about the world, something that would make it all fall into place?"

"Sure," Ryan replies, though he isn't.

"Z had been living with her long-term girlfriend, A, for ten months, and engaged in an emotional affair with a woman from the internet for three, when she became interested in Alternate Dimensions and How to Get There. The woman had sent her a link to the online forum during their text conversation one night.

"Through the forum, she learned that all of time is a simultaneous parallel on an infinite grid of moments, and that a person can leave their reality and walk right into another self, another life. There was a list of techniques for detaching from reality, rituals she hadn't gathered the bravery to try.

"One method involved taking two drinking glasses, writing on one the things you have but don't want, writing on the other the things you want but don't have, and then drinking water from the glass branded with your desires. One method involved waiting until nightfall, staring into a floor-length mirror while holding a candle, and not breaking eye contact until the mirror-self began to move in some way you hadn't. There was the 'owl method,' which advised the dimension-jumper to look for owls (both real and symbolic) appearing in their daily lives as a sign that the veil between realities was thinning—but at the time, owls were a big fashion trend, and Z's seeing them did not feel especially meaningful. Some people on the forum described slipping into another dimension by accident, and only realizing it after feeling a cosmic tingle, or a great surge of wind, but the universe had never given Z anything she'd wanted by accident, and she didn't predict it would start doing so any time soon.

"In one of the videos on the forum, the camera focused on a frame of light moving across the same white corner of a ceiling, like days and nights were passing outside. Then the camera zoomed out to a grid of black squares and hurtled back down into a bustling Czech plaza twenty years in the past. The video was nine minutes and thirteen seconds long, and she watched it in bed at the end of every night while A washed and moisturized her face, and set water out for the cat, and combed her hair into a high bun for sleep. A would crawl into their bed, say, 'Good night, Hum,' and when A's breathing got thick and murky, Z would lower the brightness on her phone screen and watch the video again.

"A called Z 'Hum,' because of how she was always around, like a second set of lungs. To A this was meant as a great tenderness, but it reminded Z of the noise an air conditioner makes as it shifts off and on throughout the day without anyone noticing.

"Z recalled a time in her youth when she used to think getting to be alone in a room with someone you loved, indefinitely, would be so glitteringly wondrous as to be unbearable. But it wasn't. She'd grown up and learned how to put on a sparkle and ask the right questions to make a whole handful of people want to get in rooms with her. But A was familiar; they'd grown up in the same place, and by the time it dawned on Z that the feeling of home she got from A could translate into something real and stable, Z was tired of wandering through the world alone and craved the real. A was safe and kind and seemed to reliably love her, so Z didn't notice the way she was arching parts of herself to make them fit together, how her natural sparkle dulled, until she looked back and couldn't remember how to conjure it, or how she'd managed to be someone like that. She sat inside herself waiting for the urge to speak, for something true to rise up in her gullet, and when it finally did, she'd swat it back down like the hand of a child.

"When A left the house to go to work or the coffee shop or the store, Z lit the green 'heart chakra' candle she'd bought on a road trip years ago, and lay on the couch with her headphones in. She listened to a guided meditation she'd found on YouTube, where a man's voice instructed her to imagine walking out of her body like her life was a window to climb through, then to pass through a glass tunnel to a circuit room made of pure light, and select another window to climb through, another life to set herself down in. When she opened her eyes to the world again, she half expected the room to be reversed, or to wake in a dusty cabin on a faraway hill. But Z always surfaced as the same self, lying on the same couch, A walking through the front door with a pizza box in hand, and Z raising her head and smiling as if she'd only been napping.

"Z and the woman from the internet, a freckled brunette named Georgia who lived in Kentucky, messaged often about the alternate lives they might at that very moment be living together, elsewheres in which the reasons and miles between them contracted like the bellows of an accordion. Z could feel those other possible paths forking off with each day that slipped out of her, with each choice she made, passing out of reach like rotted tree limbs into the lacy void.

"Georgia from Kentucky was actually Tomás, who lived in the southwesternmost squiggle of Indiana, and whose teenage daughter was daily, in the adjoining room of their two-bedroom apartment, writhing with sickness from the same malady that killed his wife five years before, her womb twisting inside her like a wrung set of branches. It's not hard to imagine how Tomás might have stumbled on Alternate Dimensions and How to Get There in his search for another way: when his daughter was sedated with the expensive pills they rationed for use only when she began to scream so loud the neighbors called the police, again, or after the dread of opening another past-due medical bill, the debt six times larger than any salary he'd made a year in his life."

"Sorry," Ryan interjects. "It's just, it seems like maybe this is a long story? Like I get the vibe you're just getting started?"

"Oh," Elaine says, feeling the first thing akin to embarrassment that night. "Yeah, sorry. Are you completely bored?"

"No, no, seriously, I'm very interested. I just wanted to know what to expect," he says. "I just want to understand what I'm in for." He smiles in a movie-star kind of way, and she can't tell if he's flirting, or if he'd noticed the fault in her confidence and was just trying to be nice.

"Okay. If you're sure? We could do something else."

"No, it's fine. I might get another drink, though, if that's okay?"

"Yeah, of course. Mixers are in the fridge and spirits are in the freezer."

"I love a good freezer ghost," he says.

"What?"

"Spirits. Sorry, it was just a dumb joke."

Elaine laughs anyway, and he both loves and resents her for it.

While Ryan is in the kitchen, Elaine pretends not to have noticed how Ryan grimaced a bit when she said the word *womb*, or how his eyes went round with some flicker of sorrowful wonder, or how tender it is to watch anyone's eyes go round with a feeling they've never had to experience before. With his face hidden behind the half wall that separates the living room from the kitchen, she feels suddenly alone in her home, as if he might've walked out the back door and released her from the obligation to be anyone.

There are parts of her own story Elaine never tells, even in the few pinched instances when she offhandedly brought up her kidnapping to an ex-boyfriend or coworker, as if just one item on a laundry list of her life's milestones. She rarely thinks about her time roped to the cold, cinder-block wall of the basement, and the man who put her there, but she can feel it passively pulsing behind her eyes, tinting her solitary moments like a purple ooze her body keeps out of view. She has no illusions of being "healed," as if that were a final destination a person could arrive at, without a whole new wave of trauma pummeling them during the course of their regular human life. But she must admit it gives her a sense of pride, how little she feels about this thing that happened to some version of her she no longer inhabits. More often these days she feels tempted, once and for all, to chalk up that part of her life to little more than an uncomfortable bout of boredom. It was over now, anyway, as all things are over eventually. But loss lives on in its hosts, a dormant sting pinning us to the empty underbelly of the world.

Ryan appears again with his already-familiar-seeming face, cheeks lit into friendly glow by the fresh tequila in his cup, and sits down on the floor in front of her.

She moves to the carpet next to him, cross-legged, spreading her short skirt over her thighs just enough to feign dignity.

"Anyway," she says.

"Anyway," he echoes.

"Z would never know any of this about the person she believed was her soulmate, of course, but it hardly mattered; surely in one of the uncountable alternate dimensions that exist unseen, stacked around us like warm sheets of phyllo dough, Georgia from Kentucky did exist," Elaine begins again.

"Or at least that thing inside Georgia that Z was suckling at, the light-drenched dollop of belonging that's produced when a person finds themselves understood by another person. It should not take the prospect of a cross-dimensional dalliance with an emotionally unavailable internet catfish to conjure this feeling of belonging, but it does, and it did.

"After very adequate sex one evening, Z lay on her girlfriend's dewy chest and stared at the chipped spot on their wall where a gash of pale blue poked through, revealing a piece of the room as it had existed before it was hers. And though she was perfectly content, she also knew she would abandon her life in an instant to be anywhere else the cosmic tunnel would take her.

"By the time Z committed to the idea of leaving her life, Georgia from Kentucky had gone silent. It had been a month and a half since their last conversation, but each morning Z still woke and immediately checked her phone, racked with longing. Some moments, standing at the sink scrubbing dishes, or driving back from the laundromat, a deep shame bowled her over. She was truly insane, she thought, to pin every morsel of hope on a person she barely knew, when she had a perfectly good partner standing in front of her every day, knowing her, wanting her.

"Even if A loved her in a way that passed through her without sticking, it was more than most people had. Even though it felt to Z like she and Georgia had known each other before time, outside of time, Georgia from Kentucky was just a person, and Z knew very little about the realities of her life. And besides, Z didn't actually know how to love anyone; she jumped from one thing to the next to see what new pieces of herself she could coax to the surface by rubbing up against someone else. She planned panicked new futures until she arrived and found them unsatisfactory, because there was no uncertainty left to gnaw on. She was searching for another way, but there was none; there was only existing, and whatever one chose to do with it.

"Z toiled over that month of silence, and then another, and another, to accept her desire as delusion: her foolishness, her ugly, childish hope—and to beat it away, though it still clawed inside her like a slowly starving animal.

"Then, after four months without a word from Georgia, there was a voice mail.

"When Z got out of the shower and saw it, her heart twisted, leapt. Thirteen seconds—mostly of background noise, feet shuffling, wind whirring, a distant intercom—but it was there, undeniable: a woman's voice. Z had never actually heard Georgia's voice before, she realized. In their first interactions,

Georgia told Z she was a caretaker for her elderly mother, who had dementia and became violently irate at any noise, so talking on the phone was out of the question. On the recording, she sounded small, vulnerable. Z couldn't make out exactly what she was saying, but after a gust of static wind, she thought she heard the words: *Get Here.*

"Z's body sparked, and a laugh pushed its way through her, a great hysterical laugh that went on for minutes, and she had to muffle her face with a bath towel to keep A from hearing. It wasn't that Georgia didn't love her, Z realized, more joyful than she remembered feeling in her life. Georgia had left, spliced into another dimension, and now she was there, waiting for Z. Waiting for her to *Get Here.*

"When A left for work that morning, Z started the water ritual. She pulled two glasses from the cupboard and placed lime-green sticky notes on them: on one she wrote *Here* and on the other *With Georgia*, but then worried the wording wasn't specific enough, so she crossed out *Here* and wrote instead *With A.* But that wasn't quite true either, and she felt guilty marking A the thing she wanted to get away from, when it wasn't really about her so much as about Z's overall lack, which happened to include her. She thought about writing *With Myself* instead, but that was obviously too maudlin, so she threw away both sticky notes, stuck new ones on each glass, and wrote *Here* and *Elsewhere.* As instructed on the forum, Z ran water from the tap into *Here* and stared at it for a handful of minutes, focusing on imbuing it with her selfhood, her spiritual reality divorced from the merely physical. Then, Z poured the water into *Elsewhere*, drank it in one gulp, and crumpled and ate the sticky note, for good measure.

"A day passed and she felt no different. Light fanned its usual colors through the window. Z checked around the house for any small indication of change: the stove knobs, the font on the mailbox, the organization of her books on the shelf. It was all depressingly familiar. She lay and waited to feel a cosmic tingle enter her, but fell asleep waiting, and then A came home, and they cooked and ate a salmon dinner, and fell asleep in their usual way, fresh faced and calves touching.

"She was, in truth, a little frightened of the 'mirror method'; the horror movies her mom liked to watch on cable had conditioned her to believe that the express purpose of mirrors was to reveal some ghost or grotesquerie standing behind you, and if there *was* a ghoul trailing her, she'd rather not know about it. She dreaded the idea of spending hours staring into her own dull, unchanging face, only to see her second self twitch to life and walk without her into the world she wanted so badly to join. That the forum claimed this was the most powerful exercise for pressing through the skin between dimensions frightened her a little, too, she had to admit. She also knew she had to try it.

"A little past midnight, Z snuck out of bed and walked to the kitchen, pretending she was only retrieving a glass of water. She paused and listened for the metallic creak of A's body shifting in their bed; when she didn't hear it, she snatched the lighter from the counter.

"The spare room was cluttered with unopened boxes of art supplies, broken gym equipment, less-than-stylish wall art they'd been gifted, stacks of DVDs they had no method for playing. Both Z and A were the kind of people who felt guilty getting rid of anything, as if objects could sense when they were unwanted and held grudges. Both women had childhood memories of receiving ill-fitting pajamas as Christmas presents and keeping them anyway, knowing they were all their parents could afford. So they sat folded in drawers for years, casting a pang of sadness every time they dressed, until they finally stuffed them into donation bags when they next moved apartments. Even with stable jobs, the worth of objects—even unnecessary ones—imbued Z and A with a kind of paralysis, and thus they regarded the spare room like a treasure cave guarded by the dragon of their guilt. As soon as they moved in together, they wordlessly began to fill it with everything they didn't love enough to live with, but couldn't yet convince themselves to let go of.

"Z sat on the floor in front of an old wooden mirror propped against the wall, lit the candle in her hand, and slowly met her own gaze. In the dark, her eyes looked wide and black in their sockets, the shadows distorting her face to a blank oval. It seemed she was looking at a Puritan: some strangely plain, ragged woman who had crawled out of another century's forest. Orange light dipped in and out of the hollows beneath her eyes, the lines where her lips joined her cheeks, the crescent shadow under her second chin. She hadn't planned to be one of those women who was overly concerned about wrinkles, but that's mostly because she'd never imagined getting old enough to have them. She recalled how her mother began to wear sequins on every piece of clothing as she approached her fiftieth birthday, and finally understood the plea behind it: surely, a woman who shimmers like that couldn't be slipping toward the grave.

"She hadn't stopped to consider what would happen to her body in this life once she fled it. Would A find it collapsed on the floor, shucked off onto the carpet like a winter coat? In her absence, would her neurons keep running some version of Z on autopilot, or would a new being enter the vacant body from elsewhere, like a game of musical chairs? She decided that perhaps it would simply be like switching the channel on a TV. No one worried, when they clicked over to the next channel, if the one before it went on existing when they weren't watching it. It didn't matter either way.

"She stared through the stilled dark, but nothing came, or changed; there was no twitch in Z's eye, no eerie grin, nothing to invite the feeling that the person in the mirror had any will of her own. She was just another woman trapped behind the glass, unable to reach herself.

"Out of resigned habit more than anything, the following night, Z queued up the usual video—light crossing the non-distinct corner of a ceiling, zooming out to the grid, zooming forward to the plaza—while A washed her face and prepared for bed. It took until the last seconds of the shot of the all-white ceiling before she caught it: a chip in the paint no bigger than a fingernail. Unmistakable. Z's fingers stammered at the pause button, and when she zoomed in, it took a long, lumbering minute to convince her of what she was seeing: a flicker of pale blue, same as the paint peeking through her own wall, showing up on someone else's ceiling in a video, where it certainly hadn't been before.

"Instinctually, she got out of bed and sat on the ground, hunched over her phone. What did this mean? Had she actually changed something? Was she afraid? Should she be? And how to press further?

"She had two choices: Stay, and be this, finally and always. Or move. Now.

"Z slid on her shoes and left. She walked fast, a jolt in her limbs, some giggle or guttural sigh swelling in her chest, and she said nothing, did nothing, thought nothing beyond the shuffling of her feet, her breath, the thick slab of night. She did not know where she was going, but she trusted her body to take her there—not *trusted*, which implies a choice—surrendered, and followed where it willed. She remembered a post she'd read on the forum that she'd shrugged off as overzealous: *To do this, you have to destroy everything you are and everything you have, so the only place left to go is elsewhere.*

"She understood now what it meant: it was not about Georgia, or A, or what the elsewhere held for her. To live in hope was to snare her to this world. It couldn't be about getting more; it had to be about giving up.

"She stopped when she reached the pedestrian bridge, an ornate set of columns suspended high up over the river, the contours of its banks receded in the darkness. She pressed her body to the smooth granite rail, felt its chill under her palm, the beads of sweat the sky had gathered on its surface. Peering over, below, the blue was there: a rush, an answer, a secret that led her, magnetic, to the water; a new blue mirror for her to slip through. To fall, and—full with belief, empty of hope—land whole."

For the half moment after Elaine finishes speaking, the room is gulped with silence. Ryan stares at her.

"So, what happened next?"

"What do you mean?"

"Did she jump?"

"If she had, how would I be able to tell you this story?" Elaine says, a weird little grin pulling at the corners of her mouth. "How would anyone know it?"

"What's the point then?"

"The point to what."

"Telling it."

"I dunno. Does there need to be a point? I just thought it was interesting." Elaine inches closer to him, her knees dragging on the carpet. Later, when he leaves and she replays this moment in her head, she will replace it with what she wishes she'd said instead: *I'm curious when and why we find ourselves straddling the thin line between faith and delusion.*

Elaine tells him, "It was just something to say."

She is shifting toward him, and he registers her hand on his knee, the spiced vanilla scent of her body heat, but he can't shake feeling like he's emerging from the veil of sleep. When she looks up at him, nearly nuzzled into his chest, he remembers why he's there.

"Anyway, sorry if that was weird or boring or whatever," she says, tossing her head, as if to wipe clear the slate of the evening. The gap between her teeth is slick with saliva, and Ryan can't remember why he found it sexy before, only that now he feels a woozy churn when he looks at it. She seems too young, staring up at him like this, like a child coming apart tooth by tooth. He feels the urge to lay her in his lap and touch her hair until she falls asleep, then quietly slip out the door.

Ryan glances down at Elaine, his eyelashes so dark and long and lovely she's almost envious of them, and he does not kiss her. She giggles and fingers the seam around the pocket of his jeans, and he does not kiss her. She reaches out to snake her hand behind his neck, and he grabs it and holds it, and looks at her, his eyes brimming with something closer to pity than lust, and she knows he is not going to kiss her.

The things she says to him then, the thorn that drags through her voice, is not for him. A gulf opens inside Elaine, and she fills it with misplaced fury. Ryan's face prickles red, but he stays; to be yelled into for as long as the moment lasts somehow feels important. He holds her wrists. When she halts and looks around, like she'd taken the wrong turn and ended up in a gully of her life that was never supposed to be lived out, he lets her go.

"I'm sorry," she says.

He nods. "No problem."

She breaks their stare to take a drink, coughs, and wipes her mouth with the back of her hand, smearing what lipstick is left at the border of her uneven cupid's bow. "Can you tell me something about you, some story? So I don't feel so stupid for having talked so long. I'd like to know about you. Anything."

"Like what?"

"Like anything. What's something you remember from your childhood? What's the worst thing that's ever happened to you?"

"Well, yikes, um . . ." He chokes, but it comes out sounding like a laugh. "This became a different kind of night than I was expecting."

Elaine bats her wet eyelashes and grins.

"Come on. I've got no one to tell."

Ryan looks down at an ash-smeared spot on the carpet, and when he finds the words to tell her about the worst thing, he does not tell her about the slant of afternoon light in the kitchen when he was six, when a man who was his father's friend pinned his mother to the wall, covered her mouth with his hand, and how her tears shined in streaks across her neck. He does not mention walking in on the too-drunk girl in high school and seeing his best friend move atop her the same way, his hand erasing the lower half of her face; and he does not mention driving home drunk that night with his brother in the front seat and speeding through the intersection, and the elderly woman who ripped her Lincoln into the side of his brother's body. How the old woman was blamed—Ryan's car technically had the right-of-way—and likely died impoverished, guilty, manslaughterer.

Ryan instead mumbles something about a neighborhood cat found straying in the woods, and how the middle-school boys prodded its orifices until it lay limp in the leaves, emanating a broken, alien whine. Elaine nods, and holds his wrists, places a thumb gently over each pulse. They sit like that.

Ryan clears his throat. She thinks he is going to stand, but he asks, "What about you?"

She knows she will be outside of this moment eventually; it will become just another smear of memory, another silent specter she hoists around. She knows this even while he's still sitting in front of her, and she does not want to let this be a memory yet.

When she'd escaped, and later found herself sitting in the concrete interrogation room with her family, she told the cops what happened to her in the basement, and her parents wouldn't look at her. Elaine could see the cops watching them and knew the carefully masked judgments: her parents were obvious on sight as devout Pentecostals, with their thin expressions, their long-sleeve, high-necked Walmart shirts, their homeschooling bequeathed on her and her siblings like the threat it was. Her brother, two years younger, broke the silence, accusing her of making it all up for attention. Her father nodded in his tight-lipped way, as if it were understood by all parties present that this was all a convenient ruse to hide the fact she'd been holed up with some burnout in a motel room for half a year, indulging in premarital sex and grainy satellite HBO. The cops shook their heads with incredulous pity, as if to shrug and say, *Sorry, best of luck with this shit show.* Her sister, three years older, didn't disagree with their brother, didn't say anything, just sat there picking her nail beds and looking wax-struck.

So, she was estranged from them, in the most literal meaning of the word. They had chosen the separation, Elaine reasoned. She'd just kept it up.

Her mother died. Elaine knew it was in the *after*—years after she'd struck out on her own, when a childhood friend's mom reached out on social media to share the week-old obituary (and what it withheld: ovarian cancer, "faith-based" treatment). But in her mind it was all one moment, one simultaneous grief, a rat king of memory flashes and sensory details: the squeak of her wet shoes stepping into the man's linoleum entryway; her sister's downcast face, scraping her cuticles in the gray interrogation room; the day, about a year after leaving her family, that the sweater she'd stolen from her mother vanished from the laundromat; the burnt oatmeal smell of the basement; her mother's long blond braid, swinging; a slicing radiating up through her and expelling her out of her body; the sickly orange daylight when she crawled out of that house; all the *befores* and *afters* snarling time around her like the opaque cocoon of a spider's web.

Ryan waits. When she smiles, he thinks it's the saddest shape he's seen a face fold into.

"When my mom died," Elaine begins, "her hair was like angels' bones, white and brittle from an eternity of home bleaching. I remember that smell, the sour, toxic ammonia. The way it ate away at the skin on her fingertips. No one ever looked at her fingertips.

"Her name was Sheryl. I don't really tell people that. I don't really tell people about her at all. And she kept her maiden name, Hart. In Irish it means *hero*. In French, it means *rope*. In English, an organ that has nothing to do with love."

With surgical precision, she tells Ryan how she held her mother's hand in the hospital as her breaths narrowed, brushed her dissolving wisps of hair, breathed that bile smell that radiated from her skin, conjuring to life all the details of her mother's death she never saw: the blue, diamond-printed hospital gown with its texture like a dish towel, tracing the pattern of the material over her mother's collarbone until, in the last days, her fingerprints left diamond-shaped bruises. She tells Ryan this as if it is the only cleaving event she's known, this usual human grief: the light of a person and what's left when it goes.

He gives her the space to let it be true, as if all a person needs to turn a wish into a story is an audience.

When they stand and walk to the door, Elaine feels very calm, very grief-stricken. She knows she will never stop waiting for Ryan to show up, at a grocery store years from now, exiting an airport terminal—that when he leaves, she will wretch and suffer and worry the memory to smooth stone in the folds of her brain, until it is not even the same shape as the truth.

Over and over in her life, she would find this fact the hardest to reconcile: a moment can change you irreparably and not change the coordinates or conditions of your life in the slightest. It can mean more than anything, and still not matter.

"Drive safe," she says.

"Thanks."

Ryan slides into the driver's seat of his truck, starts the engine, and pulls away from the curb. He feels light-headed, like he's eaten fistfuls of mud.

He knows how it will be when he reaches home: When he pulls into his driveway, tires gliding over wet leaves on the concrete. When he turns the doorknob and feels the heater's warmth rush to meet his skin, the smell of perfumed candles and dish soap, last week's chili, neglected trash. When he sees his girl-friend standing at the counter, their unborn child a flicker in her barely fledged belly bump, and she turns to him—then, he will let the weight of home flatten him. He will let guilt begin to flower.

But for this stretch of now, he is a machine slicing the night air. As he turns out of Elaine's neighborhood, he notices a large white house on a hill, the lights flowing out as if through a paper lantern. He imagines Z lingering in the definitive moment, her feet clung to wet stone, staring at the blue thrash below.

He drives in silence, and as he does, he hopes for her with all his guts: *Go*. Into the elsewhere, he prays Z can feel him reaching, that she whispers back at herself, *Go. Trust it. Jump*. And does.

ACKNOWLEDGMENTS

The fact that this book is in your hands is nothing short of a small miracle, brought on by the kindnesses of many people across many years, cities, drafts, readings, and conversations.

Thank you, first and foremost, to my incredible agent, Cassie Mannes Murray, for taking a chance on me and making all of this happen, for reading messy drafts and manic emails, and being a force for good across the publishing industry; and to my amazing editor, Emma Kupor, for making my wildest dreams come true, making these stories a million times better than I could've alone, and helping me become a better writer in the process. Infinite thanks, also, to everyone at Harper Perennial who advocated for this book—Heather Drucker, Lisa Erickson, Katie Teas, Doug Jones, and Amy Baker—and worked hard behind the scenes to help it find its readers. And a big thank you to Jared Oriel for the cover of my dreams and Jen Overstreet and Stacey Fischkelta for bringing the text to life.

Thank you to my family, for the sacrifices that allowed me to be here writing these words.

Thank you to my friends, who are my greatest loves, with special thanks to CJ Scruton, Allison Adams, Clinton Craig, Bridget Adams, Lauren Howton, Brett Hanley, Rebecca Orchard, Rachel Weaver, Dylan Hayes, Lucy Karam, and Alex Howard. Thank you to my friend Cameron Moreno for the Brunch Time Writers' Workshop, which not only helped get this book finished but also helped keep me alive through the pandemic. Thank you to my best friend, ideal reader, business partner, and cosmic soulmate Lena Ziegler, for everything, forever.

Thank you to the editors, publishers, and fellow writers who gave me early encouragement, helped guide me through the lit world, and in a very real way paved a path for this book to exist. I would especially like to thank Michael Wheaton, Jenny Irish, Brian Oliu, Nayt Rundquist, Leza Cantoral, Christoph Paul, Matt Bell, Skip Horack, Mark Winegardner, Kristen Miller, and Jared Yates Sexton. Thank you to all the writers, readers, and artists I've been fortunate to meet through *The Hunger*. Many of the most crucial opportunities in my writing career are due to volunteer readers, interns, students, and others whose names I will likely never know and are too numerous to list; genuinely, I am grateful to you for doing this work, and for giving space to my stories.

Thank you to my teachers, especially David Bell and Rebbecca Brown, who gave early feedback on these stories and have been generous resources in the years since; and David Kirby and Barbara Hamby, who showed me what a life lived in poetry looks like. I owe much to the institutions that allowed me to focus solely on writing and spending time among other writers—an incredible privilege: Western Kentucky University, Florida State University, the University of North Texas, the Byrdcliffe Arts

Colony, PEN America, and the Edward H. and Marie C. Kingsbury Fellowship.

Finally, thank you, reader, for being here. It means more to me than you'll ever know. This book is yours now, and I hope you find in it a glimmer of something you can carry with you, anywhere you may find yourself.

Grateful acknowledgment to the following publications for printing these stories in their original form:

CRAFT: "Nest"

New South: "The Dragging Route"

Passages North: "The Box" (Originally titled "Black Pear Tree and the Boxed-In Sky")

Prairie Schooner: "Instructions for Assembly"

Pulp Literature: "Anywhere" (Originally titled "One Safe Place")

Quarterly West: "A Manual for How to Love Us"

The Rupture: "Crescendo"

"Anywhere" was inspired by, and pays homage to, select poems in Richard Siken's book *Crush*.

ABOUT THE AUTHOR

Erin Slaughter is the author of two poetry collections: *The Sorrow Festival* and *I Will Tell This Story to the Sun Until You Remember That You Are the Sun*. She is the editor and cofounder of the literary journal and chapbook press *The Hunger,* and holds an MFA from Western Kentucky University. Originally from Texas, she lives in Tallahassee, Florida, where she is a PhD candidate at Florida State University.